BY HARRIET WALKER

The Wedding Night

The New Girl

THE
WEDDING
NIGHT

THE
WEDDING
NIGHT

A Novel

HARRIET WALKER

BALLANTINE BOOKS
NEW YORK

A Ballantine Books Trade Paperback Original

Published in the United States by Ballantine Books, an imprint of Random House, a division of Penguin Random House LLC, New York.

BALLANTINE and the HOUSE colophon are registered trademarks of Penguin Random House LLC.

RANDOM HOUSE BOOK CLUB and colophon are trademarks of Penguin Random House LLC.

Library of Congress Cataloging-in-Publication Data
Names: Walker, Harriet, author.
Title: The wedding night: a novel / Harriet Walker.
Description: New York: Ballantine Books, [2021]
Identifiers: LCCN 2020046005 (print) | LCCN 2020046006 (ebook) |
ISBN 9781984820020 (trade paperback) | ISBN 9781984820013 (ebook)
Subjects: GSAFD: Suspense fiction.
Classification: LCC PR6123.A426 W43 2021 (print) |
LCC PR6123.A426 (ebook) | DDC 823/.92—dc23
LC record available at https://lccn.loc.gov/2020046005
LC ebook record available at https://lccn.loc.gov/2020046006

Printed in the United States of America on acid-free paper

randomhousebooks.com

9 8 7 6 5 4 3 2 1

Book design by Caroline Cunningham

To Freda, who has blossomed alongside these pages,

and Douglas, whose heart started beating during the edits

At the still point of the turning world . . . there the dance is,
. . . Where past and future are gathered.

—T. S. Eliot, "Burnt Norton"

CAST OF CHARACTERS

The Bride, Lizzie

The Groom, Dan

Ben, Dan's Best Man

The Bridal Party:

    Effie and Anna, Lizzie's Best Women

    Steve

    Charlie

    Iso

    Bertie

THE
WEEK
BEFORE

From: Lizzie & Dan <danandlizziegetmarried@gmail.com>

To: Effie Talbot, Anna & Steve Watson, Ben Holyoake, Charlie Bishop, <ajbr86@hotmail.com>

Subject: Some news
Hi guys,

There's no easy way to say this, but the two of us have come to a decision that we think is best for us both.

We won't be getting married next week. Or ever, in fact.

We're so sorry, we know you all have your flights booked, but hopefully you can appreciate we haven't taken this step lightly.

We'll be in touch with you all soon. For now, we need a bit of space.

Love,

Lizzie and Dan

I.

Effie

Effie read the email again and looked down at her fingertips on the computer keyboard in front of her. They were pale and chewed, nails as red-rimmed as her eyes.

Un-fucking-believable. She had been looking forward to that holiday for months.

When Lizzie—happy, carefree, in-love-with-love Lizzie, lit from within by the sort of glow that comes only from the joy of somebody having weighed you in the balance and decided that, yes, they would like to spend the rest of their existence by your side—had first mentioned her plan to get married abroad, Effie had made all the right impressed, positive noises.

In fact, she had never seen the point of marrying in another country neither of you were from when your own had more than enough venues and your guests all lived in it. Lizzie even came from the sort of commuter belt family for whom home is a village with a Norman church tucked away for the precise purpose of rendering its prodigal City-worker daughters Elizabeth Bennet for a day.

Supposing the couple didn't fancy that option, there were plenty of municipal buildings near where they lived in London to choose from. Proud borough town halls built in civic red brick that would appear nice enough in the background of the photos as long as you positioned someone in front of the fire escape signs. Deliberately derelict warehouses and deconsecrated chapels gone just enough to rack and ruin to look good on Instagram but not to pose any real health and safety risks, beyond an enduring chill that storage heaters would never quite take the edge off. Wood-paneled rooms upstairs in pubs, where the groomsmen could nip down to catch the football highlights between the speeches.

Or conference suites in five-star hotels that rich tourists paid to stay in and Londoners only ever went to on somebody else's money, full of regimented chairs with covers that slipped over them to guard against the worst of the stains. Were the covers, Effie wondered, lined with something waterproof? Otherwise, what was the point in providing two different layers of fabric for the inevitable nuptial spillages of red wine, gravy, and stomach acid to soak into?

Effie noted that nobody who got married abroad ever seemed to do it in a climate colder than their own. It was always in a châteur, a trullo, or a vineyard located in some hot-blooded country, in the hope that the terroir would imbue the pallid Celts who booked them with the same body and top notes—zest, even!—it did the grapes it nurtured.

No, when the time came, Effie had always presumed she would do what most people seemed to: book a registry office, where tidy men and women in bank manager suits presided over efficient, non-Latinate words exchanged between couples who filed in and out on the hour like cuckoos from a clock.

Of course, for this to be any sort of viable option, Effie needed somebody who was interested in marrying her. She closed her eyes at the thought—briefly, but for a beat longer than a blink, in case she started crying at her desk. Again. She had managed not to for a whole month now; it was a record she didn't want to break.

Especially not now that things might finally be looking up again.

Despite Effie's initial misgivings, her best friend's obvious and utter delight had been enough to sell Effie on the idea of a wedding abroad eventually. Over the months, she'd come to see the wedding as the least important part of the holiday anyway—not that she'd let that on to Lizzie, of course.

The rest of the week Effie intended to spend nursing her poor battered soul and steam-rollered self-esteem on a sun lounger, trying to discover who she might be able to become when she arrived home again—hopefully less lonely—and unlocked the door to her flat, where nothing would have moved while she was away and nobody would be waiting for her.

Six months to the day, it'd be, by the time her plane touched back down at Heathrow. Almost half a year of desolate pain, bleak, pointless anger, and regrets. This Provençal break was going to be a coda, she'd decided: after it, she would have turned a corner.

No more craziness. No more blurriness. No more drinking the pain away as evening turned to night and night to dawn, then waking up a few hours later with a sense that the sky was falling in.

Already, these past few weeks, Effie had begun to feel less doom-laden. Upbeat even. *Excited*. She *had* hoped the wedding might have been the moment to share with her friends the reason why.

Effie knew she was reacting selfishly. As she read the email over again and took in the quiet, dignified hurt contained in its wording, her own indignation and disappointment lessened in the face of Lizzie's anguish.

Effie had suspected that her best friend of a decade was having some niggles about marrying the man she'd been with for the past eighteen months. Quiet, sensible Dan had been a port in a storm after Lizzie's last long-term boyfriend, who had been yacht-mad and permanently on some kind of far-flung gap year, with whom she had literally broken up while at sea. But what if, Effie had worried, Dan was *too* quiet, *too* sensible?

Effie had wondered if her friend was trying to breeze through her doubts by organizing the wedding at breakneck speed and with her usual enthusiasm, but she also knew that Lizzie's gusto could be a tiresome force at times. Hadn't Effie gladly borne the brunt of it for years? The elaborate homemade brunches, the "adventure" holidays Lizzie insisted her two best friends go on, the theater trips, the countless book clubs she'd tried to corral them into—Effie loved Lizzie's organizational streak, but thank goodness she didn't have to live with it anymore.

Lizzie had told her that Dan had said they didn't really need a big wedding unless it was what she wanted.

But she hadn't let on that it was serious enough of an issue to bring things to a head. Effie supposed that once you were engaged, had agreed to be on the same team, you were no longer able to kvetch to your friends about your partner's shortcomings—that sort of whinging suddenly became disloyal once you'd both plighted your troth. No, bitching and gossiping were for single people and those who found themselves in the wrong relationships. Effie knew that feeling all too well.

She reached down to her handbag where it sat by her feet, nestled among the wheels of her desk chair, and pulled out her phone.

"Just saw your email. That was brave—are you okay? Sending love, call me when you're ready."

2.

Anna

Anna opened the email on her phone before her first court session of the day and felt her stomach slide into her black leather Chelsea boots as she read it. The disappointment inside her weighed heavier even than the trolley full of legal briefs she had been wheeling around behind her for the best part of ten years.

A week of respite gone!

Surely the two of them could work it out. As the words on the screen traveled from her retina to her brain, Anna could hardly believe that Lizzie and Dan hadn't simply decided to go through with the wedding next week and then sort out whatever the problem was afterward, like normal people do. Like all Anna's celebrity clients certainly did—although whether hiring a £900-per-hour divorce lawyer within the first year of wedded bliss counted as "sorting out" was up for debate, she supposed.

Anna sighed and chewed her lip. Of all the friends to have! Trust hers to be of the honest minority who would rather the mortification of a wedding canceled, and the bone-grinding awkwardness of jilting the guests, in the face of a forever after with the wrong person. Anna had to admire the girl she had met in her first week at university for that much, she admitted to herself as she huffed her wheelie of straining foolscap folders up yet another flight of stone steps.

Anna's heart was a limp balloon. Not, it had to be said, at the prospect of Lizzie's own upset—although that was the second text message the frazzled-looking barrister would send in the wake of this bombshell—but at the idea of relinquishing the glorious week in the south of France that she and her husband had planned minutely, and looked forward to accordingly, around the fact that their three-year-old, Sonny, would be unable to accompany them.

No, the first text message Anna sent was to the only other person in the world who would be as devastated at the collapse of Lizzie and Dan's relationship—and its subsequent effect on their holiday plans—as she was: Steve, Sonny's father.

"Wedding's off," she texted her husband, thumbs flitting around the screen faster than she could have voiced her disappointment but almost as forcefully. "Beyond gutted. Reckon your mum can still take Son that week anyway?"

It wasn't that she wanted to spend less time with her child. Anna adored the solid, knee-high mass of flesh and curls that bounced around their house like a pinball, pepped up on blueberries and story books and the never-ending buzz of discovering things for the first time.

Anna shivered where she stood, from the cold but also from the memory of prying a still-moving creepy-crawly from inside her son's chubby fist before she had stepped out the door to go to work that morning. An hour later she had been seated in her law firm's penthouse boardroom at a table so deliberately and aggressively wide it made even the trusted colleagues opposite feel like adversaries. The disconnect between Anna's work and home lives made her smile on a daily basis, more often out of sheer bafflement than anything officially good-humored.

At least Sonny was out of nappies now; the months when she had cleaned up actual shit in the mornings before arriving in that glass-plated tower only to spend her day disposing of the metaphorical kind for spoiled, overgrown children who had made bad life decisions had been too painfully ironic to scrutinize closely.

And yes, she supposed she meant "ironic" the same way Alanis Morissette had.

She added the thought reflexively; it was the kind of music-journalist joke Steve would make. Steve with his jolly creative-industries job, his writing and the witty cultural observations he was paid significantly less than her to make.

Now, standing at the top of the steps across the road from her office, outside the courtroom she would be in for so long that she would likely miss Sonny's bedtime once again, Anna shrugged her arms out of her blazer, suddenly too hot for it. The sleeves were getting tighter again, and not because she'd built up so much muscle carting all her paperwork around. The May sunshine was warm but the morning air hadn't quite caught up, and it hung, like bathroom mist, around the spires and domes of London's oldest district, where its laws had been made and barristers like Anna now maintained them.

She needed some time off. God, she needed it so much. Not just from work—she regularly reminded herself that she had the sort of job most people would kill for, not for the status or the money but for the simple and unusual fact that she enjoyed it most of the time—but from home as well. From Sonny, indirectly, but mostly from herself. The person she had become.

Only last night, unable to sleep again after one of Sonny's pre-dawn wake-ups, Anna had found herself trying to turn Steve's phone off night mode in order to read his messages. She had crouched by his bedside table, inches from her husband's slack features as he snored, and paged about unsuccessfully, attempting fruitlessly to hack the tech-nerd model he had insisted on paying slightly extra for. *With whose money, Steve?*

The two of them had a long-running joke about her not being able to work it, but the gag was becoming less funny the more texts her husband received from the same number just before lights-out each night.

It was difficult for their neighbor Celia, ferrying Olwen around her shifts at the salon without a partner to share the load, so Steve tried to help out where possible. Sonny and Olwen went to the same nursery, after all.

But those same shifts meant Celia—slim, attractive, naturally maternal Celia—was around far more during the day than Anna ever could be. Around during the day and just next door to where Steve wrote and interviewed and edited from the table in their kitchen.

Stop it.

Celia never seemed to be cross or frustrated with Olwen the way Anna so often was with Sonny.

Stop it.

Really, the perpetual state of low-level chaos in which Anna and Steve's neighbor and her daughter lived was a cautionary tale; Anna should feel sorry for a woman whose husband had left her last year, not fear her as competition.

Anna *needed* this break. Just a week, surrounded by her friends, the people she had known since university, the gang who had grown into their thirties alongside her. A holiday that actually felt like one, instead of the usual kind she and Steve now had post-baby—ones that involved all the same chores, just set against a different backdrop, and made her and her husband feel like some bedraggled touring drama company permanently out on rep. Anna had had Lizzie and Dan's wedding week on the horizon for so long, she had convinced herself that it was her opportunity to rediscover who she had been when they all met, to remind Steve of the real woman he had married. The one who laughed at his jokes and didn't check her watch or her emails all the time.

Now the wedding had been called off, and that woman felt even more beyond her reach.

Anna's phone vibrated with a message again: Steve.

"Damn. Poor Lizzie and Dan. Can we get our money back? We could just go somewhere by ourselves for a week?"

As much as Anna was desperate for some time with her husband—actual quality time rather than the silent and stodgy variety they spent watching TV dramas when they were too tired to speak—she knew she would only feel guilty if they did that. Choosing to leave Sonny behind was quite different from having been forced to by someone else's wedding plans. When they'd seen the words "no children" on the invite, there had been a split second of indignation, but then—the spreading warmth of realization, followed swiftly by a giddiness Anna hadn't felt in years.

The sort that descends at the beginning of a night out, at the first sip of whatever you've chosen to fuel it with, at the prospect of not knowing when or where it might end.

If she and Steve went away by themselves, she knew that the bad-mother pangs would no doubt kick in the very evening they arrived and she'd spend the next six days painfully aware of her son's absence instead of reveling in her husband's company. She'd be haranguing Steve's mother for pictures of Sonny within hours—shots of him covered in cereal and glitter. Or mud, as it tended to be when he spent time with his grandparents. *Why did they always let him get so dirty?*

No, it was the wedding that had made such an escape possible—the idea that she was fulfilling a duty to someone else, to her friend Lizzie, rather than simply indulging her own needs.

Anna swallowed the lump of gloom that had settled in her throat. She should text Lizzie, really.

She noted that Steve's first reaction, in contrast to her own, had been for the sundered couple.

What a selfish cow I am.

It's easier for Steve to be kind; he isn't as stressed as I always am.

As Anna paged around her screen composing a message to Lizzie, the bride-to-be who had so recently become the bride-that-wasn't, her phone buzzed in her palm. An email:

From: Charlie Bishop

To: Effie Talbot, Anna & Steve Watson, <ajbr86@hotmail
.com>

Subject: Re: Some news
Hey you lot,

I've taken Lizzie, Dan and Ben off the thread. Just thinking,
I've been slammed at work recently, had this week booked
off for ages, paid for my flights, and already coughed up to
stay at the not inexpensive "Oratoire de St. Eris." It's too late
for us to get our money back, I've checked.

    I suppose what I'm saying is this: I could really do with a
holiday, and this might as well be it.

    Shall we just go anyway? And persuade Lizzie to come
with?

    C

A bird broke out in song from a Clerkenwell rooftop somewhere above Anna's head, and she thought—just for a moment—
that she might join in.

A
WEEK
LATER

3.

Effie

"... plus you know he has this hot new girlfriend now?"

Anna's voice drifted over from the front seat and Effie came to as if surfacing from underwater, hungry with dread for the last nugget of information she had just heard.

Please, no. I can't take it just yet. Give me another week. Another month.

"Who has?" Effie heard herself demanding, taut and urgent. Her question ripped through the cozy atmosphere and easy chit-chat of the car and landed in the dashboard, a quivering javelin hurled from the backseat, sharp and discordant.

This was what she had been most afraid of. In the early days of heartbreak, it hadn't been the idea of being alone forever or the prospect of picking up a life that was in pieces and trying to reassemble it—like gluing a smashed vase back together without ever having seen it whole—that pulled her awake in the middle of the night, cold and shivering with loss and residual disbelief.

It was the thought of her ex-boyfriend finding someone else. The idea that someone else might make him a different, more genuine shade of what she had mistaken for happy. That some other Effie—but crucially not Effie—was doing everything with him and for him that she had once done; and that—this time—it felt right to him. Even though, to Effie, things had never felt more shockingly, paralyzingly, chaotically wrong.

Effie might have felt more positive recently, but her hurt was still raw, her heart still porous and vulnerable. Six months was not quite long enough to get over six years with someone. Despite the promise of happiness on the horizon, Effie was still not ready for this.

Anna shifted in her seat and her face appeared around the headrest in front. "Charlie has," she said, sighing and scanning Effie where she sat. Her keen eye, honed over years of close friendship, discerned a dullness to her friend's skin, a lack of shine in her usually twinkling gaze. There were shadows under her eyes, and the cotton skirt Effie was wearing stopped at her knees, displaying pale thin shins mapped with coffee table–height blue and purple bruises. "Charlie," she said again, quietly.

Oh thank God. Anna turned round again and Effie went back to chewing the skin around her fingernails and looking out the window. As they hurtled toward the airport, the receding city gave way to liminal business parks that looked like corporate greenhouses and were guarded with spiked metal fences.

They had had to move their flights back a day—officially because something had "come up" at Anna's work, but the truth was that the friends had engineered the delay to avoid the pain of waking up at the château on the morning of Lizzie's big day with none of the planned preening and no white dress to put on. Instead, the morning had been like any other and they would arrive at the Oratoire just before the sun went down on what would have been the wedding date itself.

"Do we know her, Charlie's girlfriend?" Effie asked gamely.

Anna's left arm was dangling from where she held the passenger-side grab rail in the car's ceiling. Effie's mother always clung to it during car journeys, too.

Effie had been ready for years now to ride up front next to the father of her child, the safest and softest cushioned carapace money could buy and its oblivious pudgy cargo anchored with seatbelts behind her. Instead here she sat, surrounded by the crumbs sprinkled from Sonny's own safety throne when Anna had removed it that morning, fretting at a scab on her leg like a surly teen.

Anna replied to her question with a laugh. "Only that she's called Iso and she's—what?—Charlie's first proper girlfriend since . . . you?"

Effie snorted. She had barely been a girlfriend, let alone a proper one. They had coupled up briefly during their first term at Cambridge, those russet-leaved weeks when freshers try on new personalities like hats to see what suits.

Charlie and she—with their nearby rooms off the same tiled corridor, their shared kitchenette and penchant for curling up and watching films late at night while others in their year marauded around the pubs and cobbled streets of their university town—had settled into a routine of mundane domesticity so quickly it had scared her. Effie had ended it before Christmas that term, determined to see something more of university life, and Charlie had become a friend instead.

In fact, Charlie had become a rogue—*our* rogue, the three women who knew him best called him, to differentiate him from other, less special lotharios and exonerate his comically clichéd treatment of the women he lured into his orbit, kept around for just long enough that they fell head over heels for him, then quickly tired of.

Anna and Lizzie had joked for a decade now that Effie had broken Charlie and turned him promiscuous with that early rejection, but Effie knew that he too had felt a jolt of unease at how immediately the two of them had become so middle-aged together. Then, that sort of banal intimacy had upset the natural order of things; now it was all Effie craved.

"I wonder what's so special about this one," Anna continued.

"The hotness, I imagine," said Effie sarcastically.

"No wonder he was so keen to go on this holiday," Steve said from the driver's seat, glancing up at the mirror as he signaled. "He probably can't wait to show her off to us."

Anna laughed—once, and tersely, because she couldn't remember Steve ever having shown her off to anybody. "Makes a change—he usually keeps them hidden, in case they get the wrong idea: meeting the friends means it's serious, after all."

"That's true—Dan didn't even introduce us to Ben until the engagement party," Effie piped up from the backseat, her voice light but loaded. She met Anna's brown eyes in the passenger seat's visor mirror. Steve changed lanes, apparently unaware.

Ben was Dan's best friend and erstwhile best man. He and the groom had been to some godforsaken authoritarian boarding school together, where they had formed the sort of brotherly bond that had been strengthened by cold showers and early morning army drills on frozen rugby pitches. Charlie had taken him off the email chain earlier that week: they hardly expected the best man to join them—Lizzie's mates—on a holiday that had once been his best friend's wedding.

And hadn't he been worth the wait? Effie turned back to the window and warmed herself with a smile that she knew Anna couldn't see in the mirror.

Effie had only met Ben a couple of times in the months after the engagement party, and had tried to be friendly—he'd be escorting her back down the lavender-bordered aisle after the ceremony, after all. They had gotten along fine at the party: the two of them had spent much of it with their heads either bent together or thrown back in laughter, chatting by the bar, while James had looked on sourly from the sidelines. But in the weeks afterward—after James had finished with her—Ben had been aloof, occasionally acerbic, and—frustratingly at the time, although Effie was prepared now to admit she had been at one of her many low ebbs—entirely uninterested in the face of her slightly desperate attempts to flirt with him.

It was several months later that Effie found herself sitting opposite the best man in a busy pub not far from the school she worked at—which, happily, took up most of her time these days. Ben had met her at the gates long after Effie's beloved girls had filed out, ducklings in boater hats, and gone home. He was all plans and secret projects for a video he wanted to make and show during the speeches on the couple's big day.

It was to tell the story of Lizzie and Dan's relationship, a montage of their moments together, starting with how they'd met on a dating app and ending with messages from those who hadn't been able to make it over to the Oratoire—once a medieval convent, now a lavish, Instagram-friendly rental property—for the ceremony. As he explained it to Effie, asking for her opinions, her ideas, how she might be able to quietly corral Lizzie's network while he contacted Dan's, she had seen the rather brusque man she'd come to expect thaw before her eyes, watched all his stuffy reserve evaporate under the heat of his boyish enthusiasm. They ended up having a rather lovely night in the pub, as they planned and plotted, drank pints, and swapped stories.

It had turned into a rather lovely morning as well.

Since then, Effie and Ben had seen a lot more of each other. The gaping wounds that her ex, James, had left—in her life, her future—were beginning to heal. She still felt sad, still caught herself staring for minutes at a time into the past as though it was a view from a window. But for the first time in months, Effie also felt optimistic. Loved, even. Though that word had not been uttered yet—it had only been a month.

But Ben was so open, so genuine, so keen to make plans and put things in the diary with her—plans she was only too glad to accept, after realizing those pages had gradually emptied without her noticing toward the end with James—that Effie wondered whether it might not be long before it was said.

It was in this spirit that they had decided to keep their relationship—or whatever it was; Effie felt superstitious about labeling it—under wraps until the wedding. Let's not distract from Lizzie and Dan's day, Effie and Ben had reasoned to each other one morning as the sun crept onto the pillow they shared, like a hand reaching in through the curtains. They would tell the others after the ceremony.

In the week since Lizzie's email, Effie had seen less of Ben. They had both been busy mopping up their friends' tears but, even in this, they had been thrown together.

Ben had offered to help cancel various deliveries; refund wedding favors and gift-list items; send back chairs, tables, and the like; have floral displays taken down and trellises dismantled; return the unlucky rings so they could be cast into Mount Doom and smelted down for the next unwitting fingers. As best man and de facto maid of honor, he and Effie had, between the two of them, ensured that the mundane disassembly of the wedding had not entirely fallen on the already overburdened shoulders of those currently busy with the far bigger task of unpicking the life they had planned together.

At least I didn't have to cancel a wedding.

Effie imagined herself in a white dress and veil, crying and begging as she had indeed done, only this time in front of an audience in florals and wide brims with carefully matched bags and shoes, rather than in her pajamas on the stairs of her flat just before the front door had banged shut. She shivered the memory away.

After a few nights apart, Effie's entire body was looking forward to seeing Ben again. The time they'd spent together had so far been the giggling, wine-flushed, last-people-in-the-restaurant sort—and what inevitably came afterward. She had been more than a little bleary in the classroom at Coral Hill Prep of late, after chatting into the dawn with Ben while tracing the whorls of hair on his chest with one finger.

Muted in her palm, Effie's phone hummed, and she felt her insides wriggle. It was from Ben: "See you soon, gorgeous."

She blushed enjoyably in her seat: there would be more chance for that this week. But Effie was also looking forward to spending daylight hours with her new boyfriend. They had gone out for breakfast together one weekend, walked in the park, but since they were single thirty-somethings with efficient and established lives, one or the other of them eventually had to head off to something else. Effie craved the sort of uninhibited, languorous, limitless hours that come only with being in a foreign country and having taken one's watch off. Strolling through a market town, cycling through vineyards, simply lying by the pool with Ben, making small talk.

The pool. She had studied it endlessly on the website's photo gallery over the past six months: on her phone, from her desk in the staff room, in bed, in several pubs with countless glasses of wine in hand. Lapping azure water overlooking rolling fields of lavender and sunflowers demarcated by avenues of needle-pointed cypress trees: a Hockney air-dropped into Cézanne country. Effie stretched her thin limbs and aching joints in the car at the very thought, at the baptismal qualities she had projected onto it, and warmed in anticipation of unfurling beside it as soon as she arrived. She had been almost existentially cold for half a year.

"Have you heard any more from Lizbet? How is she?" Anna was asking from the front.

Effie stalled as the car flew along. She didn't want to describe how their once bubbly, golden hair–tossing friend, whose white teeth were always bared in a shriek of laughter, had become sad-eyed and silent, a watchful lank-haired supplicant who wished only to rewind to before the breakup.

"She's doing okay," she replied, from the backseat. "Up and down. You know."

Anna did know. She had picked Effie up only too recently, and Lizzie had done similar for her years before she had met Steve. Women spend half their party decade either in this coma or sitting at its bedside, Effie thought, waiting for their friends to wake up. When they do, the prescribed medicine is booze and solidarity, a pile of handbags on a dance floor. Rehabilitation comes in learning how to smile again, how to dine alone, how to talk to strangers. How to spend a Friday night in with only one's soul for company.

They all knew the stunned desolation of brokenhearted grief, all felt their friends' hurt like a memory of their own. At university, Anna and Effie had practically scraped Lizzie off the floor after one such rupture. For several days, Anna had coaxed soup into her mouth, while Effie persuaded her up and out of bed, into an exam hall to answer the questions that would move her life on in the right direction, past this painful and unforeseen bump in the road. Effie knew that Lizzie counted the favor she had done back then as above and beyond the call of duty. She supposed it had been—she had made Lizzie promise to tell no one, not even Anna—but Effie had done it gladly.

It hadn't taken that long for them to come round from breakups in their twenties, but in your thirties. . . . Effie had found that it was different, more difficult. Once people began to swap their urban family of flatmates and pals for the cozy little biological units they were creating at home, there were fewer—if any—who could offer the necessary hours of vigil. The only single woman among her friends after the breakup, Effie often faced the prospect of a whole weekend devoid of plans, and it sent her spiraling into a breathless crouch of despair every time. She found solace in books and daytime cinema trips, but only had to imagine herself at the Singles 'n' Salsa night in the pub at the end of her road and the panic would come again.

She knew she could always turn up at Anna's house, where the background thrum of toddler patter, the washing machine, and something from Steve's obscure vinyl collection might drown out the internal static for an afternoon. Effie delighted in Sonny's company and lavished attention on him as though he were her own blood. Childcare came naturally to her, and she recognized a wistfulness in Anna's gratitude.

But Effie also knew she was an addendum there. If she and

Sonny played a game or painted a picture, he always wanted to tell Mama and Dada he had won, to show them what he had made. Effie yearned to be so crucial to somebody, at the center of a little world. As much as she wanted the company, she didn't like to highlight how much she needed it.

Effie had gone round to hold Lizzie's hand the evening after the email. Dan had already moved out of their pretty garden flat on the most superficial level, meaning his underwear was no longer there but his books and CDs were. Effie remembered this stage from when James left: every well-thumbed page, creased spine, and half-remembered romantic lyric was a ghost in the room, each a soft-focus Then that existed in filmic palimpsest with the shitty, unflatteringly lit Now. She'd thought that stage was bad, but she had found the empty spaces on the shelves once they had been removed even worse.

"Spray his belongings with your favorite perfume before you hand them over," *Cosmo* had educated them all as teenagers. "He'll be overwhelmed with memories and want you back."

It hadn't worked for Effie; it had just made James cough.

Lizzie had been distant and distracted when Effie arrived— but that was to be expected. Effie knew how having your life canceled without notice could change a person. She had tried her best to persuade Lizzie to come on the holiday with the rest of them, to spend what would surely be the most difficult week of her life with the people who knew her best—but Lizzie had been reticent. Even talking about the place she should have been married in had made her cry fresh tears.

"I can't, Eff," she'd sputtered into a tissue. "It would be all I thought about."

"But won't you be thinking about it here too?" Effie had gestured around the empty flat. "You'd be surrounded by your friends there—here you'll just be by yourself, wondering when Dan's next coming round to pick up his stuff."

Eventually Lizzie had acquiesced: she would come with them

to the Oratoire de St. Eris, the place she had chosen as backdrop for her future with Dan now recast as square one in the new journey her life would take.

Effie had been glad. As the single elder stateswoman, she knew the importance of company, and she'd wanted to make sure Lizzie would have it on request. Before she'd left the flat that evening, Effie had even offered to stay the night, but her friend had waved her off from the front step. As she walked away down the road, Effie had guiltily admitted to herself that the prospect of one more friend—*one more than none*—whose future felt that little bit less mapped out had felt reassuring. It had been a little soon to make the point to Lizzie that they would have each other, just as it felt a little soon to press Ben on the specifics of whatever it was they had together.

Effie had gone straight from there to the pub to meet him— not that she had told Lizzie that. Effie knew that, eventually, Lizzie would be delighted for her and for Ben—she knew how difficult Effie had found the past six months; but the news that a friend is having depression-busting, chandelier-rattling sex with your ex's best mate wasn't exactly what Lizzie needed to hear right then. Effie felt more reckless and spontaneous with Ben than she ever had done with James; that night, flush-faced and with a corona of pillow-static hair, she had told him of the plan to whisk Lizzie away with them, to soothe the rawness of her hurt with the company of her oldest friends.

The last six months hadn't been difficult for just Effie. She and Anna had noticed a transformation in their friend over that time too. Lizzie had always been strong-minded and successful; she spent her days making the sort of trailblazing adverts that talking heads ended up commenting on in state-of-the-nation clip shows. She knew her rights and her worth like she did her target demographics, but she had surprised both of them by diving into the planning of her "Big Day" like a Victorian wallflower working on her trousseau.

These days, they met up less frequently than they had in their twenties and, just like their drinks when they did, their time together felt watered down. In recent months, Lizzie had been quieter than usual—withdrawn, almost—and, when Effie and Anna had managed to coax her out of herself, able to talk of little other than the wedding. She asked their advice about readings, place settings, and favors, with none of the sarcasm Effie might have overlaid or Anna's resentment at how much time her own nuptials had taken up. Lizzie was almost obsessive about the wedding—to the exclusion of her old personality, in fact.

But she didn't seem excited about it, either. Lizzie's wasn't the sort of bridezilla monomania or self-importance that bulldozed or hijacked every other topic of conversation between the three of them. It seemed as though she couldn't let herself talk about anything else, didn't trust herself to. When Effie and Anna shared stories about what sort of day they'd both had, what their weekends looked like, Lizzie simply shrank into the cushions of whatever sofa they were sitting on or remained blank across the table they sat at.

Effie had first noticed it after the engagement party: Lizzie had become so bland, so docile. A blushing bride but somehow lacking in enthusiasm too. Lizzie was no longer mischievous; she no longer laughed. She had once called something "wedmin" over brunch (Effie watched Anna repress a shudder), without even pausing to pull a face.

Lizzie had deployed the same determination she always brought to all things professional and planned the wedding like an automaton: the dress had been chosen with minimum fuss (neither Effie nor Anna had been invited along); the venue—lavish and far away—decided on swiftly and without too much agonizing. The invitation, a hand-finished fold-out card filled with multiple inserts detailing logistics and a single sprig of Provençal lavender, had arrived with little pomp and just the right amount of ceremony. Lizzie had diligently—robotically, even—gotten on with all of it.

So what had changed her mind?

4.

Anna

"She didn't want to talk about it." Effie's voice from the back of the car wavered slightly with an emotion that Anna knew her fragile friend shared. As much as her heart went out to Lizzie—Lizzie, who had stepped back from bride to mere woman again—it was Effie, still, six months on, who concerned her most.

The head of his own digital marketing agency, Effie's ex-boyfriend, James, had constructed his entire identity around being ahead of the curve; James had always known the best bars, owned the best albums before anyone else did. He had a collection of prized T-shirts emblazoned with the inscrutable logos of cult Japanese fashion brands, of record labels and microbreweries—Anna could rarely tell one from the other—that reached out to the like-minded souls he passed in the red brick Shoreditch streets near his office (*sorry, "workspace"*) and meant nothing to the pedestrians James considered to be beneath his notice.

She and Effie had both been through breakups before, but this one . . . Anna pulled a strand of her dark hair in front of her face and rolled it between her fingers. This one had been life-changing. Effie had thought she and James would have children together, grow old side by side. He might not have been sold on getting married, but they had been together nearly six years; the rest of them had all assumed it was a done deal—despite the fact that they might privately have wished Effie could meet somebody who was more appreciative of her.

Instead, Anna had answered her phone during one of Sonny's cute but terrifyingly brutal toddler football sessions one Sunday morning to hear Effie lowing like a dying animal.

"He's gone," she managed through the pain. "It's over."

Anna hadn't even been able to get to her until two days later, and the fact had shamed her. In the old days, she would have been round with tissues and wine within the hour, but an inexcusably clichéd combination of childcare and court prep meant that the heartbreak Bat-Signal had gone unanswered for forty-eight hours solid. Effie had said she didn't mind, that she had work to get through as well—but was that proof of how busy and grown-up they both were or of how dislocated they had become?

Between them, Anna and Lizzie had made time to check in on their friend but, as the weeks and months passed since the bomb had gone off in Effie's life, Anna found she no longer had the stamina she once did for friend emergencies. She didn't have enough evenings free, between the ones she spent either hunched low and late, scribbling at her desk, or rushing out of the office in case she could make it back in time for Sonny's bath. She couldn't keep in her yawns as Effie re-trod the shock, the incredulity, and the anger over bottle after bottle, well beyond Anna's strict ten P.M. bedtime. She couldn't manage the headaches the next day in the office as the love fermented to spite and the yearning distilled to fury. She couldn't help Effie every minute of the day as they and Lizzie had all done for each other in the past. When they did manage to meet as a three, Lizzie had seemed barely able to concentrate on what Effie was saying anyway.

Anna felt Effie's text messages buzzing in her pocket as she met clients, turned her phone facedown when the calls came during briefing sessions with her juniors. *How did she have time to ring during the school day anyway?* After a decade of devotion to Coral Hill Prep and teaching its precocious preteen girls with the type of enthusiasm that couldn't be faked, Effie was now one step away from being headmistress at one of the most prestigious primary schools in London. Anna couldn't imagine the pushy mothers, for which that particularly leafy, southwest quadrant of the city was famous, standing for anybody being anything other than full Mary Poppins when in loco parentis with their highly competitive, socially engineered charges.

So Anna yelled her advice out over speakerphone as she danced around the kitchen with Sonny's potato waffles or soaped the paint out of his hair in the bath. Each time, she acknowledged briefly to herself—and hated—that her life no longer felt broad enough to encompass all of Effie's feelings as well as her own.

A text message more than two inches long was an indulgence to her parental mind, and further evidence that her friend's was unraveling.

Married for a year longer than Sonny's tiny life span and with Steve for three before that, Anna had forgotten how distant memories, unearthed emails, the gradual joining of dots could precipitate aftershocks of emotion that felt as new and disorientating as the original landslide of a relationship ending. She could no longer recall how thinking back over a conversation in a new light somehow intensified and renewed what had happened all over again. An entire relationship could be recast in a moment, a love story rewritten in a second—but Anna did not have the energy to talk Effie down every time.

Instead, her responses had become copy-and-paste jobs, her patience stretched translucent. But now that she saw Effie for the first time in a few weeks—really *saw* her—Anna realized that her friend was still struggling under the weight of a decision taken about her future that she had not been consulted on.

After James's departure, Effie's complexion, always light and prone to rosiness, had become a blotch of blue-toned gray pallor. Her baby-soft hair was thinner, her athletic build now nearly skeletal; her joints were bony hinges and her sternum a ridged xylophone beneath her T-shirt. In a past life, wearing the contented pudge that came of being in long-term, loved-up, if not exactly red-hot relationships, the two of them would have joked about the cheese-rind skin and wine-coated teeth that accompanied glamorous, emaciated sorrow, but now—one of them wasting away under her own sadness, the other bloated with domestic grudges—there seemed little to laugh about.

Anna was pleased to see that some of her friend's former glow had been restored recently, but she still wasn't back to full strength.

I'll speak to her properly this week. This holiday will be just what we both need.

That was why she'd also begged Lizzie to come with them, so that she might lick her wounds in their company rather than alone, in the flat she used to share with her now former fiancé.

As Anna glanced out the window and Steve began to slow to pull off for the exit toward the airport's vast expanses of car park, there came the sound of two phones, hers and Effie's, vibrating in unison as the same message arrived to them both simultaneously.

It was from Lizzie: "Are you at the airport yet? Running a bit late—eek! Can't wait to see you both."

5.

Effie

Ben was waiting there for her after the security checks. Broad and beaming with a nervous smile that made Effie's own slightly jittery stomach lurch like a stalling car, he bent to kiss her cheek before greeting Anna and Steve. He had carefully saved a table large enough for the whole group, took coffee orders as the three of them schlepped their wheelies out of the way, and went to the bar as they settled in.

"I'm sorry—you're seeing someone?" Anna said to Effie, once he was out of earshot, eyebrows raised practically to her hairline and her voice well above its usual pitch. "And it's best man *Ben*?"

"We . . . just hit it off about a month ago," she replied, embarrassed but earnest. "He's kind of great." And when Anna pressed her—on the when, the how, the what it all meant—she added: "Let's just see, shall we? Even I don't know yet."

Ben handed the drinks around carefully, remembered perfectly who had asked for what, refusing repayment. Deliberately lingered as he brushed Effie's fingers with his own when it was her turn to take a steaming cup. He settled into the chair next to hers and wiggled his eyebrows at her when Effie next summoned the courage to look up into his face.

Across the table, Anna waved at someone behind them: Lizzie, sprinting across the departures lounge, looking just as she used to coming back from college hockey practice when she would stop by Effie and Anna's rooms for a cup of tea, dressed in a gray marled sweatshirt and navy jogging bottoms with her hair pulled back into a rough ponytail.

Already the shaken and shell-shocked woman Effie had put her arm around earlier that week seemed more herself again; she even managed a triumphant smile as she heaved her handbag down onto a chair. But it faded, replaced with confusion—and something else—when Lizzie registered the man at Effie's side.

"Ben?" she asked bluntly, her voice hoarse with feeling. Lizzie's face was suddenly full of color, her eyes threatening to brim over with glossy tears. "What are you doing here?"

Ben's expression stuttered like a blinking bulb. Anna, too, looked taken aback, her face stricken by a horrified half-smile, the body's betraying impulse to laugh at awkwardness, to smooth away the edge it had introduced.

"It was my idea, Lizbet," Effie said hurriedly, leaning across the table so that Lizzie was looking into her friendly face rather than Ben's flustered one. "I asked him to come."

Lizzie's mouth moved as though in silent recital of some unknown text, her eyes searching Effie's as though reading words in a foreign language.

"We were going to leave it until after the wedding so we didn't distract from anything, but . . ." Effie's voice cracked a little at the reveal. "Ben and I have been seeing each other for a little while."

She turned her head to smile at him and saw that his face had begun to relax too. Effie felt a rush of tenderness for him: he had been so thoughtfully reticent about whether he should come this week, considering only Dan and whether or not his oldest friend might need the company in London instead. Effie could have been more careful of her friend's feelings too, she realized.

"I'm so sorry, Lizbet," she said. "We didn't mean to give you a shock."

"Surprise!" Ben laughed nervously.

Lizzie's breath tumbled out as though she had been kicked in the stomach. "Well!" she laughed—a little too loudly—and Effie noticed the tears remaining in her eyes. "I didn't realize I'd be the seventh wheel at my own wedding party. . . . But still, what a treat to go away with you lot again."

She didn't want coddling or fussing over, she said, just good company and a change of scene—where else to go than on the holiday she had so carefully planned every minute of for the past six months, she joked.

The rest of the group collectively blushed and smiled, unsure how to reply but nodding as though it really was funny: a bride heading to the venue where her wedding no longer was. Effie found she suddenly felt nervous: she knew a change of surroundings could be a good thing, but she was fairly certain that the scenery involved should be new and invigorating, rather than one intended to have been the backdrop to cherished photos that would now never be taken.

"All right, gang?" A smooth, treacly voice interrupted her thoughts: Charlie. He and Iso were standing behind her chair, smiling down at the rest of them with impossibly bleached, rich-person teeth that sang out from already-tanned skin. "Everyone, this is Iso; Iso, these are the reprobates I warned you about."

The woman standing next to him turned her own full-beam smile on the group and waved, directing her gaze carefully to each of them in turn as they introduced themselves.

"Just a turmeric latte for me," Iso said as she took a seat and Charlie went to the counter.

A *turmeric latte*. Effie had been wondering whether it was too early for a gin and tonic.

Iso, Charlie's new—*first proper*—girlfriend was, not to put too fine a point on it, completely gorgeous: long, tumbling waves of dark hair, big, brown, Bambi-lashed eyes, and a café au lait tan that spoke of a regular holiday regime far away from the Home Counties, which had shaped her cut-glass vowels and consonants.

Her long, tanned legs in denim cut-off shorts stretched out beyond the table and crossed delicately at the ankles.

Effie felt exhausted just looking at her. She saw it in Anna's reaction too—the primal slump that happens around women so ineffably beautiful that they make one feel almost evolutionarily redundant by comparison. The worst part was that Iso looked a lot like Anna used to—before the big job and the baby had taken their respective tolls.

She seemed nice enough—friendly, quick to smile and to giggle, eager to chat, none of the standoffishness or the arrogance that so often comes of growing up attractive. And her awkwardness around Lizzie was noticeable, too: as someone so clearly in the first flush of whatever she and Charlie had going on, Iso kept looking at Lizzie as though she was a specimen, a case study in it all going wrong.

Over another round of drinks (a beer each for the boys, peppermint tea for Effie—it *was* too early for gin, and she still had a slight hangover from the wine she'd drunk while packing her suitcase), Iso told them that she was an "influencer."

"Is that like a fixer?" asked Steve.

"No, mate, no," Charlie jumped in earnestly. "She doesn't buy drugs for rock stars. An influencer is, like, someone who knows what we want before we do, and shows us how nice life could be." He winked at Iso across the Formica table.

"For a fee," said Anna briskly, fiddling with one of the ties on the embroidered peasant blouse that Effie knew she had been persuaded into buying after seeing one of her competitive mum friends wearing it on Facebook.

"That's right," Iso said smoothly, uncrossing and recrossing her golden haunches. "I'm a content creator who uses products and clothes to inspire my audience as they follow my adventures around the world."

That explained the tan, at least, thought Effie. "Wow," she said. "How many followers do you have?"

Iso dimpled into her yellow drink as she took a sip. "Nearly seven hundred thousand. But it's really not about the numbers—it's about creating a community."

Effie had met Anna's eyes for less than a second, just to confirm that they were both thinking the same thing.

A few hours later, across a narrow sea and a patchwork of asphalt and farmland, the rental car and its passengers barreled along through the French countryside. Excitement rose in each of their chests, along with a feeling of having been liberated, like actors faced with a run of scenes for which they weren't needed onstage. This was a chance to return their bodies to a natural, unmannered state; for their minds to abandon the usual rote; to wipe their faces of all the expressions they assumed simply to get themselves through the day.

After they had collected their bags, picked up the keys to the rental car, and clunked its doors shut behind them, there had been a collective exhalation. A Zen state of calm contentment descended, perked up now and again by the familiar landmarks of Being on Holiday: the serried ranks of vines on either side of them, automated sprinklers spinning and zapping crops with bursts of water. The roadside shrines, signs pointing visitors toward the local, bottle-lined *caves de dégustation*. Swimming pool showrooms and garden centers with their driveways full of birdbaths and plaster-molded seraphim.

"Who buys all these amphoras?" Anna asked as they passed a fourth outlet replete with neoclassical patio accessories.

"Am all phora good-looking garden," joked Steve in a hokey French accent, and she batted lazily at the arm he wasn't steering with as the car rumbled on.

Lizzie was quiet, jollied along by the other passengers. Anna and Effie took care not to make eye contact too obviously whenever their friend's words trailed off and a veil of introspection clouded her features as though she was remembering words spoken, decisions taken. In the driver's seat, Steve set his sights firmly on the hairpin bends ahead and the mopeds that emerged suddenly from its grassy sidings as though loosed deliberately to test his reaction times.

The sun settled into a low afternoon sky as if staked there on a picture hook, throwing yolk-yellow rays over the granite protrusions they climbed and the limy rivers they crossed. Effie felt her heart buoy—still a relatively recent occurrence after what seemed like years. Her shoulders unhunched and her neck lifted like the stems of the sunflowers they passed. She could tell, from the way the dust swirled in the light and the noise of the crickets through the windows, that the air when they stepped out of the car would be a warm embrace on her bare skin. Not that she was cold anymore: where she sat in the middle of the minivan's backseat, she could feel the heat from both Lizzie's and Ben's thighs where they pressed either side of her own.

"Plenty of fabulous scenery for Iso's Instagram account," Anna remarked drily as they bombed along a smooth tarmac road with medieval hilltop villages strewn to its left and right. Charlie and Iso were making their way to the château in a sexy and antisocial two-seater soft-top, while the rest of them had piled into a rather more family-focused people carrier.

"Are we on holiday with a celebrity, then?" Steve asked from the driver's seat.

"No!" Effie and Anna both replied quickly, while Lizzie paused to weigh it up.

Ben pulled out his phone and typed Iso's name into the app's search function, watched as her profile page and its grid of exotic destinations, tasteful bikini shots, and artfully placed succulents loaded up. "I don't know," he said. "She looks pretty famous to me—this cup has got three thousand likes!"

On his screen was the turmeric latte from the airport, its bilious foam somehow rendered almost sparklingly golden against the gray marble tabletop. Except the table had just been plastic printed to look like veined stone. Nobody clicking on that photo would know that Iso hadn't been in the sort of upmarket café that had highly polished counters and thick cotton napkins—or, Effie reflected, that she had been surrounded by a group of nobodies. *Is anybody really how they seem on the internet?*

Effie saw them all through Iso's eyes: the jilted bride, a hungover scarecrow, a pair of tired-looking, hip-once-but-slightly-past-it parents, Ben, and . . . Charlie. He hadn't changed—ten years had barely touched him. Charlie was like that faux-marble table: unweathered by events. Where on earth had he found Iso?

Effie's own heartache had put a limit on how much joy she could feel for other people before tipping over into the sort of self-pity that razed everything in its path like a forest fire. She had been glad, after James had left, that he had waited until a little while after Lizzie had gotten engaged—that she had been able to enjoy her best friend's happiness in a moment of sheer jubilance that was untainted by the state of her own love life.

Although, of course, the comparison had always been there, really—at every friend's wedding, every engagement party, every ring-finger photo, every "I said yes" group message. James hadn't wanted to get married, said it wasn't for him. Who needed to be given a piece of paper that told them how they felt? Over time, Effie had persuaded herself that she didn't want that piece of paper, either. That is, until Lizzie was in line for one.

Effie didn't remember the engagement party very well; she had drunk too much in a way that had started out enthusiastic and become embittered. That night, when they got home, she had started a conversation with James that she expected to turn into a fight but instead had simply turned into a shrug of resignation. The next morning, he had told her they wanted different things. Shocked, with a stabbing headache and the all-too-familiar sense that she couldn't quite remember what had happened the night before, she had tried to persuade him otherwise, had begged him to reconsider.

But he had gone, immune to her pleas. He had closed the door behind himself, and except for a series of tragically procedural texts around moving out, and a few apologies sent in response to her late-night calls (unanswered) and rambling messages (mortifying when read back the next morning), that was that.

Throughout the snotty cuddles, the hand-holding and the hair-stroking of those difficult first weeks, Lizzie had assured Effie that nothing had happened at the party, but Effie couldn't deny the uncomfortable feeling that her oldest friend had seemed to be holding something back ever since.

Now Effie looked over at Lizzie's familiar heart-shaped, freckled face, the ghost of worry playing across it almost imperceptibly. On her other side, Ben was still gazing at his phone, still scrolling through Iso's archive of covetable lifestyle ephemera. Effie leaned into his solid, cotton-fresh frame to better scrutinize the pictures and left Lizzie, frowning into the window next to her, to her silent reflection.

It was what Effie's father had always called "golden hour" by the time they arrived at the Oratoire de St. Eris. The turreted building, made of pale limestone, absorbed the warm orange of the late afternoon sun from its hilltop perch like a cat on a windowsill.

Beyond the driveway, cut into the hillside below it, steps led down toward a shimmering rectangle of pure cyan. The pool! Effie's heart leaped even before her eyes were drawn from its crystalline depths to the landscape beyond. She tilted her body left and then right to take in the panorama, and ran one hand through her flyaway hair as it lifted slightly in a sultry but welcome breeze.

For the first time in months, she felt she was on neutral ground, a new place and a blank slate: somewhere that had never witnessed her in any state other than how she was right now. Her home city, her regular haunts, the school, even her flat—they all still held traces of her as she used to be, of her happy, of her in a couple. All of them were tainted by memories. Sometimes she felt she was wading against a current just walking down her local high street; already here she felt unburdened by her own sad history.

Enough of that. Effie would leave here one half of a new couple: a fresh start with a delightfully unmapped future ahead of them.

6.

Lizzie

I still couldn't believe I'd had to cancel our wedding.

We weren't *that* kind of people; we were *us*. Reasonable and refined. Above the sort of brute transaction that pits terror against trust in return for silence. For cooperation.

The first time he threatened me, I thought it was a joke. A bad one. I couldn't believe he would ever treat me like that, but then he did.

I couldn't believe he had taken those photos either. Taken them, saved them, readied them to share at the click of a button with everyone I knew, and with even more I didn't.

I'd never seen myself asleep before. I don't think I'll ever look that peaceful again; I certainly don't sleep anymore.

I couldn't believe that the thing that had made us so special together—the intimacy, the tangled limbs and pink cheeks, the private language of daylight on skin as the dawn interrupts—had become a weapon. Couldn't believe a man I cared so much for—so much that my body had ached for him when he wasn't near me—would do this to me. That was the first time I thought I was going mad, but not the last.

He said those images would become public property if I didn't play along, didn't do what he asked. So I did.

I kept him sweet. I smiled when I felt the hard pinch of fear in my gut. Laughed my way through the awkwardness and the nerves. Pretended it was normal, fine—told myself it would be. I chatted at dinner, never went to bed angry. Blurred out the reality and gave my life a gloss. From the outside, everything looked perfect.

I could teach that stunning influencer girlfriend a thing or two about filters.

7.

Anna

The countryside unspooled in every direction around her: the house overlooked the valley below it. Grids and stripes of fields crazy-paved in a spectrum of greens, red tiled roofs, and avenues of trees—all of it lay before the house like a rug in front of a fireplace, and it existed in a permanent chatty buzz of crickets and far-off, hee-hawing donkeys.

Thank God we're here. Anna cupped her hand to her forehead to shield her eyes from the low-hanging and insistent sun and surveyed the site—the venue, as they'd been referring to it for so long. Now, stripped of the wedding, it was just a place again. But what a spot! High soaring birds, their wings open like books, flew across the sky as she took in the view. An appreciative sigh caught in her throat—not only from the dusty car journey but also because, as she relaxed properly for the first time since Sonny had been born, she felt tears of relief spring to her eyes.

I'll be a different person by the time we leave—one who has infinite patience with her husband and can balance work and a child without feeling guilty about either.

Sweating slightly and anticipating the moment when she'd be able to swap her clothes for swimwear, Anna strode toward the wooden front door within its Gothic archway, solid and dotted with fortifying lead pins. The metal ring handle was sun-warmed in her palm and the latch squealed as she lifted it, but the door swung open smoothly into the château's main room—the Great Hall, a tennis court in length or more.

"Oh my God," Anna breathed, raising one hand to her chest as she looked around. "Effie!" She called her friend's name without taking her eyes off the scene in front of her—and again, louder: "Effie!"

Anna heard the scuffing of trainers and the crunching of gravel; the noise stopped as their owner came to a pause behind her. The long room in front of them was dim after the brightness of the garden, and it took a moment for Effie's eyes to adjust. But, eventually, there was the interior, laid out like a banquet before them.

"Ohhhh fuck." Effie's words were low and slow. She brought her hand to her forehead in a subconscious mirroring of Anna's pose. "Oh dear."

Golden rays bounced off the glassware, cutlery, and lanterns lined up on the pair of long tables in front of the two women. On a wooden trestle near the hearth stood an impossibly white, three-tiered cake decorated with dewy yellow roses and freshly foraged curlicues of ivy.

At the other end of the room was another sturdy medieval fireplace the height of a grown man, with a pair of crossed swords pinned on the chimney breast above it. The hammerbeam roof—a much-vaunted original feature that was mentioned countless times on the website, as Anna recalled—was made of dark timber, but light streamed in from the windows that looked out onto the courtyard.

Set at the bottom of a U-shaped quad, the Hall opened out through a pair of double doors onto a lavender-edged terrace. Beyond, the vista spread itself languidly like a diva across a piano, the sky vast and empty. The terrace, however, was busy with chairs—the wooden folding sort, arranged into rows that gazed back at the house as though filled with an expectant crowd.

Spotlit in the fiery sun hung a garlanded archway above the doorway, a trellis wreathed in lush flowers and dripping vines. And in front of that—at the top of a short flight of steps down onto the patio—was a small stand. An altar, if they were calling a spade a spade, as Anna always preferred to. On top of it lay a thick bound book with vellum pages, and on top of that were two small hoops, glinting in the afternoon sun.

"Well, bloody hell," said Steve as he sauntered up behind them to gaze in as well. "That's what I call a welcome."

"It isn't a sodding welcome, Steve, you idiot," Anna spat.

The venom that she thought she'd left at home with her barrister's gown and childcare duties but that had apparently been bubbling away just below the surface the whole time boiled over once again. She realized she was holding the doorframe so tightly her knuckles had turned white.

"It's Lizzie's wedding," Effie said, finishing the horrified train of thought for her.

8.

Effie

There was no time to hide what the Hall held as the woman who was supposed to have been the center of its attentions turned from the valley view toward the others at its doors.

"Don't wait for me to start exploring!" Lizzie called, one hand raised to shield her eyes from the glare of the sun as she strode back from the ridge's edge to join them.

"Lizbet, it, er, looks like they might not have got the message," Anna called, attempting a warning before Lizzie reached them, but it only served to increase the other woman's curiosity—and her pace.

Lizzie's manner since climbing out of the car had been what Effie had silently registered as contemplative. Her face was clouded with the poignancy of arriving at the venue she would have left as a wife, but Lizzie's features had, like everyone's, lit up as the beauty of the estate—its harmonious setting, ancien régime charm, and easy balance of the rustic and the elegant—had dawned on them. Now, as she saw her friends gathered at the entrance of the Hall, uncertainty settled into the crease of her brow again and a question formed on her lips.

Before she could ask it, there came the purr of an engine from the direction of the road and another car joined theirs on the gravel. As they watched, Charlie and Iso climbed out and emptied its trunk, the former carrying a businessman's hard-cased silver carry-on in one hand and an expensive Scotch-grain holdall in chocolate-brown leather in the other.

The perfect couple right down to their luggage: complementary rather than matchy-matchy,

Effie's keen sense of tragedy focused on the fact that they looked so at ease as a pair. She wondered whether Ben would carry her bag up the stairs for her later without her asking him to; currently he was taking in the view of the valley below them, and she was glad to see that he seemed as enchanted by the place as she was. Effie worried sometimes that he seemed more worldly than her, more used to the sort of luxury they were now surrounded by and therefore less easily impressed than she was.

Lizzie turned to greet Charlie and Iso where she stood, a few yards away from the doorway and still out of range to survey the scene inside the Hall.

"Not bad, huh?" She smiled, hamming up with a tragic expression the sadness Effie knew she was feeling, as Charlie reached her side and Iso stepped along neatly behind him. The younger woman had one hand securing a knowingly picture-perfect straw sun hat atop her dark waves as she turned to look at the vista, and the valley, behind her.

"You can say that again." Charlie set down the bags and put a friendly arm around Lizzie. "Have you fought over who gets the best bedroom yet?"

"Not exactly," Anna said. "You see, there's been a—"

But as she spoke, Lizzie pivoted, walked over to a small window in the thick wall, framed by a pair of cornflower blue wooden shutters, and peered in. Effie and Anna saw her suddenly grow rigid and still as she took in the Hall. "No—"

The exclamation came quickly: a sharply exhaled breath, as though she were winded by the sight of what was inside. Of the decorations, the sparkle, the promised conviviality. Of the setup, a carefully stage-managed scene, waiting for a troupe of players to arrive. The cast had returned from their coffee breaks, but they had suddenly been assigned different roles. Now none of them knew their lines, nor where they were supposed to be standing at curtain up.

"Is this some kind of joke?" Lizzie cried as she crossed to where the others had gathered at the doors and jostled them aside. "How could this happen?"

She stood in the center of the archway, her shadow long across the cool flagstones she might have danced on.

Lizzie's wedding breakfast had been laid out in scrupulous, immaculate, tasteful—*so tasteful*—detail. The former bride was silent for a moment before the tears came, and when they did, they were the ugly, guttural sobs Effie knew so well. Yet when Effie stepped forward to offer some comfort, Lizzie shrugged her off. Her sadness was tinged with what looked like a sort of fury, her blindsided shock a wellspring of emotion.

"We canceled this!" she shrieked, sobbing even harder. As she lifted her hands to her face, as if to veil herself from the view, Effie noticed that Lizzie was still wearing her engagement ring. "We canceled all of it!"

She looked hard at Ben, and Effie shifted uneasily on her feet next to him with the thought that, between them—distracted by each other as they had been—they might have left some crucial element of the day un-revoked, un-refunded. Un-canceled.

Stemming tears and providing a soft cushion for spiky indignation was now as much a habit for Anna as arguing a case in court; she offered her embrace to Lizzie so instinctively that the tear-smudged woman accepted it before her temper could get the better of her.

"Go and get her stuff from the car, Steve," Anna asked her husband softly, her earlier flintiness with him worn down by the damp emotion seeping into her cheesecloth blouse.

Charlie had the good grace to back off and take Iso with him, giving Lizzie the space to cry it out and calm down. Together the two of them wandered to the edge of the bank that led down to the pool.

Effie and Anna helped their friend inside. Sniffing now, and juddering softly with the hiccuping coughs of pain's aftermath, Lizzie cast her eyes over the unwanted splendor as they passed through it on the way to the stone staircase that led to the bedrooms.

"I canceled this," she whispered again, Effie and Anna on either side of her, as they wove through the choreography of a party as yet un-thrown.

The centuries-old stairs were worn smooth and bowed in the middle. In another life, Lizzie would have appeared at the top of them alongside Dan before dinner, one hand looped through his arm, a posy of meadow flowers in the other, wearing her ivory gown and a serene smile.

As salt from Lizzie's cheeks dripped onto the treads as they climbed, Effie reflected that she did not have much advice to give. What had she learned in the past six months to keep the sadness at bay, other than to ensure that any wine bottle in the vicinity was as empty as she felt?

It gets easier? *It doesn't.*

Time is the best healer? *But the most bitter medicine.*

You'll meet someone else? *But also, maybe not?*

Effie wondered guiltily whether Ben would manage downstairs in her absence, then caught herself: he would be fine; he was a confident, well-mannered grown-up—the very opposite of James.

At the top of the stairs, the three women emerged into a long, terra-cotta-tiled corridor of bedrooms with whitewashed walls and small mullioned windows. Pushing at the first wooden door they came to, they were greeted by a scene worthy of a brochure: all soft white drapes and Carrara marble, complete with four-poster bed and a scattered welcoming of red rose petals across the pristine coverlet. Effie had unwittingly led them into the bridal suite, fully prepped for the happy couple's first night as husband and wife.

"Oh Christ," muttered Anna, and Lizzie breathed raggedly out, jaw set, her neck tense and veined, her body rigid, like that of an animal sensing the crosshairs trained on it. Anna redoubled the support around Lizzie's waist and continued their progress along the hallway.

On the bride's other side, Effie braced her portion of Lizzie's weight and, with it, something like guilt. Guilt for having been so pleased to arrive here with Dan's best man, guilt at not having told Lizzie about him sooner. But Lizzie hadn't been angry with her, Effie told herself, she'd just been surprised—and, now, was drained by the shock of the setup in the Hall. Effie remembered her own bittersweet feeling when she had heard the news that Charlie had finally found love—it was hard to celebrate someone else's happiness from the depths of despair.

The second door they reached yielded a smaller double bedroom, with a carved wooden bed that was still canopied but less ritualistically dressed than the last. Provençal ocher and ceramic blue danced in wreaths along its curtains; a spindled chair sat against one wall next to a simple wooden wardrobe. It was a lovely room, Effie noted almost dispassionately as they entered: sympathetically refurbished, sophisticated but not too flashy. Authentically local-feeling, a replica in soft furnishings of the entire holiday pretense—a rustic make-believe with AC units and electric cooktops—of living like early modern villagers in these parts for a week.

She wondered how long it had been since these old walls had contained as much anguish.

"This will do," Lizzie managed, and unfolded herself from their care. She went to the window, a tall oblong set in foot-thick ancient stone, opened it, and unlatched the external shutters, then quickly creaked them closed against the warm sunshine outside. The transition in the room to total darkness was so sudden Effie had to grope along the rough wall for the main light switch.

By the time she found it and pooled the room in yellow glow once more, Lizzie had moved back toward them.

"Lizzie . . . ?" Effie began nervously.

But Lizzie only rummaged in her handbag where it lay on the chair, addressing them both without looking up.

"I'm just going to go to bed," she said wearily. A metallic crackle announced that she had found a blister pack of pills. Popping two out, Lizzie turned her apologetic face, blotched with unhappiness and drawn with fatigue, to the two other women. "These will see me through until morning, and I'll deal with it all then."

When neither Effie nor Anna moved, she spoke again, quietly and more firmly, but her manner was also less jagged: "Please. I'm fine. I just need to sleep now."

Effie remembered another time, years ago, when she had left Lizzie to rest, after stroking the hair from her feverish forehead as she settled, her heart tugging at the pain contorting her friend's lovely young face.

There was little for it but to leave her once again to the warm tide of the tablets she had taken. One foot numb, then the other, followed by a cozy sensation of being beyond caring anymore. An attitude that would rise up through the torso like a blanket tucked in by a watchful mother, soothe the ache in her chest like a longed-for embrace. Effie had also taken comfort in it; the gradual slowing of the whirring cogs in her mind, whether with a few drinks or a couple of heavy-duty painkillers left over from a nasty ankle sprain the year before, had been a highlight of most days for her until recently.

Halfway down the stairs, at around the point Lizzie and her father might have stopped to pose for the photographer, Effie heard the click, not of a camera shutter but of the bedroom light switch, as their friend retreated into the darkness.

9.

Anna

Outside, the late afternoon sun still twinkled jauntily—insistently, like a drunk friend who didn't know when to leave—on the perfectly arrayed scene below.

"Any idea who we ring to sort this out?" Anna asked as she trailed after Effie through the trappings of the phantom wedding breakfast.

"Not really," Effie replied, eyeing the lavish settings with regret. "Lizzie's right—we already canceled it all once. I suppose we could try Dan? Bad enough that she has to deal with it—I don't really want to bother him as well . . ."

It wouldn't be an easy call, Anna thought, as she pulled her mobile from her pocket and stepped over the threshold, outside into the sun. *No signal.* However they fixed the mess, it wouldn't be by phone—not from here, at least.

The two women walked the wrong way down the aisle and crossed the terrace toward the steps to the pool where Charlie, Iso, Ben, and Steve occupied four of the sun loungers that lined one edge of the lapping azure water. As Effie drew close, Ben stood up, then hesitated, still a little awkward about how to greet her in front of her friends. She headed for the point where his chest melted into one of his strong arms, and when she reached it, he crooked it around her in response.

On the slatted square table between Charlie and Iso's recliners stood an open bottle of champagne, green glass beading with condensation in the sunshine, its contents already carefully shared out between six crystal flutes sourced from the *placements* inside.

"Seemed a shame not to put it to good use," Charlie called to them as they approached.

He and Iso had scoped out the kitchen that lay to the back of the Great Hall and come across an anteroom piled high with box upon box of supplies for the wedding: bottles of the grape and grain variety, great bales of party food, one fridge stocked as though a hungry army were scheduled to pass through, another full of chilling bottles, their round, green bottoms facing out in uniform rows.

From the ground by the side of his sunbed, Charlie lifted a plate of cold meats in greeting. The local earthenware was hand-painted with bucolic dancing figures and fruits in stages from lusciously ripe to deliquescent, its surface fanned with slices of *saucisson, crudo* ham, and varieties of cheese so hyperlocal they practically counted as next-door neighbors.

Anna felt a familiar swell of authoritarianism rise within her and, with it, an annoyance that even without her child, it was still as much a part of her daily routine as brushing her hair. She ground her teeth—of course it would fall to her to explain to them that this really was not on. That the setup had been in error and was therefore not to be abused as a freebie. That the best-laid plans had been carefully undone with tears and regret, emails sent in sad resignation, the alcohol budget refunded and reallocated. That the food and drink indoors—enough for five times their number—were not to pass their lips but to be handed dutifully back to whoever had provided it in error for a wedding that was no longer happening. Of course she would have to be the party pooper once again.

Anna had noticed, since she had become the only mother among her university friends, that she had taken on, along with the unasked-for and often uncomfortable mantle of Responsible Adult, the role of a sort of bellwether for bad behavior in her friends—rare though it was that she was out late enough to witness it these days. On Sunday afternoons, the gauge for whether a second pint would be replaced with a third. At the end of a dinner party, whether the dessert forks would be swapped for taxis home or for rolled notes. If the latter, as the night descended with Anna having neither partaken nor scolded those who had, she would invariably become the subject of ever more anxious and apologetic, placatory looks cast in her direction.

It was as though she were an elderly relative or some kind of religious icon whose beatific visage might crack at the merest suggestion of sin.

"It's because you're a lawyer!" Steve would prod her when she complained about always having to be the sensible one.

"No," she always replied, shortly, her jaw set in irritation at being rendered everybody else's Plimsoll line for squareness. "It's because I'm a *mother*."

And he would do his sacred martyr impression at her—the same one he did when she sighed too loudly over the washing up: hands mock-clasped in prayer, eyes lifted to the heavens—until she cracked a smile. Which seemed to take longer and longer these days.

Anna looked at her husband now, eyes closed on the next sunbed along, his fingers laced across the stomach beneath his faded rock band T-shirt—softer now than in years before, like hers—and his skinny legs crossed in front of him. Steve could fall asleep anywhere. He regularly did so on the floor of the nursery while gently shushing a chatty Sonny back to drowsiness in the middle of the night, to the effect that Anna usually had to step over—and take over from—his inert form.

Anna stayed resolutely silent. Her noiselessness prompted Steve to open one eye, as if in expectation of chilly disapproval.

On the sunbed next door to his, Iso—already accessorized with a fizzing glass, round John Lennon sunglasses, and a lazy smile—had managed to change into a bikini with impressive alacrity. It wasn't, as Anna had assumed it might be, the sort of swimwear earned in the gym and woven from dental floss, but a sophisticated black two-piece, high of knicker in a retro Bettie Page style, with a plain bandeau top knotted into a twist at the front.

Not as tarty as I thought it'd be. Just as stunning as I expected though.

"Do you really think we should be . . . ?" It was Effie who said it in the end, and Anna's heart leaped: a rare chance to play good cop in her designated role as one half of the fun police.

But Effie's concern was not for the invoices as yet unsigned nor the deposits that might be unreturnable in the event of their indulgence, Anna realized. Her worries were for Lizzie, dosed into docility indoors.

"I mean, isn't it a bit harsh? To be glugging the stuff we were supposed to be cheers-ing her with?" she finished hesitantly, wringing her hands in an effort, Anna thought, not to grab the nearest flute and swiftly drain it.

Guilt flitted across Iso's features like the shadows of the clouds across the valley floor below them, and she looked at the glass in her hand as though it were tainted, then glanced at Charlie for reassurance.

Charlie sat up and removed his own sunglasses. "I wasn't about to suggest a toast!" He looked pained. "But there's absolutely stacks of it in there. They aren't going to miss a couple of bottles. And besides, it's our holiday too."

The blunt narcissism of the self-righteous was weapon enough to cudgel Anna's misgivings into silence. She had been waiting long enough for this break, and how often was it—*after all*—that the mother of a toddler found herself next to a pool, totally unencumbered, with an endless supply of free champagne at her disposal? She could excuse practically anything on those grounds.

Was she really prepared to reason herself out of enjoying her holiday, just because her better judgment told her to? Anna spent the greater part of her working days listening to the old men of the judiciary hand down their reasoned opinions—surely she was allowed to disregard the spinning arrow of her moral compass on holiday.

"That food'll only go off in the heat if we leave it," Steve volunteered, sipping from his own flute and winking at his wife.

He has a point.

Anna and Effie looked at each other, one stern-faced but her severity melting away like the droplets coursing down the side of the green bottle in front of them, the other already shrugging a half-apology for what she knew she was about to do.

Effie reached a slender wrist over to the table where the glasses stood, took one and passed it to Anna, then picked up another for herself. She raised the honey-colored liquid so that it filtered the warm Luberon sunshine onto her face into an even deeper gold.

Lizzie's sadness was not hers to wallow in; Anna had come away in order to feel better about her own life too. She proposed the toast to herself and her future privately, silently, and drank deep, the warmth on her skin replicated in her throat, her stomach, her heart as the champagne worked its magic.

10.

Lizzie

My friends never even knew anything was wrong.

That wasn't exactly new. Effie and I had kept what happened at university from Anna for years—were *still* keeping it from her. Not because I thought she would have done any differently or told me and Effie not to do it, but because I couldn't bear her judging me for it. The sense of fairness that runs through her like words in a stick of rock wouldn't have been able to simply tell me that it was okay, that I'd only done what I'd needed to, and that Effie had, too. And unfortunately, that was all I was capable of hearing back then.

Anna had studied Law—a big, solid hulking course that spread across her daylight hours like the giant tomes she so often had cascading over the desk in her student room—while Effie and I had done English, an altogether more ethereal sort of studying that also involved lots of books but focused more on the abstract discussion of them. Over coffee, perhaps, or cake. Discussions we had in cafés, on the sofas in our shared set of rooms with cigarettes nipped between our fingers. On the green banks of the river where the columns of our college mirrored dapples of sunshine on the water. Discussions that often weren't really about the books at all in the end but about music, clothes, films, boys.

To put it bluntly, Anna had to go to lectures, and we didn't. She had to get up early every morning, and we didn't.

By the time we met up with her again for dinner every night, Effie and I would have had a whole day together. Sometimes we'd go shopping, others we'd drink cocktails—lurid pink ones that were in fashion at the time because well-dressed New Yorkers ordered them on TV. That's why Anna never knew about what happened: because it took root late at night and unfurled during the day. By the time it had run its course, we were all sitting our finals and there was no point dwelling on it anymore.

After the engagement party—oh God, the engagement party—I knew I must have been behaving strangely, because Effie—whose near-constant battle with hungover anxiety had become something of a joke since we'd all turned thirty—asked whether she'd said something that had hurt my feelings. I assured her: no, nothing to worry about. Even if she had, I wouldn't have had the spare emotion to be upset by it.

Anna looked at me as though I was letting the side down, egging me on to bitch about a wedding I was organizing as if I wanted it, even though I knew life would never be the same if it went ahead. I couldn't: if I started talking as though anything was less than perfect behind the facade, I didn't know what else might come out.

I had originally thought the wedding would fix the problem, return him to the man he'd been before; but in the run-up the threats got worse. The cruelty, the panic, the mental torture. The constant worry on the horizon. It was with me always, even when he wasn't. I realized that it always would be unless I did something about it.

That was when I stopped obeying him.

He didn't like that, me being free, making my own decisions. What he had—those pictures—no longer had the heft they might once have done. They lost their value, some of it at least. They could still wound, but they weren't terminal.

Until he told me what else he had done.

By that point I felt so dirty, so soiled by them and by him, that I didn't have much left to lose. So I canceled the wedding.

I gave it all away. The love, the trappings of it. The Big Day and the lifelong company. In exchange for my freedom. The liberty to live again. An exoneration from the worry-load of guilt I felt at having let it all happen to me. To us.

It wasn't until I saw that room, dressed and readied for the day I had convinced myself I no longer wanted, that I realized: I'd made yet another mistake.

Stupid Lizzie, caught off guard. *Again*. As if that wasn't the reason it had all kicked off in the first place.

I'd been blind time and again. Of course he wasn't going to let me go that easily.

THE
MORNING
AFTER

11.

Effie

A noise that might have come from her, but she wasn't sure. Then consciousness. But no air.

Effie's mind raced as she fought to catch her breath. Something clamped over her mouth let neither life in nor protest out, but allowed only an impotent sucking against the seal that was preventing her lungs from filling.

As her oxygen-starved semiconsciousness cast around in confusion, she dragged her eyelids open to a pure and bright white light so intense it was more feeling than sight.

I must be dead.

So why am I still in such pain?

Effie wiped her face with a heavy, sleep-numbed hand and peeled from her cheek warm flakes of skin that tore off in great layers and then clung to the ends of her fingers. One further clumsy swipe and cool air rushed into her open mouth and dry, desperate throat in a gasp that sounded like a horror movie corpse being reanimated. She was not dead; every fuzzy and frayed nerve ending spoke of how alive she was.

Alive—and in a state of terrible, terrible suffering.

There was more skin peeling from her bare arms and legs, flaking off and bubbling as if from giant sores.

What the—

Effie shook the bridal suite rose petals from her hands and brushed them off her chest, her cheeks. The one that had stoppered her mouth as effectively as any gag lay on the pillow next to her, damp and crumpled.

Oh Christ.

Effie had had mornings like this before, where the weight of existence took a demi-second before reattaching itself, and she experienced a momentary lightness—the brief float of a sheet being shaken out and straightened in midair above a bed before it gently kisses the mattress once more. Then—the reserves of optimism emptied, the well of memory refilled—Effie's earthly heaviness would resume.

It had been at its most intense right after James had left, when her old life still existed as living history in the borrowed moments between sleeping and waking, before she remembered he had gone. As she outgrew them, the thump back down to earth grew less bone-shattering with every day; with Ben by her side, waking up was no longer anything to fear.

Except he wasn't next to her this morning.

Without moving her pounding head, Effie pieced together the room. White sheets, white canopy, white walls. White light gleaming in shafts through the windows—she must have left them unshuttered. A white bridal suite, for a white wedding that hadn't happened.

How had she ended up in here?

Her mouth was dry, her tongue a rubber bath mat suckered to its roof. Her eyes felt gritty, and her vision swam with pressure flecks when she rubbed at them. Day-old mascaraed lashes cracked and broke clean off under the friction of her fists. Effie's joints ached; her limbs were heavy. Her heart, tentatively stretching itself awake for the day, returned to its senses and sank that little bit lower into her chest when it, too, realized just how hungover she was.

Effie looked around herself at a too-familiar scene: yesterday's clothes piled on the floor next to the bed, flung there as an indistinct consequence of actions that she knew, logically, must have happened in order for the garments to have ended up where they had, but one that she couldn't quite remember being active in. Imagine, yes, but not remember.

In the last six months she had sometimes lurched awake in rooms with the knowledge that something had happened there—an abstract sense of past action, lingering like the final note sung by a lone voice—but no further details. Sometimes there were showreels, teasers almost, to accompany the rooms: flashes of time out of sequence for her to attempt to edit into a narrative. Tears. Fury. Blinkered first-person perspectives of shouting and laughing, their sound muted and the words muffled. Brief and blurry glimpses of light switches, bathroom tiles, faces, mouths. Crying. Retching.

And there were the rooms she woke up in alone, but with the feeling that someone had recently absented themselves, like the March Hare dashing off. A scent, perhaps, or an abandoned item of clothing—a tie, a sock, a cuff link. And a humming, a thrumming; a guilty throbbing or dull, insistent ache between her legs that she felt she could not possibly have signed up for in those moments of half-life, given that she sometimes awoke knowing neither where or even who she was anymore—nor who she had been with—but which she had more than likely invited or embarked upon willingly enough before the blackout curtain fell mid-act.

No, I don't do that anymore.

Nevertheless, Effie eyed the dent in the pillow next to the one her head was resting on. A crater in the linen that contained within a few stray hairs—short, dark; *dark?*—and an empty glass on the bedside table adjacent to it. And then she remembered— some, not all.

Drinks by the pool. *More* drinks by the pool. At some point, drinks in the pool; at another, music. Indoors now and laughter. Swaying to a beat, now spinning, and then collapsing. Words of comfort, screeches of hilarity, then darkness and now here. At Lizzie's wedding.

How much did I drink?

Stuttering into life, Effie raised herself on bony elbows and saw her skinny naked body reflected in a ghoulish pale blue against the white, white sheets and under the harsh tones of morning in this white, white room. Her hip bones rose like sleigh rails on either side of the empty stomach slung taut between them. James used to cup the one closest to him in his palm as she woke up. "Too nobbly," he'd say, when she was working too hard and eating too little. They were sharper now than they ever had been.

"Ben?" she tried to ask the room, but her throat was too dry to disturb the silence.

Water.

Effie swung her feet to the floor and stood, allowing the room a moment to finish swaying around her before she took her first steps. She hooked her feet back into yesterday's skirt and T-shirt, pulled them up and over her, then walked slowly—padding and plodding as though bowed by age or infirmity rather than the stacking sensation of shame upon shame that she was beginning to feel—out of the room and onto the terra-cotta-tiled landing.

The house was silent but for the holiday half-sound of light cotton curtains swirling on currents of warm air as it met the building's ancient coolness. A door creaked somewhere in a breeze, the sonorous timbre of mature timber only ever heard in old buildings, across flagged floors with no plush carpets to guzzle up the noise. Outside, the tinkling hum of a garden sprinkler puttering water across the lawn to quench its thirst and the low, long-distance hum of an engine in motion—a lawnmower, Effie assumed before remembering that she was no longer in the city. A tractor, then, or an airplane, something mechanical whose buzz and drone matched precisely the one beginning to kick in at the point where her skull sat on the stem of her neck.

She approached the top of the stairs, moving gingerly with her head down, shoulders hunched against the day and its insistence on time passing as usual despite a slowness she felt emanating from her very bones. The ancient coldness of the stone steps seeped through the bamboo soles of her flip-flops, and when she looked up and over the balustrade into the Hall, she wondered, briefly, whether she was looking at a scene from its past, some great and boisterous banquet abandoned by lords and ladies long finished their wassailing.

The two tables that ran the length of the large room were strewn with the wreckage of festivities—dishes started but not finished, dobs of cream and sauce all over. Glasses lay upended on them; the many empty bottles that hadn't smashed had rolled and come to a stop on their sides in the channels on either side between them and the thick stone walls. One of the benches had been knocked over and left lying where it fell; a smashed vase and the wildflowers it had contained lay not far off. The tablecloth hung asymmetrically, as if grabbed on the way down, a magic trick aborted.

Farther along the length of the room, one of the elaborate freestanding candelabra ringed with brass sconces leaned drunkenly against the sandy-toned stone wall, its candles melted down haphazardly and standing askew like crooked teeth. A few yards away, another lay on its side, ivory wax cooled into fragile stalactites where it had spilled from the holders.

The trellis arch stood firm over the double doors, but the flowers that had yesterday sprung from it in beauty now hung blowsily down, their fullness pointing at the steps below as if avoiding eye contact.

Effie took the final few stairs into the Hall slowly, absorbing the mess with eyes that were wide yet bleary and panda-rimmed with sleep-smudged makeup. As her foot connected with the floor at the bottom, there was a loud clanging noise, like a metal gong from within a doorway just a few yards beyond where she stood—the kitchen.

If she had seen the room before now, she had no memory of the occasion. A high-ceilinged stone space that was part rustic pantry and part luxury condo, with wooden pulleys that dripped bundles of fresh and drying herbs alongside an eight-hob range of the sort TV chefs practice posing in front of. Leaning on it with his back to the doorway in which Effie stood, still and cautious, was Charlie. His dark head was bowed and his breathing labored; each exhalation ended with a small moan—whether of pain or sorrow, Effie could not tell.

As she stepped into the room, slowly and feebly, her foot connected with an empty wine bottle. It spun on the floor with a grating clatter before slowing to a halt along a line as straight as any arrow, pointing directly at the man its disturbance had frightened so much he had leaped several feet and turned, apparently in midair, to face the intruder.

Charlie's face crimsoned from ashen to puce and then settled into a pale shade of green. "Oh, it's only you," he groaned weakly, swallowing thickly in a way Effie recognized to be a precursor of a day's worth—or more—of drinking-related illness.

A beat then, and his face colored again—briefly this time, like the dimming of a bulb whose glow falters momentarily—before he spoke, gruff now and self-conscious.

"Look, Effie, there's no need to mention—"

"Oh my God!" went up the cry—Lizzie's cry—in the Hall, and the two of them sprang toward the door. The instinctive movement left them both reeling against its frame as their heavy bodies caught up with sprightly reflexes honed in the years before they had ever really felt their hangovers.

"What the fuck?!"

Lizzie stood at the top of the flight of stairs that led into the Hall, her white cotton nightgown a mockery of the dress she should have worn to survey the room. Her bird's-nest hair suggested deep but tormented sleep. Her arms were crooked in question marks by her sides, her fingers spread wide, claw-like.

She looks like a horror movie prom queen.

"What the fuck, guys?" She sounded broken, but her face was savage with rage. "Why would you—? How could you have . . ."

Effie followed Lizzie's glistening, tear-filled eyes as they traveled around the room and could see that her friend felt its ravishing like a physical blow.

"My wedding, this was my fucking wedding," she continued, clarion sharp against the silence of the others. "The one I had to cancel, the one that has broken my fucking heart! Could you really not have restrained yourselves?"

Effie understood only too well that the destruction of the tableau stood as a leitmotif for the emotional turmoil within. Her own flat had been a mausoleum of pain after James; she refused to wash his coffee cup for a month, had preserved his clothes in the heaps he'd left until he came to collect them. She'd slept in a T-shirt of his until Anna pointed out that she was trying to have sex with a ghost. Now here was Lizzie, phantom bride at a *Mary Celeste* of a reception. As she surveyed the scene, she clawed at the place on her chest where her heart was, as though trying to dig it out and stop the pain.

"I haven't even got the refunds back yet," she said, quieter now, voice deadened by the weight of realization dawning. "I probably won't now. Do you know how much this will cost? You're like a bunch of sodding teenagers. You just don't give a shit, do you? Did you just decide to have my wedding without me?"

Shamed, Effie scanned the room once more. She hadn't noticed, on first dull-eyed inspection, that in among the listing lamps and spilled drinks were the usual marital rites the guests might have reasonably expected during their stay at the Oratoire for Lizzie and Dan's nuptials.

Now she saw that the tiered white cake had been cut into and a thick, solitary slice extracted; the bone-handled knife used in the disfigurement lay discarded nearby. Effie realized that the floor was scattered with what she had at first glimpse assumed to be rubbish but could now tell was a sprinkling of dried petals—the petals left out in baskets as confetti. Some way off, behind the altar on the terrace outside—in the middle of an aisle now obstructed by knocked and fallen chairs that had meant to accommodate another eighty or so guests staying in the town at the bottom of the hill—a bundle of carefully selected and deliberately folksy-looking wildflowers lay on the stone flags. Surrounding it were several dead heads and petals that it had shed on impact, as if hurled.

Lizzie's bouquet.

Beyond the back row of chairs, Anna had been standing silently on the terrace, eyes closed and chin tilted, bathing her face in the morning sunshine. As voices rose within, her lids snapped open and she strode back toward them, twisting through the melee of chairs and through the open doors. Her capable, toddler-strengthened arms were folded across the white cotton T-shirt she wore with a pair of navy shorts. She looked considerably less haunted than the rest of them, Effie thought, as Anna took in the scene with the detachment of somebody not appraising it for the first time.

"Lizzie, I—," Effie began confidently enough, then halted, as if suddenly chastened. "I'm so, so sorry."

From the other end of the terrace, climbing the steps that led from the swimming pool, Ben loped toward the open doors. He wore the same clothes as yesterday and an expression of sore confusion that seemed etched into his face as though onto a statue. His feet were bare, his lips slightly gray.

Effie dragged herself from Charlie's side in the lee of the kitchen doorway along one wall to approach Lizzie. She walked bowed, with the morning's weakness but also in penance, regret.

On the opposite side of the room, the altar stood, framed by the doorway, still serene and seemingly undisturbed by the chaos surrounding it. A tide of spilled . . . something had licked around its wooden base, but it stood otherwise untouched, upright in the morass like the crow's nest on a sinking ship.

A rustling sound came from one of the open doorways at the other end of the Hall. Steve made his entrance, bare-chested with his lower half wrapped in a purple towel, blinking himself awake and into daylight with what looked like a difficulty similar to that which Effie had experienced upstairs. His eyes tracked guiltily to Anna by the altar, her face pulled into the sort of wordless query only couples can exchange.

She stood behind the podium, stony-faced. In front of her, the teak shelf was empty—the thick-paged guest book now lay at a drunken angle on the long table nearest to where Effie stood, hunched and swaying slightly. The pair of golden rings that had sat in its crease and caught the sun yesterday—*was it really only yesterday?*—were gone.

Shouldn't Dan have had the rings ahead of the ceremony?

The thought was so fleeting, given what Effie's eyes took in next, that she never voiced it, had forgotten it in the time it took her to breathe. On the textured vellum of the wedding book, somebody had entered the first and only message in celebration of the wedding that hadn't happened. Block capitals, tidy but arresting, in the black ink of the Sharpie left for precisely that purpose, and in the purposeful handwriting of a "Back in five minutes" shop sign, a "Deliveries round the back" note: functional, anonymous. Which made what it said even more strange.

Effie blinked. She rolled her vision over the square letters once more, noting the varying gaps between them, the seasick slant of the lines that gave away the late, lush hour at which they were written. She felt a butterflying nervousness settle into her stomach. It mixed there with the resident nausea into a gluey, anxious curdle.

"'Congratulations,'" she croaked. "'You deserve each other.'"

As she read the message aloud—more in an attempt to disprove the fruits of her own literacy than to alert anyone else as to the book's contents—Iso appeared in the doorway behind Steve.

Luminous, tanned, and glamorous in even a state of bedhead—the edge only slightly taken off her sleekness with a telltale smearing of eye makeup just like Effie had woken up with—she was clad in a matching shade of lavender beach towel to Steve's, wrapped around the middle of her from sternum to upper thigh, and nothing else. As she heard Effie mouth the words into existence, her dull and semi-somnolent expression leaped into fresh urgency. In its wake came the seconds-later reverb of creakiness and pain that Effie and Charlie had experienced in the kitchen.

"Did someone get married last night?" Iso croaked.

The woman's every move was followed by almost a million people, but Effie could see that the most recent activity, like her own, had failed to upload. The young "influencer" was experiencing a Page Not Found moment, a 404 error message in the depths of her brain. She put one hand to the top of her head, as if that might stop the pulse there beating like a Taiko drummer, scrunched her thick dark hair in a fist, and looked at her other hand, clenching the purple towel to her otherwise naked body, as she noticed Steve similarly wrapped next to her.

"Oh my God." Iso's voice was a rusty gear in need of oiling. "Did *we* get married?"

12.

Anna

Iso's words hung in the Hall like confetti above their—*aching*—heads, then fell to earth not with the picturesque quality of the floral gauntlet that each new couple runs after their ceremony but with something rather more like the reality of it. On every nuptial showreel, in between the smiling shots harvested for the albums, the silver frames, the profile pictures, are the unfortunate stills where the well-meaning blizzard dive-bombs the bride's and groom's eyes and clogs their throats like a cloud of Highland midges.

Across the room, Anna saw Charlie's face crumple in confusion. At the other end of it, her husband stood rigidly beneath the stone arch of the doorway and trained his unblinking eyes on the woman he had promised never to forsake for anyone else, whose forehead he had cooled with flannels for two days during childbirth, whose subsequent pelvic-floor issues he knew like an old friend, whose salary paid two-thirds of his mortgage every month.

She knew Steve couldn't really have married a complete stranger—on holiday, with no vicar, no celebrant, no certificate—but, for once, it wasn't the legal issues Anna was sifting through. No, it was everything else that might have happened. The thought of Steve pretending to marry another woman—even as a joke—was almost as horrifying to Anna as the idea that he might potentially have consummated this new union while in the haze of more free alcohol than he had seen at even the biggest rock band's album launch.

Just as she knew that Steve's hands would be clammy and cold right now, Anna also knew how he often had to grapple with big, not-quite-memorable nights upon waking, had sometimes been forced to ask colleagues and friends to fill in the blanks—who hadn't? But those blanks had never before contained quite so much potential. Everything she had suspected him of doing with Celia—things they had not done together for so long—Anna now pictured happening with Iso, and her own hands began to tremble.

Anna thought once more of their wedding day as she weighed Iso's question in the balance, set the beautiful young woman's words against the ballast of Steve's horrified expression and dumbstruck pose. He had been in tears as he'd made his vows to her, even though he was the one who spent his life propping her up and soothing her fears. When it came to it, she had remained dry-eyed in the face of her usually lighthearted husband's own emotional collapse.

She was tearless now too, but inside she felt like a crumbling building, as though great chunks of masonry were falling away from her core. She had thought they might revisit some version of their youth on this holiday, had hoped that whatever fiction she had created between her husband and the woman who texted him late at night had been just that. But if Steve could wake up naked with someone he had only just met, there was little doubt where he had already smoothed away the sharper edges of his conscience: number 68. Celia's house. The final bricks holding Anna up crashed down within her.

Is this how betrayal feels?

In response to the apparent infidelity unfolding in front of the fragile audience members—*unfolding like a loosely wrapped beach towel*—Anna could only summon a great and primordial weariness. It was one she could no longer remember being without. There was a certain "dust to dust" inevitability to Steve cheating on her: the reflexive disappointment that being with a man—any man—eventually came to, because they were all so consistently untrustworthy.

When did I become so cynical?

"Errr, no?" When Steve finally answered Iso's question, he sounded high-pitched and strangled, like the time he'd forgotten to set up the direct debit for Sonny's nursery fees and their son had been barred from daycare for a week. A week that, because Steve had been away at a festival for his music magazine, Anna had had to cover at the last minute, a week of trial by toddler as well as by jury.

Seeing him there with Iso, Anna weighed the endless drudgery of care and career that was her constant companion against her husband's consistent ability to shrug off that burden and wear the guise of his younger years without it pulling or digging in the way all her own clothes did. She felt her heart wither toward him, wondered whether he might actually have broken it beyond despair and beyond repair.

Still, Anna's skeptical nature couldn't quite believe that the worst had happened. She knew only too well how her husband wore his guilt: Steve was not in repentant mode but enervated—and rightly so—by the prospect that his wife would be angry with him regardless. He and Iso clearly hadn't got married, but what else had they been up to, with their matching hangovers and coordinating nudity?

"It would be more convincing if you hadn't framed your denial as a question, Steve," Anna replied, unfolding her arms and stepping slowly over the threshold into the bedraggled Hall.

13.

Effie

Christ, imagine being married to a barrister.

Effie felt Steve's regret and damp-palmed confusion as if it were her own. Her stomach heaved at the palpable awkwardness that now permeated the space like some kind of unwanted, cloying room spray. Yesterday it had been coming off only her and Lizzie; now, it seemed, everyone had had a squirt of the tester.

Steve cleared his throat. "No, look, Anna, *of course* we haven't got married. Don't be ridiculous, I would never—I wouldn't— Look, we just didn't. . . . Nothing happened, okay?"

That he could barely look at his wife was an unfortunate by-product of her standing with the day's bright sunshine behind her rather than shame or mendacity, but he seemed aware, as he blinked his eyes to the floor once more, that it didn't look good.

"Then who wrote the note? And why?" Charlie asked weakly.

By the table, Effie stared at the letters again. No identifying curlicues or tells, just incontrovertible black on white. Nobody raised a hand or spoke to claim them.

She looked around the room.

Lizzie was asleep and Anna must have gone to bed too.

Steve and Iso are both naked under those towels.

Effie glanced over at Ben, who stood queasily just beyond the

Hall, bracing himself against one of the paned French doors and shivering.

Ben genuinely looks like he might have slept outside.

She swallowed drily, thinking of the flashes of memory, the blank spots in her timeline. The dent next to her in the bed. Dark hairs, not blond. Not the hair of the man she had brought here in the hope of cementing whatever it was they had together—the thing that had given her reason to smile again.

What have I done?

"Look," she said feebly, "it doesn't actually mean anything happened." Effie took in the scene again: the cake, the bouquet, the bottles, the glasses, and the smeared plates. "We clearly just . . . overdid it." And she steadied herself with one hand on the table-top.

"Well, thanks a lot, guys," Lizzie said, the pitch of her voice high and ragged: a semi-scream that came from the gut. "I came here to try and get away from all this . . . *shit*"—she gestured at the tables, the food, the flowers, the incontrovertible fact of a wedding party well and truly thrown—"and you celebrate while I'm fucking asleep." She wiped a heavy hand across her face. "What time did you even go to bed anyway?"

"You didn't hear us come up?" Anna asked quietly.

Lizzie shook her head slowly. "Dosed up, remember."

Bed. Effie tried to remember the fact of having gone to bed, something she knew she must have done because she had woken up in one. But there was no recollection there—only a worried whirring that echoed around her head as her empty mind flicked through its Rolodex of likelihoods.

Charlie.

She felt a settling sensation in her bowels, like snow shifting in a drift. Charlie, standing only a few feet away from her, wore the tragic look of a man who knew he had let himself down. What had he said when she'd walked in on him in the kitchen? "There's no need to mention—" And then he'd been interrupted.

Charlie, who she'd known for so long, had been with once,

long ago, for a clutch of weeks that added up to just a few minutes over the life span of their friendship but that now felt more relevant than they had done in years.

Charlie, with his short, dark hair, just like the ones she'd found on the pillow next to hers. In the honeymoon suite, where the newlyweds would go after they'd been married.

Effie lifted her head where she leaned on the table and retched efficiently into the ruined plate of hors d'oeuvres nearest to her. As she wiped a long strand of bile from her chin, she caught his eye and the look was almost symbiotic. A fellow sufferer . . . and what else? He darted his pupils away before she could search his face for clues.

Lizzie was still standing at the top of the stairs, a player in the eaves waiting to be lowered into the action on a wire. Now she descended for the exposition. "What on earth did you lot do last night?"

"We had some drinks—" Charlie began.

"A lot of drinks," interrupted Effie.

"Ben kept pouring shots," Anna said, and Lizzie's expression hardened.

"We danced," murmured Iso.

"Yes! We danced!" Effie agreed, relieved to at least be able to corroborate something.

"We carried on drinking." Steve's eyes were big brown pools of contrition, directed toward Anna, his alcohol buddy and hangover soulmate for seven years who knew just how badly affected he could be by both. "What *was* that cocktail you mixed up, Ben? I felt like I was on drugs."

Ben's voice came out like a gargle of stones. "Called a shambles," he said. "Vodka, champagne, Red Bull." He shrugged guiltily. "Fun, but lethal."

"Then what?" asked Effie. Her hands and upper arms were shaking as she tried to re-tie her hair into a ponytail, away from her face, where a slick of anxious sweat was building on her forehead, the bridge of her nose, the nervous zone on her upper lip.

"Then I went to bed, you lot carried on, and whatever happened . . . happened." Anna spread her hands, waiting for them to enlighten her. "Lizzie, did you really sleep through the whole thing?"

The question almost sounded accusatory: directed at the one person who couldn't have had anything to do with their antics.

"I was out cold." She cleared her throat and shrugged her shoulders in quizzical mode. "Should I be jealous? Clearly, I didn't have half as much fun at my own wedding as you lot did."

Lizzie took a few more steps into the rubble of the night before. "You know, part of me thought you might have tidied some of this away so I didn't have to see it all again this morning. Demolishing it instead was certainly one approach."

The set of her face was frosty and thoroughly unimpressed.

Though Effie winced at the acerbic tone, Anna held Lizzie's stare for a moment, opened her mouth, and then closed it again. She tapped the fingers of one hand along her jawbone, then tried again. "Well, I think we need to contact whoever set all this up and tell them to come and collect it. Do you have their numbers?"

"I told you: we already canceled it all. Me, Dan, Effie, Ben. We called them all." Lizzie's tone was frustrated, bordering on disgust.

Anna softened and began walking toward her friend, still ignoring her husband, where he stood in the doorway to her right.

"I know," she said. "And I'm sorry. I know this must be . . . very weird. And upsetting. All our fault—we messed up. But is there somebody we can get in touch with to sort out the . . . ?" She gestured around the room. "All this?"

"I'll try Marie?" Ben spoke up, querulously, from the opposite side of the Hall. Marie was the woman Lizzie and Dan had paid to knit all the strands of their day together on the ground from her office in a nearby town. "Think I got some reception over there yesterday."

He pulled his phone from his pocket and strode farther off

across the terrace, toward where the landscape lay on the horizon.

"Should we call Dan?" Effie asked quietly.

Marie had been Dan's find, Dan's contact. Dan's responsibility on the list of things to be undone. He had been the one to call her, to explain that they wouldn't need the long list of things she had been working through for them. Lizzie hadn't been able to face it. Now she set her jaw against the specter of the man she had once wanted to grow old beside: too painful to have on this holiday, in this room, in her head.

Ben returned from the end of the terrace, shaking his head. "No answer," he called. "Barely any reception, but just enough to get her voicemail."

"Look," Anna said gently to Lizzie. "We'll get in the car, drive to the nearest village, and you can call Dan."

Both Charlie and Steve cringed at the prospect of taking the wheel in their current state. But it was Lizzie who seemed most anxious at the suggestion, and simply shook her head.

"No," she said quietly but adamantly, the haunted look returning to her pale face, the blood draining beneath the freckles. "I can't speak to him right now. Please don't make me."

Anna narrowed her eyes, but Effie moved in a few paces to stand next to the heartbroken former bride and laid an arm around her shoulders. "Don't worry, I'll call him," she offered.

14.

Anna

Anna picked up the keys to her and Steve's rental car from the terra-cotta bowl painted with gaudy ripe lemons that sat on the sideboard at one end of the cool, dark Hall, then wrested open the front door of the house, which led straight out to the limy track where the cars were parked.

Amid the wreckage of the wedding night, Anna's thoughts had found a clarity that her heart hadn't. They needed to track down this Marie person, to tidy up and to find whoever's job it was to clear and take away the bacchanalian mess, and then to sit down and thrash out among themselves what had actually taken place.

For that thrashing to happen, she would need to speak to Steve, and she found she had absolutely no wish to do so right now. Her heart, her blood, their history told her he had done nothing wrong, that he never would—and yet, he had still ended up naked with the most attractive woman either of them had encountered since their relationship had begun, seven years ago. On this, the holiday she had so hoped would bring them back together.

Out in the midmorning sunshine, Effie's pale, sweat-beaded face reminded Anna of the night Sonny had come into the world.

She had clung to Steve then as though he could stop her from passing out with the pain of it, the sensation of a drawbridge deep inside her being slowly winched open. Anna, whose medical notes declared that she had had a "normal" labor—an "easy" birth, as the doctor who had stitched her back up afterward told them (*easy for whom, exactly?*)—had looked into Steve's face with every turn of the handle within, every notch of agony, and thanked a God she didn't believe in that if she was going to die, she would do so gazing at someone she loved so much.

Hot tears formed behind Anna's eyes, and she breathed them away again. The very fact that Steve had upset her so much also cheered her.

I still have feelings for him, after all.

So Anna channeled her nervous energy—the adrenaline that was making her hands shake and her mouth dry despite constantly swallowing—into simply leaving the house and reaching the car.

Yesterday it had been a charabanc delivering them all up for a frothy excursion like exuberant day-trippers; now Anna felt she was leading Effie to it as a policeman might a criminal to the squad car. Pale and thin, Effie looked like she might need to vomit (*again*) before she climbed in. Anna benchmarked her suffering against her friend's: slight headache, potentially broken marriage, but thankfully not the sort of hangover that leaves you foaming at the mouth with every step taken.

Small mercies.

She was so focused on Effie's quaking progress toward the passenger seat that she might easily have missed him, but Effie's neck jerked so quickly at the movement she had to steady herself with one hand on the car's roof.

Ben jogged out from the Hall in their wake. "Let me come with you," he panted, the exertion having propelled some of last night's alcohol out onto his skin in boozy droplets that Anna could almost smell from where she stood. "If we're calling Dan, perhaps it's best I deal with him."

Fair enough, Anna thought as she unlocked the car.

She had expected to enjoy the stubborn refusal of their phones to register any more than half a bar of reception. The château's lack of Wi-Fi was so pronounced it had to have been deliberate, she supposed, to foster intense rest and relaxation among the Oratoire's many guests. But she felt increasingly nervous of it— she was keen to check in on Sonny at home. The house's remoteness would have been lovely had any of them felt like they were on holiday; instead, it seemed as though they were all on trial for something none of them had any memory of doing.

15.

Effie

Dan's phone was dead.

Ben listened to the high-pitched pips at the end of the line for just as long as it took Effie to realize that she no longer had the strength to hold herself upright. As he let the phone drop from his ear, she slumped forward in the passenger seat of the car.

"No answer," she panted to Anna. "Let's go back. I've got to drink some water."

"Yeah, I need to put more clothes on," said Ben, still shivering in shorts and a T-shirt in the backseat despite the brightening sunshine. "Frozen to the bone."

Anna eyeballed him in the driver's mirror.

They had driven as far as they needed to in order for his phone to grasp enough network coverage and put the call through from golden Provence to dreary London. Next to a vineyard laid out so neatly it looked like an even-handed embroidery sampler, Anna turned the car around in a lay-by and drove them back to the Oratoire.

Effie was not in such dire straits that she had forgotten to wonder whether her phone would suddenly burst into life with backed-up texts from James once it had found reception. The mania had lessened since she'd started seeing Ben, but she still spent too many days willing the screen to light up with his name out of habit.

It remained stubbornly silent but for a message from her parents asking whether she had arrived safely. Effie replied promptly; she knew they worried about how chaotic her life had become, how the stable orderliness she'd once lived by had been undone overnight like a ship overturned in a gale. She just hoped nobody at work had realized that yet. Effie loved her job, adored her girls, but she had not done them justice recently.

As Anna spun the car in a horseshoe, from one side of the road to the other, the phone in Effie's lap gave a tardy shudder.

James. She had deleted her ex-boyfriend's details from her phone, but his very facial features were visible to her in the digits she knew by heart anyway.

"Are you around for a chat? Something I need to tell you."

Effie knew her ex well enough to understand what this meant: the full stop at the end of a sentence that she had long hoped had just temporarily trailed off rather than been fully reconciled. As much as Effie might hope James was getting in touch to say he missed her, it seemed more likely he'd found a new girlfriend and was gearing up to break the news as gently as possible.

Effie couldn't speak to him there and then, not just because Ben was in the car but because Anna had driven them back into the black spot that surrounded the house for what seemed to be a two-mile radius.

She felt winded and battle-weary, but also in that moment, as the mostly empty people-carrier bounced along the stones and potholes of the dusty and otherwise deserted trail that led up to the château, strangely wired—as though she had drunk several very strong French coffees.

She had something to tell James too, she reflected, not without a rising feeling of triumph: she had a new boyfriend, after all.

16.

Eighteen Months Earlier: Lizzie

I was single for eight hours before we met. Just long enough to fly to Bangkok to begin the process of coming home—and growing up. Walking off that beach was like shedding a skin that had never really fit me properly; I was more myself the minute I took it off.

I had never really enjoyed traveling the way Guy did. I preferred my holidays finite, with the prospect of returning to real life at the end of them. I wanted a job and a home, a family. Guy said that was *bourgeois*, but I was more interested in climbing the career ladder than the rigging. People like Guy can afford to be bohemian, just like men can afford to drift along without making up their minds for significantly longer than women can.

Guy had a filthy laugh and long, dark hair like a pirate, and although the *Dark & Stormy* was no *Jolly Roger* exactly, she exerted a pull over him as strong as any mermaid. He could hear her siren call from every mid-ranking London desk job I persuaded him to try in the name of building a future together like a normal couple. But eventually, all the plans we had to save for a deposit, maybe get married, start trying for a baby were lured onto the rocks and smashed to smithereens.

I grew tired of turning up to everything alone with nothing to show for my relationship but a suntan and a new shell necklace. Tired of watching other people's lives move on, with promotions and rings, mortgages and cashmere baby bonnets, while my own life sometimes fell off the GPS tracker app Guy installed on my phone—to help us feel closer, he said—for days on end.

By the time we approached Langkawi, I'd been on the boat with Guy for a week and he'd been away—this time—for nearly two months. I watched through binoculars as on the sands, straight-backed hotel waiters in ironed shirts and pressed slacks set up yet another table for two in the low evening sun for dinner, drinks, and a proposal by candlelight. The couples dining at those tables would stagger back love-drunk to a room festooned with rose petals, not caring that this was—as Guy scoffed from his seat by the tiller—a standard romance-by-numbers package worth £85 and added to their bill at check-out, but reveling in the tangible prospect of each other, for ever after.

I knew then—although I think I had always known—that the only official certificate that would ever bind me legally to Guy was the skipper qualification I'd studied for last year.

In the end, stepping off the yacht alone and booking a flight home was the most adventurous thing I had ever done. The staff of the paradise resort Guy had dropped me at booked me a taxi to the airport while I cried in the foyer.

I felt brimming with purpose, driven to get on with the rest of my life. I suppose that's why everything happened so fast when I met the first man who happened to be wearing a suit rather than a pair of board shorts.

I landed in Bangkok in midafternoon and the next London flight left in the morning, so I followed a tide of twenty-year-olds into town and booked myself into a clean-looking hostel, the only person there with a smart wheelie suitcase rather than an unwieldy but characterful rucksack and an armful of Buddha beads. The showers didn't exactly have doors on them, but it was only a twelve-hour stay.

I decided to go on a date. With myself. A walk around the market, to enjoy being alone rather than fearing it or resenting it.

Women are taught from such a young age that their own company is always the second-best option, that dining alone is embarrassing, to be done furtively and quickly from behind a book or with headphones on. But I now know that women adopt these distractions not to hide the fact of their aloneness but to conceal it from those who enjoy disturbing them. Never other women—always men, who see our privacy as public property.

I took over for Anna often enough during her maternity leave—a few hours here or there with Sonny simply so she might spend some time by herself—to see how much of a pleasure those snatched minutes of being unaccountable were for her. I realized then that time alone is as precious as gold—it just looks shinier the less you have of it.

Once I trained myself not to cling to my phone for company in Bangkok but to look up—at the gilt on the temple roof and the gills in the fishmonger's stall—I felt more in the moment than I had done for most of mine and Guy's relationship. It is difficult to focus on going for a walk on Hackney Marshes when your heart and your other half are somewhere in the South China Sea.

Alone in the market streets of Bangkok, I watched crabs climb over each other in hollow polystyrene bricks, jumped out of the way of tuk-tuks, and graciously accepted a garland of flowers over my head but declined the lurid green liquid that came with it. I breathed deep the smell of rotten eggs, petrol, and fish guts and, somehow, felt cleansed.

After about an hour, I downloaded a dating app. I know. But I'd had a couple of beers in a rickety lean-to bar, buzzing with younger, hairier backpackers in their sociable, enviable groups. I don't think I really meant to meet anyone; I was simply exploring the potential. Scrolling through my possibilities felt a more exotic proposition in the spicy hubbub of the Khao San Road than I knew they would from the sofa in my flat, tabbing between men who would probably ghost me and my local pizza delivery service. Besides, all these men were based in Thailand, and I'd had my fill of long-distance love.

I just wanted to see what I might be missing out on.

I chose a picture for my profile and carefully cropped Guy out of it. I flicked through lives like I was dealing cards, a croupier on a bamboo stool. Barely pausing for any of them, I realized that the fascination was not in the caliber but the quantity. It was like reading the phone book, but with pictures.

"Laughter," "fun," "socializing"—were any of these really hobbies? Yet more dispiriting: "protein." Things that seemed to me to be fundamental at best were touted as talents or achievements. Jobs became characteristics, personality types reduced to bare chests. "Enjoys food," another profile said, but didn't we all? Was this what I'd given up my pirate for—a future full of men with smiles like party tricks for whom it was enough to eat and commute? Then again: Wasn't this exactly what I had wanted Guy to do?

It didn't take long for me to close the app in desolation at the dregs it offered up, and begin to reminisce over the better times I'd had with Guy. Fat tears dripped into my straw-colored lager.

And then a little *ping*. A light on the screen I had just turned over in disgust. A wink across a room: a match. Or at least the offer of one.

Tapping through to the profile, I noted bright eyes and a smile. A rare clothed torso, and a name, an age. "I came for the cocktails and stayed for the corporate lifestyle," the tagline read. It ended with a little forehead-slapping emoji: "Doh!"

A joke! And a funny one! Sarcasm seemed to be an endangered species among this live-laugh-love-and-eat-food cohort. I clicked back to confirm the match immediately, and he messaged me right away—a whole stream of comments, popping onto my screen like bubbles in a glass of champagne.

-Hi! I know everyone says they don't normally do this, but I really don't. You seem different from the usual crowd on here though?

-I hope that doesn't sound creepy

-Oh God, it does doesn't it?

-How about just: would you like to go for a drink?

-(sorry)

I laughed aloud, but everyone else around me was either arm-wrestling or doing shots or some contorted combination of the two, and my peal of delight went unnoticed.

-Not creepy, and sure! I'm on the Khao San Road, where are you?

There was a pause and the dots of him typing his response.

-Oh no, you're in literally the worst part of Bangkok. Are you new here?

-Kind of . . .

-In that case, dinner's on me—meet me at the Banyan Tree in an hour?

17.

Effie

By the time Anna, Effie, and Ben returned, Lizzie had gone up-stairs to shower. In her absence, furniture was apologetically righted, chairs penitently folded and tucked away in the Hall's cavernous and secretive corners. Flowers were carefully picked up from the floor and rescue attempts made on the displays, the dirty plates; the cake on its pedestal was whisked away to stay fresh in the fridge. The group moved slowly, the survivors of some great military push. The Hall was busy with battlefield debris, full of wedding.

They stacked and carried, tidied and scrubbed until they heard the midmorning siren wail in the fields: the call to lunch for the laborers picking grapes or scything wheat, digging trenches or plucking fruit from the vines that snaked around the house. Effie imagined the farmhands retreating from the midday sun in aerial view, moving through their verdant lanes like Pac-Man, and she felt her still-empty stomach chomp in protest.

She liked the sensation of being excavated from the inside: a warm churn of righteousness, the intensity settings of which she alone could control. The low hum of hunger matched the din in her head and softened it, distracted from it—when the thoughts became too loud, she simply doubled down on fasting, cranked up the stomach acid to drown them out.

She had always done it, sought agency through her intake and by mastering her meals—or lack of them. As a teenager, Effie had realized that her emotions functioned like a microwave on whatever food she laid eyes on—able either to warm it with joy to a heartiness she could let herself take pleasure in or to nuke it, blanch it, boil it in misery until it became something she would not allow past her lips. At first, it had been more instinct than aesthetic, but when she realized the effect her moods had on her waistline—and on the circumference of each thigh, the bony lumps on top of each shoulder—the two had become inextricably linked: happy+fat or sad+thin. As much as she tried to break the chain—Effie would have been delighted with happy+thin, for example—it seemed to have been forged from sterner stuff than she. And so her silhouette—recently, her increasingly etiolated Nosferatu shadow—had become a barometer for her baseline satisfaction, every bulge or hollow a visceral synecdoche for what was going on in her head.

Her stomach rumbled again as she scrubbed red wine marks from the burnt-orange floor tiles in the Hall, and looking up from her crouch, Effie noticed more shards of broken porcelain beneath one of the long tables. Crawling farther in, she recovered a serving platter, smashed into little pieces.

Clasping them to her breast, she maneuvered herself back out from under the table, and as she did so, a warm pair of hands cupped her hips and moved slowly up along her torso.

"Can I join you in there?" Ben's voice asked huskily, and Effie thought she might crumble like one of the shards in her hands. "I smell of booze and bleach, but don't let that put you off."

She slid farther back and into his grasp, twisted to kiss him as her face reappeared from beneath the tablecloth, and worried belatedly what she might taste like.

"We lost a night together," he said in an undertone that

wouldn't reach Charlie and Iso, who were clearing the other table. "That bloody sun lounger wasn't a patch on being in your bed."

Effie blushed and swallowed the butterflies that had replaced the hunger in her belly.

"Five more left," she murmured back, and he leaned into her lips once again. "But right now, I need food."

The others were casting around for tasks and, finding none left to do in the Hall, also began to mutter about eating—but as Effie pulled herself upright, there came a screech and the banging of a door from the upstairs landing, in the direction of the bedrooms.

Whatever it was Lizzie held in her shaking hand when she appeared, ashen, at the top of the stairs was too small to see at a distance, even though the former bride held it out away from her in disgusted horror.

"This is fucking sick," she called, her voice trembling as much as her outstretched fist. "Sick! What the fuck did I do to deserve this?"

As Effie skittered closer and reached out an arm to guide Lizzie, her teary eyes making her steps unsteady, down the stone staircase, she peered into the other woman's palm.

The bride figurine from the top of the three-tiered cake, in her sculpted ivory crinoline, and the groom in his black tie.

There was little about Lizzie's wedding that was bridal in the frilly sense; she had an allergy to anything remotely naff, so even the traditional elements had been streamlined and modernized according to her stringently clean-lines tastes. But the cake decorations had been Lizzie's one piece of kitsch: she'd found a website that promised to 3D-print the bride and groom's faces onto a pair of tiny statuettes, using their passport photos. Gleefully, Lizzie had scanned in hers and Dan's mug shots—"he looks like a murderer in his!" she trilled over the phone to Effie—and she cackled uproariously when the tiny imitations came through and, predictably enough, looked nothing like either of them. She regaled everyone with the story, and even made a photo of the little "Dan" face, with its vacant expression and painted-on beard; it became the one that flashed up whenever her fiancé called her.

Now, though, Effie had to agree that the figures in Lizzie's hand looked nothing like her and Dan, but that was mainly because they had been—quite carefully and ruthlessly, it seemed—decapitated.

"They were on my pillow." Lizzie's voice quavered as she shrugged Effie's arm off her shoulders and stepped away. "Left on my fucking pillow."

Effie looked again at the statuettes, their heads so neatly struck—*sawn?*—from their bodies like doomed Tudor queens. It had been done too precisely on each of them for it to have been anything other than expressly intended.

Effie shuddered: she knew angry drunk people were capable of horrible things, and they had all been very drunk.

But who had been this angry?

18.

Anna

Anna felt a chill in the bottom of her stomach when she heard the scream. Scrambling from the kitchen into the Hall, she saw Lizzie's anxious, blotched face, the headless figurines held in one palm out in front of her. Anna reached an arm to her, but she found she didn't have the words to soothe this woman she loved so well and felt she now understood so little. The woman who had made the biggest decision of her life—to cancel her wedding—without telling her two best friends first. Without even warning them it was about to happen.

"God, how horrible." Behind Anna, Steve stepped into the room—ever kind, ever mindful of everybody else's feelings—from where he had been rinsing dishes at the kitchen sink. "I'm so sorry, Lizzie. For what it's worth, this would have been an amazing wedding. You must have worked so hard on it."

Anna's heart clenched to a tiny dried-out raisin.

The only thing you cared about at ours was whether we had the right audio cables for the DJ.

Which font on the invites? Which flowers? Which tablecloths, which napkins? Which blackboard for the seating plan? Which cousin is it your Auntie Joan can't stand? Anna had simply stopped asking Steve in the end, so that she wouldn't have to see him shrug. He didn't know a ranunculus from a hydrangea, and he didn't care. The fact that she didn't either hadn't seemed to matter after a while: one of them had to, so the wedding became her job, just the way the supermarket shopping, the Christmas cards, and the thinking three steps ahead for Sonny would eventually, too.

If her marriage were a contract she was looking over for a client, she would tell them to run for the hills.

None of it mattered on the day, of course. Anna had barely thought of the hours she had put in, stenciling chalk foliage, stamping placement cards and calligraphing menus; barely thought of the spreadsheet, the to-do list, and the invoices to pay as they and their guests enjoyed the eye-wateringly marked-up fruits of her unpaid labor. It was only as she'd read Sonny his fairy tales recently, then stayed up half the night working on his nursery school Book Day costume, which they had all forgotten about, that she'd realized who in her and Steve's relationship was the elves and who the shoemaker.

That Steve had managed to run Celia down to the fancy dress shop in the car that afternoon to get supplies for Olwen's costume and still not thought to do Sonny's led to a full-blown row. But he was reviewing a gig for work that night, so Anna had glued the tinfoil sword together after she'd put their son to bed, Anna had attached feathers to the makeshift Robin Hood hat after she'd finished reading up on her latest case at work, and Anna had felt utterly taken for granted all the while.

She brushed yet more scattered petals from the kitchen table now and remembered the surprise of the confetti on her wedding day: that such a moment could feel like such an onslaught. And that was even before she'd encountered her divorced cousin standing at the end of the human walkway deliberately throwing sharp grains of easy-cook rice right into her face.

As the photo-op debris had drifted to her feet, encased under her skirts in a pair of icicle-gray satin ballet slippers (the closest she'd come to "something blue"—it hadn't matched her color scheme), Anna's bridesmaids had struggled to pull the petals, grains, foil hearts, and paper Cupids free of the carefully tonged tendrils of curly hair in which they had nested, to brush them from where they had pebble-dashed the gauzy sleeves of her elegant gown, and to surreptitiously excavate them from the line of her cleavage before they showed up in the photos like a lewd joke.

Anna had felt a welter of emotions that day, but the confetti shower left her shaken with its vague hint of aggression and the niggling feeling that, had the guests been holding buckets of slops, they might have emptied those over her and Steve too. Perhaps she had imagined it, but somewhere just beneath the goodwill and drunken euphoria of their guests had lurked the subtlest note of resentment at their happiness. Anna struggled to pinpoint its provenance, but had registered it anxiously nonetheless.

She looked at her husband as he returned to the suds and the dirty plates in the sink. She wasn't ready to let him back into her heart yet—not until he had explained to her what on earth had happened for him and Iso to have been so thoroughly divested of their clothes at the same time and in the same place. Anna picked up a serving dish of tapenade from the side and plastic-wrapped it vengefully, before carrying it across the stone room to the larder.

"You can't seriously think I would do that to you?" Steve followed her into the coolness of the little pantry, and pleaded with her. They were surrounded by white shelves neatly stacked with dry goods as bystanders to watch them question the vows they had made.

"I'm not the one not being serious," Anna sighed. "*You* showed up semi-naked this morning, not me. What on earth am I supposed to think you were doing with her in that state?"

At this, Steve was forced to admit that he had no idea what he had been doing, what had happened. "But what about trust, Anna?"

"What about it?" she said, thrusting the greasy bowl of tapenade at him. The wine-like fumes from it brought acid to the back of his teeth, and by the time he swallowed it away again, she had pushed past him and returned to cleaning-up.

It hadn't exactly been easy for him, she reasoned, adjusting to life—*and wife*—after a baby. Steve prided himself on sidestepping the usual pitfalls of modern masculinity that Anna's friends railed against in her all-female group chats; she knew that as the two of them sat together on the couch, he read the messages as they came in, peering over her shoulder, his eyes slid right over in his skull until they watered and felt like he'd stretched them out on their stalks.

The other mums in her toddler group complained about their husbands' socks everywhere, about their sleeping in, their pawing at them as much as the little children did. Of requiring far more attention than even the most grisly teething baby.

Steve didn't do that. He waited passively—often in vain—until Anna showed him physical affection, and he tried to take his cues from her. He woke up and washed up, did nursery runs so she could get into the City early, before the crowds she so hated sharing trains with. He wrote his articles at home so he could also cook and clean, to make up for the travel he sometimes had to agree to for work. She knew that he loved her, simply but doggedly.

Still it never seemed to be what Anna wanted, and she wondered—with a regularity that made her angry with herself—whether in fact she'd prefer him to be a dick, a bore, an ungrateful, unheeding brute to her, just so she'd have something real to rail against. Instead, Steve seemed happy to be a punching bag when Anna needed him to be—he could see what her job did to her head and what Sonny had to her body (a body he nevertheless considered with near-religious awe when he thought she wasn't looking). He wanted to make it up to her, and he wanted to be her friend, at least sometimes, too.

Anna could see that the fact that she had all too readily assumed the very worst about him and Iso although those kitschy purple towels had hidden the details of it had made Steve indignant. She found that reassuring: irritation was better than guiltily accepting his wrongdoing. Less reassuring was the fact that Steve clearly didn't remember the full story.

Iso was attractive; that was not in doubt. What an attractive woman could do to even a comatose man was a question for the biologists. It wasn't like he was used to that area being regularly disturbed.

Ha! Not for months.

Anna had sensed in her husband, in the years since his small son had been born, the horror of temptation—at a bare shoulder here, a glossy lip there, Celia's laugh and the way she tucked her hair behind her ear. If they walked past a beautiful woman in the park, he would look at the ground like a medieval friar while Anna held herself so straight she felt brittle in the wind. Other people's sexiness hung in the air between them like a reproach, a veil they had to communicate through. Even hours later, Steve's guilty adrenaline coursed in waves like an aftershock around the body he had promised in eternity to his wife—the very same flesh he offered forlornly to share with her every so often, and was consistently rebuffed.

Shaking the thoughts from her mind, Anna laid out a lunch consisting of the same platters they had spent the morning clearing away. Given the toxins still coursing through them all—now topped up with the nervy unease the violently dismembered cake couple had sown among the group—nobody felt particularly excited to see the food again, but a few hours' work had fostered appetites in even the most unsettled stomachs.

Rustic olive-painted plates were piled high or low, depending on how weak their owners still felt, then taken back through to the tables in the Hall. The wedding party, as Anna had come to think of them all, sat along each side of one wooden table on benches recently straightened and picked at dried-out crudités—as much a victim of the previous night's excesses as they were—in silence.

As the sun rose and, with it, the heat of the day, the crickets outside the pale house increased their volume to an earsplitting pitch, until the surly diners could no longer hear their own thoughts. It was a reprieve of sorts.

As they chewed their food and mopped it up from their plates, scooped the dregs of the wedding spread into their mouths, the recognition of another noise dawned on each of them slowly, like moonlight over a hilltop. They looked askance at one another as if to check they were correct, as if their senses had become as tricksy as their memories had over the past day or so. As if they could no more trust their own instincts than they could the other people in the room.

The rumbling came from outside, a low grumble peppered with cracks and bangs every so often, like scratches on a record or the looping pops of one left to rotate long after its tracks have played out. It became louder and more regular, until it crescendoed near the door at the far end of the Hall—where the rental cars were parked.

The pops had been the stones on the dusty drive crunching under the weight of wheels, the rumble an engine as a vehicle—a new one—pulled up once more outside the Oratoire.

"Are you expecting anyone?" Anna asked pointedly of Lizzie, her gray eyes boring into the woman whose canceled life event had brought them all here and had now cast aspersions—and a fair share of doom and gloom—over each of them.

"I don't know, Anna," she replied tetchily. "I don't know what's going on. It isn't my wedding anymore. I'm not the one inviting surprise guests."

Lizzie looked at Ben briefly, then testily at Effie, and Anna sensed from her friend's expression that lunch had begun to co-agulate guiltily in the bottom of Effie's stomach.

"Maybe it's Marie," Effie offered, with groggy enthusiasm at the potential arrival of someone who might seem to be in charge.

"Maybe she's come to collect all this stuff," ventured Steve.

Once the wedding's architecture was gone, Anna thought, the shadow it had cast over the holiday might lift, too. Her nightly circuit of their house to stuff Sonny's cuddly animals and pull-along toys into their storage boxes, to reunite his pens with their caps and each shoe with the other, often acted like calming yogi breaths on her mood.

Steve stood, wiped his mouth with the back of his hand, and softly burped some of the hungover indigestion away from where it had bubbled up, listening as the noise appeared again in re-verse: from loud to quieter, a regular purr to one pitted with the fits and starts of the loose shale on the driveway. The car—or whatever it had been—was leaving again.

They continued to watch the front door, all turned toward its blank and pocked medieval panels as though they were a televi-sion screen—or, at least, a window that might give some clue as to what was going on beyond it. As the only person to have fought off the postprandial stupor—which was technically also a pre-prandial stupor—and to have successfully launched himself up-right, Steve made his way from the table toward the door in the archway.

"Might as well see if we can tell who it was," he said as the noise receded further.

But as he drew closer to the dark wood, there came a shrieking noise as the rusty metal ring of a handle was lifted on the exterior and turned—with some reluctance, it sounded like, from the wail of complaining iron. A chink of light appeared on the stone flags beneath, an acute angle of white on gray that grew longer and larger across the floor, before slanting toward the rows of expectant faces still seated at the table as surely as a needle on a compass.

The door to the Great Hall swung open and revealed a figure within its Gothic frame.

Bracketed by the bright lunchtime sunshine behind, the figure's face and hair color were hidden in shadow.

In his seat at the near end of the table, Charlie addressed the newcomer.

"Hello?" he asked.

19.

Effie

Lizzie sat very still. Her arms framed her body, clamped to it and rigid; she was anchored by hands that gripped the wooden bench as tightly as claws.

Her eyes were fearful, but as they adjusted to the light, the scenario, the incoming visitor, the strain between them that had caused her delicate brow to rumple into a solitary vertical wrinkle relaxed. Her forehead was ironed smooth once more.

Lizzie breathed out, brought her hands to her chest in a gesture of relief.

"Bertie!" she giggled, and the sound was the first unforced laugh—the first easy, uncomplicated cheeriness—they had heard all day.

Lizzie climbed delicately out from behind the table and made her way toward the rosy-cheeked, ginger-haired man in the doorway. His shirtsleeves were rolled up his forearms; he had a sun hat in one hand, a useless iPhone and a paper map in the other. A small silver suitcase stood by his side.

"What are you doing here?" Lizzie smiled, approached him swift and fleet. She dropped a kiss on each of his cheeks, reached her arms up his solid torso to the height of those wide shoulders and folded the new arrival into a hug.

"Congratulations!" he boomed, his voice a male equivalent of hers—soft but strong, wealthy and well-to-do, but rounded by life. Friendly and guileless.

At first Effie felt a tug of confusion, and she tried, through her hangover, to fathom who he might be speaking to, who he might be congratulating.

When nobody replied, his expectant face fell slightly. "Lizzie, I'm so sorry I'm late," he offered earnestly. "My plane was delayed. . . . Some kind of bloody electrical storm. I can't believe I missed it. I'm so so sorry."

Almost immediately, the truth dawned: he had come for the wedding, the one that was supposed to have happened yesterday—Lizzie's. And Dan's.

"You didn't get the email," Lizzie gasped. "Oh my God, Bertie, you didn't get the email!"

There was a pitch of hysteria to her—her throat cracked with emotion and her shoulders began to shake—but it became rapidly obvious, as she leaned on the newly arrived Bertie for support and tried to gasp her next breath, that she was laughing rather than crying.

Effie saw across the table that Charlie's features had brightened in mischief at the mistake, too; she found her own mouth tugging upward at the unfolding awkward but delicious gaffe that had given them some light relief from their own problems.

"Oh Christ," said the man Lizzie, now writhing in giggles, was leaning on. "What have I missed?"

He set his belongings down, took a seat at the head of the table, and listened while they explained to him. The fact of the wedding—the textured Provençal invitation had dropped promptly into the chrome mailbox at his apartment block a few months ago—then the undoing of it: an email sent a week ago that he had not received. Their arrival at the Oratoire and what it had contained. The parts they could remember and those they couldn't. The situation they had found themselves in this morning and the one he had just arrived to, fresh and unburdened.

Effie found that usually, with even the very worst hangover, the fact of relating the events that had led up to it—of spreading the pain, diffusing the shame—could ease some of the next-day anxiety. But explaining the scene to Bertie assuaged none of the nagging culpability she felt.

As they described to him what they had awoken to, Bertie's face performed an entire routine in mime, from disappointment and suspicion to shock—then sympathy. Simple, earnest worry, and pity, for the woman at the heart of it: Lizzie, his favorite cousin, who he hadn't seen in a year or more.

"We were so close," Lizzie said, as if to him but for the benefit of the group once he had been introduced to all of them, in turn, around the table. "But then he got this bloody job so far away, and we never see each other anymore."

Bertie cleared his throat. "Well, ah, that actually is about to change," he said with a modest grin. "Because I'm moving back at the end of the summer."

"Where from?" Anna asked from farther along the table, as though he were one of her witnesses. Effie saw that she was making a character sketch, deciding how useful he might be for the task ahead.

"Shanghai," he offered. "Seconded there by my firm. Privacy law. That's why I didn't know the wedding was off—I didn't get the email." He spread his hands and turned to his cousin. "I can't access that account over there, Liz—the Chinese have got this giant firewall, so I use a different one. Didn't Mum tell you?"

Lizzie's exasperated expression told them all they needed to know about how *au fait* Bertie's mother was with the tech legislation of the country in which her son worked.

"She only ever shows me your postcards," she said with a smile, then studied her hands in her lap, morose again.

"I'm so sorry you had to call it off, Lizbet," he murmured, and reached out to hold one of them.

"We call her that too!" Effie exclaimed. It was the first time she had spoken since Bertie had arrived.

He was looking at her along the table with the sort of friendly compassion she had missed lately. Anna and Lizzie had been so busy these past six months; Effie didn't blame them for it—it was a fact of thirty-something life. They had done what they could—a couple of nights each with her every week for the first month or so after James had gone. But then, back to their own lives again.

Effie had heard about Bertie for years but never met him. Lizzie's bright, slightly fusty, but unwaveringly loyal cousin was the only other person who knew about what had happened at university. He had done as much for Lizzie over the holidays that summer as Effie had in the turbulent weeks that led up to it. Meeting him finally was like finding a missing bookend of a pair: together they had held up the bride before, and they could do so again.

She noticed the effect that fresh masculinity in the group had had on Ben. He seemed stirred by Bertie's presence in a way that smacked of jealousy. Effie doubted her instincts at first, but then he shifted closer to her on the bench, laid a hand over hers on the tabletop, then draped an arm around her shoulders as though they were high school boyfriend and girlfriend. He was marking his territory, and the realization made Effie pathetically grateful. The attention made her feel more alive than she had since James had left.

Not that Ben had anything to worry about: Bertie was dressed much like Effie's dad did on holidays. *Chinos!*

Effie reached one hand up to her hair, wiry and straggling where she had dragged it into a ponytail without washing it that morning, and from there traced the dry skin of her nose, the flakes of last night's makeup still on her cheeks. Of course Bertie seemed sympathetic: she looked like a vagrant.

"I should shower," she said, to nobody in particular.

"We all should," Anna replied. "We'll feel a bit more human after that. Then we can figure out what to do with all this . . . stuff." She gestured around the hall at the trestles and stacked flatware.

"Before we do, has anybody seen the rings?" Lizzie's voice piped urgently. "Only they cost an absolute bomb. They were on the"—here, she swallowed thickly and grimaced—"altar yesterday, right? I really need that refund."

"They were," Effie said. "I saw them there. But not this morning."

"I'm sure they'll turn up," Anna said quickly, reassuringly. "They have to be in the house somewhere."

"Well, look, I can help with all that," Bertie offered. "Fresh pair of eyes and all that. Fresher than some." He met Charlie's bloodshot gaze and took in his burgeoning five o'clock shadow. "But I'll need some food first. Is there anything here, or do we need to go to the shops?"

The prospect of facing the platters once more was too much for Iso, who groaned and heaved her light frame from the bench, then skipped through the doorway behind the table, into the utility room and lavatory behind it—from where the delicate sounds of the wedding breakfast's third reappearance echoed through to them.

Bertie directed a mock grimace in Effie's direction; she sensed again in him a kindness and human interest her life had been sorely lacking. Ben had brought the heat back into her life, but Bertie reminded her of the importance of warmth. They were different things, she realized with a start.

Given the tremulous state she had woken up in, and the blur and rising dread of what she might have done the previous night, Effie needed another friend—a friend less mired in their own problems—almost as much as she felt a pressing urgency to be away from the house and the various men she'd arrived with.

Lizzie shook her head in answer to Bertie's question. "No proper food here," she muttered. "If only the hog roast had turned up. Though I suppose we should be grateful that it didn't—one less thing to try and get rid of."

"And we'll need more than party bits to see us through the week," Effie conceded. "*Le supermarché* it is."

"You're a saint," Ben said before she could suggest that he accompany them. "I can't face it, I'm afraid, but I'm sure you don't need me tagging along."

It wasn't quite the perfect boyfriend reaction she had hoped for, but she smiled the niggle away; as intoxicating an effect as he had on her, Effie needed some space.

"Come on," she said to Bertie. "I'll drive."

Effie worried, as she stepped out into the sunshine on foal-like legs, that the offer to shop had been an act of hubris she wouldn't actually be able to carry out. That the alcohol still coursing round her body would bring her out in a cold sweat, persuade the digestive juices back into her mouth once more, and frustrate her goal of getting out of the beautiful holiday home that had begun to feel a bit like a tomb.

The warm, golden air slapped her like a heavy-duty duvet being thrown over her head, cozy but stifling, and she was glad when the car's efficient air-conditioning kicked in to temper it. Effie found that the act of driving—something she hated and habitually avoided wherever possible—distracted her from the tides of nausea deep within and the ebb and flow of remorse crashing away on top. As they left the château and the bars of reception ticked up on her phone screen, she wondered briefly whether James might have been in touch again.

"So," Bertie said, stretching his khaki-clad legs out in front of him once Effie had found her way off the tracks and winding narrow lanes near the house to what constituted the closest main road into the neighboring town. "Heavy night, was it?"

"I'd rather not talk about it," she replied neatly, nudging the car up a gear as the road flattened out in front of them. She had so far avoided mentioning to anybody where she had woken up, or the suggestion that—for some of the night, at least —there had been somebody lying beside her.

It wasn't just Charlie's request to her in the kitchen that had persuaded her not to air the general outline of what she suspected had taken place between them; it was the disappointed, judgmental look she knew she'd receive from Anna if she did. Anna, who couldn't remember what being single felt like. Who had forgotten how to appreciate the luxury of sleeping next to someone—the same someone!—every night. Who had met Steve so long ago she'd never used a dating app, never even opened one up, let alone had her flaws clinically assessed by men of indistinguishable age who sent uninvited pictures of their shriveled cocks. Anna, who clearly disapproved of Effie's being with Ben because of his link to Dan, but who had the luxury of no longer needing to market herself like a secondhand car surrounded by models fresh off the lot.

"What a place!" Bertie breathed as they drove through the countryside. "What perfect scenery."

How at odds with their environment the seven pale and rueful faces must have looked when he walked in, staring back at him from where they huddled in the dark around the table like creatures of the deep, when there was glorious French sunshine to bask in only yards away behind the door. Effie began to laugh at the image, and when she explained it, Bertie did too.

"I'd sort of forgotten what British drinking culture is like," he said. "There are plenty of other expats in Shanghai, but I realized pretty soon that I didn't like most of them."

They had exported their native need to get regularly and destructively sloshed with them, he explained, just as they had shipped their grand pianos and artworks to their new homes.

"I like a couple of beers of an evening—perhaps a few more on very special occasions," he told Effie, and she squirmed with internal shame. "But, ugh, none of those sticky shots."

Effie felt him contemplating her as she sat at the wheel, wondering perhaps what it was this nervous, skinny woman was so keen to get away from—and whether she realized she'd never be able to leave her own thoughts behind.

With the car parked and a coin found to activate a shopping cart of proportions usually reserved for the Christmas haul, they stood at the entrance to the supermarket. Even the discounts looked exotic.

For Effie, French supermarkets were a happy place. They reminded her of childhood holidays spent exploring the aisles, the new tastes and aromas they promised. Oregano and citronella. Sea-creature floats she and her brother would take to the beach once and puncture immediately. Pristine, perfect stationery she'd beg her parents for so she could keep a holiday journal, but that she'd invariably ruin with the first clumsy strokes of her juvenile handwriting.

Now she was fascinated by the gadgets—a salad spinner, a twist-in lemon juicer—that here were considered fundamental to human existence but that at home would be puzzled over and prodded like something washed ashore. Effie loved the newness of foreign brands, trusted the generosity of packaging she had never seen before over the crabbed, penny-pinching labels she recognized from England. There was a sense of bounty to shops in France: the brimming bins of plump and plentiful produce here were quite different from the insipid, uniform groceries available from the shop at the end of her road in London, where gray commuters fumbled even grayer fruit and veg into polyethylene bags under blinking strip lights.

Effie felt her headache begin to recede from simply being in the presence of so many antioxidants.

The picking of fruit, the counting of portions, the meal planning, the meat selecting, the demi-fluent translation of cooking instructions and serving suggestions made for an easy and companionable hour or so, and Effie almost forgot the circumstances that had thrown Bertie and her together, the confusion that awaited them back at the house.

"What made her do it?" Bertie asked Effie somewhere between the cheese and an admirably comprehensive zone devoted entirely to breadsticks. "Why did she call things off?"

Effie looked up from the packet she was reading. "She hasn't said. Nothing specific, at least—just says they had their doubts." She unhooked three baguettes from where they stood in a sort of baker's umbrella stand and added them to the trolley. "There's something, though. Something happened. Lizzie was different after the engagement party, but she won't talk about it. Not to me, at least."

"Then I won't press her on it either," Bertie replied. "But that reminds me . . ."

He looked left and right. They had finally—after at least three tunnels of wine, along which Effie had felt her lymph nodes begin to shrivel—reached the no-man's-land end of the supermarket's hangar, where children's clothing and sports equipment jostled for space on the shelves with televisions and smaller white goods. Bertie craned his neck to see to the end of the next aisle, then pulled the now-cumbersome and willfully wheeled cart with him down a dark aisle decorated at one end with a spray of cheap gardening gloves.

"Here we go!" Bertie selected a large ring-bound notepad from a display. From a nearby shelf he picked up a pack of indelible marker pens, which Effie knew, even through their plastic wrap, would smell of her office back at the school.

She frowned at him. "Are we going to start taking a roll call every day?"

"This"—he smiled, tossing the pad onto the mountain of food that would feed their number for the next week—"is how we work out where those wedding rings have gone. Who saw them last, where, and when. Helps me think better. We'll build a time-line that will tell us everything you drunken sots have forgotten!"

He beamed at her, arms spread wide and pleased with himself, and Effie had to concentrate on not bursting into tears, just as she had practiced every day at her desk these past six months.

Bertie's enthusiasm was so wholesome—his entire personality so sensible—that he reminded Effie of the shame she had felt on waking that morning. She had yet to tell anybody what she remembered of last night, and the fact of it made her feel dirty and soiled all over again. All the self-loathing of the morning and the anxiety—of the half-year she had spent living under that feeling as though pinned to the spot by it—washed over her once more. The desolation, the sadness, the drinks, and the regrettable, sordid dealings they had led to.

It was all Effie could do not to cling to Bertie as if he were a life buoy, a kindly flotation device in the shape of a grown-up.

They paid for and bagged up their shopping, then drove back to the Oratoire, in silence.

20.

Anna

Anna was spying on Iso when she first noticed Lizzie's behavior. Watching, waiting. The former bride was frozen like an animal caught in the open, stock-still until the moment of threat has passed.

After taking a deliberate time-out from suffering stonily along-side the others to go and sit on the bed she had slept in—*alone*—the previous night and cry in a quiet and businesslike way, Anna dried her eyes and moved over to the window, from where she could look down at the scene by the pool from a distance.

Her husband was asleep on one of the loungers, wearing his faded paisley swimming trunks with yet another grotty old band T-shirt, one flip-flop hanging off his left big toe over the edge of the sunbed. He had tried to talk to her again after lunch, after Effie had left with the cousin.

She had brushed Steve off again, hadn't wanted to discuss it until she knew she would be able to speak to him without a torrent of unrelated resentments shooting forth and knocking him off his feet. It didn't seem fair to pelt him with the issues she thought she'd left at home with her little boy. Then again, what had last night crystallized but her well-developed sense of losing him to another woman? Had whatever happened last night happened because he was full of his own complaints too?

Anna looked down at Ben, handsome but slack-mouthed in sleep on another lounger. She had seen the way Effie opened like a flower in sunshine when he looked at her, how his company and attention had given her friend back the warm coat of confidence she had been lacking in the months since her breakup. Anna hoped he wouldn't let her down.

She shifted her gaze to Charlie, sitting on the edge of the pool with his feet dangling in the water. He had managed to soak up the ambience like bread in oil; his olive skin was already a shade darker, and his chocolatey crop of hair seemed almost jet black, just like one of the locals. A beautiful man, but a flighty one. Anna smiled affectionately as he slipped under the water, part athlete, part clown.

Then she regarded Iso, splashing serenely nearby, lying on a hot pink inflatable she had brought with her in her suitcase—"a great prop for photos," she had explained before persuading Charlie to blow it up for her.

How he hadn't brought up a lung—or yet more of the half-digested wedding breakfast, given the state he was in—while doing so had been a mystery to every onlooker. Yet more curious to them, though, was how this woman, the one who had woken up naked with somebody else's husband, had managed to charm her still-devoted boyfriend into doing her this favor. Their relationship seemed—so far—unpunctured by recent events, much like the inflatable; although Anna knew from a brief and testy sojourn at a holiday camp with Sonny and her parents last summer (while her three sisters had been abroad with their spouses) that those things never stayed intact for long.

She had gone with Sonny's grandparents to Oakwood Lake Cottages because Steve had been away covering yet another music festival—one that, before Sonny, they had been in the habit of going to together but that he now "reported from" alone.

As if he were on the front line with a notebook and pen rather than crowd-surfing and bar-hopping. Holidaying with her parents rather than her husband had felt like a teenage regression—Anna had spoken to them in much the same appalling tones as she had during those difficult years, and she had been mortified by her behavior by the time the holiday was over. But it had been necessary to go: sheer survival tactics in the face of a week of solo child-care.

How on earth did Celia manage it, day in, day out?

By borrowing my husband all the fucking time.

"It's not the same without you," Steve regularly mewed on his return from these work jaunts, grizzled with late nights and beer. But he still seemed to have the same partied-out look they'd both once worn, the same pinprick pupils. The same rolling hangover after four nights on the trot—four nights she'd spent bathing and wiping and soothing their son.

Now, on his sunbed, Steve briefly roused, then turned over and rocked himself back to sleep exactly the same way Sonny did.

Anna watched as Charlie sluiced away the previous night; the remorse that had hung around him for most of the day was washed off by the tepid bath-like water. He submerged his head and came up refreshed, breaking the surface between Iso's tanned feet where they dangled from the floating airbed. Her painted toenails matched the pink of the inflatable, Anna noticed. Everything matched, from Iso's toes to her hairbands, her shoes and her bags, right down to her underwear. Right down to the matching towels she and Steve had been wrapped in.

On another lounger at one of the narrow ends of the pool, moved there by its occupant into this more solitary position, lay Lizzie, earbuds in and nodding to the beat as she read her book. This she held at a precise angle above her body so its shadow would not interfere with the more serious work of tanning as she followed its plot.

Anna smiled indulgently. Of the three of them—Effie with her

Celtic coloring, she with her granny's Irish blood, which began to steam in temperatures above seventy-three degrees—Lizzie was the sun worshipper, the lizard. That was partly why she and Guy had lasted so long. Anna could have told Lizzie that Guy was bad news, though she already knew it; but he was bad news with a yacht.

Lizzie seemed delighted to have met Dan so soon after it had all finished with her ex: one final, exasperated row under the stars and then she'd arrived back at Heathrow, burnished as a terra-cotta goddess and lighting up the arrivals hall like a neon sign. Anna wondered yet again what it was that had changed her friend's mind, what had brought them all here in such altered circumstances.

What exactly had happened last night, and what it was she had seen.

Looking down at Lizzie again, Anna wondered also whether something of the woman she knew was resurfacing. Anna had never seen Lizzie angry the way she had been that morning—nor did she want to see her that upset ever again. But Christ, it was an improvement on Lizzie's barely there–ness of the past few months.

Canceling the wedding must have been the right decision after all.

Her gaze lingering, Anna realized that Lizzie wasn't turning the pages, that behind her sunglasses she was scanning not the words in front of her but the view beyond. She had positioned herself at that end of the pool in order that she might see all of the action in the water. At the top of her arms, shiny with sun cream, the sinews were tensed and taut; her glistening haunches were ready to take flight.

Who was she looking at like that?

From the window, Anna couldn't make out where the beam of Lizzie's gaze landed, but she had a good idea. She shook her head, silly with suspicion. Lizzie was heartbroken, traumatized: that was why she was tense.

What am I even doing up here?

Lurking, and looking. Spying on her friends like some lonely, dirty thing. Staring at them all as if searching for clues, for the secrets they didn't even know they were hiding.

And the ones they did.

21.

Eighteen Months Ago: Lizzie

I answered his messages on the dating app (probably far too quickly if we were playing by London rules, but we weren't), threw some coins onto the bar for my beers, and marched back to my hostel, where I attempted to create a dinner-date look from the beach clothes in my case.

Since Guy and I rarely ate anywhere more formal than a crab shack on those yacht trips, the best I could manage was a black camisole and some sort of artistry with a sarong for a skirt. I had to hope the staff at the hotel wouldn't pass comment on my Birkenstocks, and I thought again of the waiters I'd watched through Guy's binoculars, aligning napkins and tealights just so to manifest romance.

I felt like a student again, quixotic about what might happen in a time zone I didn't belong in, an existence that didn't feel like mine. I had felt the same life-out-of-life sensation at university when I had met someone who had promised to be an escape route from studying and the library rota but had soon turned out to be a reality check of a rather different sort.

Blood on water. I shook my head clear of the memory: not right now.

I could hardly breathe as I walked into the foyer, a little late, rather frazzled from the Bangkok city heat and following pavementless roads with no names but clusters of wires like washing lines hanging from every telegraph pole. The hard pebble of sadness that had lodged in my chest that morning transformed into excitement; my palms were sweating and my mouth dry, but I felt almost giddy.

Until I realized that the tastefully lit reception area was empty.

I swung my head left and then right, and the stone in my lungs was threatening to shatter with disappointment when a concierge in a striped waistcoat and white shirt gestured to the lift with a smile: "He's waiting for you on the top floor, madam."

It took a few dragging seconds to call the lift—I could feel my pulse beating behind my eyes—and as I waited for it to arrive, my back turned on the front desk staff, I was overcome with sweaty mortification that they had taken me for a call girl. My mother would almost certainly have agreed with them. Then, as I stepped into the mirrored box, I saw it illuminated on the interior panel: bar and restaurant, floor 61. The lift moved so quickly I felt like I'd left my stomach behind on the ascent.

I was amazed at the calm up there—no wind, barely even a breeze, and none of the car horns or scooter revs from the street. Lights on the tables twinkled like stars in the firmament, and the low murmur of voices rose like prayers.

As I stepped from the lift, all that separated me from the edge was a transparent wall of glass, and as I climbed a short flight of steps to the bar, the view to my left was of the city spread out in miniature below me, as if seen from the window of an airplane. It was like walking out into the heavens, but for the distant chinging of low-level, reassuringly bland house music from the bar.

I felt even more light-headed at the height and the proximity of the drop. Falling had never seemed so easy.

"Lizzie?" There he was at the top of the stairs, suited and slightly sweaty himself, collar open and eyes glittering at me. A blush of red that wasn't sunburn surfaced on his cheeks, along with a nervous half-smile as though we were doing something naughty.

I had to keep reminding myself that we weren't.

And that my plane left for London in ten—no, nine—hours.

From the start, there was no awkwardness. We fell into conversation the way people fall in love: swiftly and incidentally, zapping between topics like synapses flashing in the brain. The books we'd read, the films we'd seen. TV shows we both loved. His traveling days and mine—soon over—and our eagerness to repatriate, take our feet off the gas, the search for something gentle—meaningful but instinctive, homely. Not so much a quest for spirituality as the search for someone to share a bag of crisps with.

"A big one or a small, though?" he joked. "Not enough crisps for two people in a small one, and I'm looking for a woman who understands that."

I laughed and gazed at the lights spread around us. Other skyscrapers, like trees in a forest, emerged from the night as if on a heat map, their outlines invisible but for the red lights they were dotted with to warn planes of their hulking presence in the dark. The river wound sluggishly off in the distance, under a suspension bridge beneath which traditional wooden boats passed, garnished with blinking fairy lights. Despite the breadth of the view and the fact of all that humanity below, the air remained so still and so silent as to convince me that the two of us were alone up there.

"I've never been anywhere like this," I told him. "I grew up in the countryside. In a wold."

The word "wold" became raucously funny for some reason— the champagne and the cocktails, I suppose, but also the great breath of relief we had both exhaled at having found each other.

"God, there isn't much out there on those apps, is there?" I giggled sadly. "One of the other guys on there had listed 'eating' as a hobby."

He mimed strangling himself and twinkled at me. "That's exactly why I messaged you, actually," he said, serious now. "I've been on a few terrible dates in my time, but I saw your picture and I thought, 'This woman—no, this *goddess*—aspires to more in life than simply digesting.'"

This time I laughed so hard I thought I would fall out of the sky.

My plane was now leaving in seven hours, and I planned to spend all of them with him.

22.

Effie

Invigorated by his swim, Charlie offered to cook dinner.

As Effie counted out cutlery from the drawer, she watched beneath her eyelashes as he shook the vinaigrette into life from where it had settled in its glass bottle. Iso had presumably assured him that nothing had gone on with Steve—*could Charlie say the same to her?*

Effie knew that her own doubts would subside if she didn't prod any further—just like the oil trickling down the insides of the stoppered bottle in Charlie's hand, eventually coalescing once more at the bottom into something manageable, before settling and lying tidily, undisturbed. Where they would pose no problem to her and Ben.

The others ferried bowls of fresh salad and baskets of bread to the table outside. It and eight metal chairs were the sole occupants of the patio now that the wedding guests' folding seats had been removed. Charlie himself carried the large plate of barbecue-tender duck breasts across the terrace from the grill, with no small amount of ceremony. He was one of those men who took pride in the fact that he could cook, not because it was a life skill but because it was an all too rare accomplishment among most of the well-to-do, hands-off men of his acquaintance.

Effie knew he prized it like an eccentricity, a quirk of nature, unaware that there were other men—men like Steve, for example—who cooked regularly and without pomp. Admittedly also with less red meat and fewer esoteric glazes, less swagger, far fewer utensils, and an altogether less intensive load for whoever would wash up in their wake, but with the laudable aim of feeding their families and their loved ones, rather than simply to show off their place in the modern gendersphere.

She understood that cooking gave Charlie a sense of himself: skilled, modern, a catch. Tonight, it had helped him shrug off the greasy coating of self-loathing his hangover had left him with. The sun had melted some of it, and the pool had rinsed off yet more. His performance in the kitchen had been cleansing, and the wine currently tinkling into a glass—"Why not?" he had asked with a shrug when Lizzie had suggested opening a bottle. "We're on holiday!"—had been a rebirth of sorts.

"Charlie's so amazing in the kitchen," Iso purred as he set the dish down in front of them.

The nervous, shivering man Effie had encountered in that very room nine hours earlier had been replaced by the usual Charlie, smooth and self-confident. Even Steve and Anna seemed more relaxed; they had tended a salad, side by side, at one of the thick marble worktops in the kitchen, and the efficiency of the production line they formed spoke volumes even though they had exchanged no words.

As Effie set the table with Ben, she laid some of her inner turmoil to rest, regulated her feelings and breath with napkins and cutlery. When they had finished, Ben coaxed her to walk the perimeter of the grounds with him, stopping to kiss her as they took in the view across the valley from the pool.

"It's surprisingly hard to get you on your own with all this lot around," he said as they stood entwined and silhouetted against the beginnings of sunset in front of them. He threw a glance at the house and waved back to Lizzie where she stood, alone, on the terrace, looking out at the horizon too. She didn't return his salute.

When they reached the table, the sight of yet another sweating green bottle sheathed in cooling chrome raised Effie's pulse briefly. Her mouth dried and her stomach flipped at the thought of consuming anything from within it. She'd have no trouble turning down a drink this evening—her first day without alcohol in she didn't know how long. Quite when she had come to rely on it so much was yet another thing she couldn't remember; but it was something she and Ben had rather bonded over this past month, a shared hobby.

Is binge-drinking a hobby? Remembering Bertie's abstemiousness, Effie flinched at the knowledge that she'd drunk as much the night before as most people consume in a week.

At the head of the table, where the corner of the terrace jutted out over the slope down toward the pool, Bertie sat with the new notepad open next to his plate. He tapped his pen on its first blank page like a street hawker of bad portraiture and was received about as enthusiastically.

"What," asked Charlie, looking up from a plate of food that he'd describe as exquisite even though he'd been the one to make it. "Is. *That*." He held his knife and fork accusingly in clenched fists resting on the tabletop.

"Please." Anna sounded queasy. "No games. I can't take some stupid team thing tonight."

"Don't worry." Bertie reassured her with a smile. "This is how we find those wedding rings. We're going to pool all your memories to come up with a rough idea of where they might have gone. What's the last thing you all remember?"

Anna didn't seem any happier at this suggestion.

Charlie cleared his throat and spoke again: "Come on, mate. It was just a big night, wasn't it? What is this, *Big Brother*? We don't need to retrace our steps—this isn't a whodunit, nobody got offed."

Effie couldn't help thinking about the message. *You deserve each other.*

She was the one—she now realized with a sickening intensity—who stood to lose the most from whatever had happened last night. She felt shame pinching at her edges as she contemplated forfeiting what she had with Ben over some stupid, drunken incident with Charlie.

You deserve each other. They had both come here attached to other people, after all.

"Well, Lizzie could do with finding the rings," said Anna lightly. "Besides," she added, looking pointedly at her husband, "if nobody has anything to hide, it shouldn't be a problem, should it?"

Her tight smile shifted to Lizzie. Steve, meanwhile, was so intently focused on his plate that the light from the table's candles reflected in the sparser patches of hair on the top of his head. It was short and sober now, but he had for years kept it in a longish, face-framing, music-writer mod cut that Anna had seemed to loathe and desire in equal amounts.

Effie remembered that when the time came a few years ago for Steve to face the fact that his crowning glory no longer renewed as lusciously as it once had, Anna had met him outside the hairdresser's afterward with a miniature of Jack Daniel's in a plastic bag from the newsagent's.

"You'll always be a rock star in our house," she said, and she'd toasted him with one of her own.

Anna thought her husband's heart might break over the loss of that haircut; Effie knew he'd rather go full buzz cut than hurt the woman who had mourned it with him.

Steve cleared his throat.

"I'll go first then," he said, "seeing as we all know where I woke up. In the library, on the sofa opposite Iso, in a towel, with my clothes in a heap on the floor."

Bertie began writing on the pad. "Very good, Steve—thanks, mate. Who's next? Iso, perhaps—Steve says you were in the same room as him . . ." Anna snorted, and speared a pink slice of meat. "Did you see the wedding rings?"

Across the table from Effie, Iso shook the hair that framed her face from her eyes as she finished chewing. "No, sorry."

"I fell asleep on one of the loungers by the pool," volunteered Ben, shrugging charmingly and laying a warm hand on Effie's bare thigh. "Woke up bloody freezing."

"Now me!" cried Lizzie, who seemed to have enjoyed her first glass of wine and had poured herself another. "I went to bed as soon as we arrived and woke up sixteen hours later to find my own fucking friends had held my own wedding without me. How's that?"

She spat the last syllable and took a swig. The others looked at the plates and shifted their feet beneath the table.

Bertie made a note—his writing spidery, Effie noticed, like a doctor's. An adult's. Her own was embarrassingly rounded for someone who liked to pride herself on being so cynical.

"Perhaps this isn't doing much good," said Anna, quietly. "We all drank pretty solidly until about two A.M.—then I couldn't keep my eyes open, so I went to bed. Whatever . . . happened, I'm sure those rings are still in the house. They'll probably turn up when we pack up to leave."

The tines of Anna's fork clinked against her teeth as she ate another mouthful just to give herself something else to focus on. The stiffness round the table suggested that the end of this holiday, when it came, might not be met with as much disappointment as a return flight usually is.

"Perhaps you're right, Anna," said Bertie, putting his pen down. "Unless you remember seeing them, Effie? Where did you end up last night?"

Thickly and painfully, Effie swallowed the morsel she had been chewing for what felt like hours. It was as big as a cannonball against the rawness of a throat that had been stripped by digestive acid for much of the morning. She flicked a glance at Charlie, but his gaze was resolutely on the glistening remnants of the meal cooling on the serving plate in the middle of the table.

"Me?" Effie tried to sound insouciant, as if the next part was oh-so-casual. As if she'd planned it "for banter," as the sports teachers at Coral Hill so often claimed of their lame practical jokes. She considered using the phrase now, and decided against it. "Oh I, err . . . woke up in the honeymoon suite."

Wish I had a glass of wine to wash that down with, she thought, but she managed to stay her hand from reaching toward the bottle.

The table was silent, its length framed by two rows of intrigued faces staring back at her like jurors along the bench, and Bertie at its head, desperately trying to arrange his face into something more neutral than the curiosity that had briefly trespassed across it.

"Really?" said Ben, almost admiringly.

"The honeymoon suite?" Anna cried. "What on earth took you up there?"

What—or who?

In the seat to Bertie's left, Lizzie tried to conceal her hurt at that white, future-filled sanctum having been defiled. She gulped another mouthful of wine, and when she eventually spoke, her voice was low and sad. "Fuck's sake, Eff. Did you have to?"

Effie glanced up from her shame just in time to see Ben's eyes shift to her face from Lizzie's.

"Okay, never mind!" Bertie cut in, and Effie was grateful to him for at least the third time that day. "The rings will definitely be around here somewhere, like Anna says."

At the foot of the table, Charlie raised his eyes slowly and meaningfully, in that way that he had. The way that Lizzie, Anna, and Effie all remembered admiring during the brief window in which they had fancied him when their paths first crossed his at university. That window had closed after a matter of weeks—first when he had taken up with Effie—and then been sealed afterward, by which time they were more like sisters, and he had proceeded to parade a steady stream of more attractive women back and forth along the corridor they all shared.

The look had always suggested that he had something much

more important to be getting on with. Charlie had done it over bars and books at them, across board games and birthday cakes, for as long as they had known him. In the olden days, it had been accompanied by a smoke ring, perhaps, or a wink, but this time it seemed uncharacteristically serious. One second passed, then two—then finally the right-hand corner of Charlie's mouth ticked up as though attached to a puppeteer's string.

He gave a wry half-laugh. "Well, I woke up in one of the back bedrooms all by myself. No memory of even going upstairs. Christ, I was obliterated."

He returned his gaze to his plate, mopping at it with a hunk of baguette. Iso continued to look at him long after he had finished speaking.

"Just to say," she began quietly, then cleared her throat. "Just to say, my clothes weren't actually in the room with me and Steve." The rest of the table looked at her, a perfectly symmetrical face floating in the dark among the glasses on the table, the flickering night-lights reflected in the dark pools of her eyes.

She's so beautiful. Effie's heart pinched for Anna, and she felt a dim nausea that was unconnected to the hangover she had gradually shrugged off over the course of the day.

"My stuff was all out here, on the table near the pool," Iso continued. "I went for a swim—I know that was stupid of me, late at night and under the influence . . ."

Here she held both palms up. "I'd forgotten about it, but once I charged my phone this morning, I saw on the camera that I got Steve and Ben to take some pictures for me."

Effie's stomach slid to her feet. Of course Ben had been enlisted to take those photos: with his looks, he was far better suited to Iso than to Effie. She tried to smile brightly as he awkwardly attempted a neutral expression, but the home truth sank into her skin like butter on hot toast—even as his hand continued to lie warmly on her leg. Under the table, he began to trace circles on her thigh; despite herself, Effie felt the hairs on her neck stand on end in response.

"Pictures?" Anna squawked. "Of you naked?"

"No!" Iso replied quickly. "Well, yes, but not so you can see. Just me in the pool, nothing that would break the rules on Instagram, you know."

"You can't show nipples," Charlie offered darkly.

"But they're all really blurry because they were both so drunk. So I got out and Steve and I fell asleep on the sofas. Separate sofas. Nothing more."

Steve looked hopefully at his wife, and she offered in return a cold contempt that was even more unsettling than her earlier anger.

"Well," Bertie said, and then: "Well. You're all still recovering. Not feeling quite—"

"Average to low, is what I'm feeling," Lizzie interrupted him. "So, on that note, I'm going up to bed."

As she pushed back her chair and carried her plate inside, Effie wondered whether she should go after her friend, to apologize for sleeping in that misused, petal-strewn four-poster. But what would she say to Lizzie's inevitable line of questioning? She still didn't know the answers herself.

Effie also considered chasing after her to apologize for bringing her ex-fiancé's best friend on a holiday that was supposed to be about moving on. She had noticed the two of them, Lizzie and Ben, orbiting each other as though they were repellent ends of magnets: never quite coming together, politely avoiding any interactions beyond the most phatic, staying carefully out of the way or folding themselves closed should they have to pass one another. Effie felt suddenly slightly ashamed at the prospect of sharing her room with Ben that night.

Later, with the dishes washed and the kitchen wiped down, the group began to disperse for the night as the moon rose, large, white, and looming over the ancient building and the valley below. The terrace looked as cold and hard in silver by night as it did warm and golden under daytime's touch.

As Effie crossed the Hall and climbed the stairs to bed, she was overwhelmed by the weariness she had thus far staved off. This natural tiredness had eluded her for as long as she had been determined to turn in to bed half-cut and booze-wired, and she reveled in the warm heaviness that had been earned as surely as the hangover it was replacing, rather than induced by a gulp of pills.

Earlier in the day, Effie had selected a more suitable room for the rest of her stay, one toward the back of the house that was furnished with two twin beds, given that the double rooms were all taken. *The one Charlie must have slept in last night.* She hoped furiously that he had been telling the truth, but the hairs on the pillow next to her. . . .

Sleeping in either single bed would be a depressingly solitary experience, but a less loaded, less incriminating one than last night's choice. The door to the honeymoon suite had remained firmly closed ever since she had scurried in and straightened the sheets—beat the clefts out of each of the pillows—earlier that afternoon.

Now, at the top of the stairs that led back into the Hall, Effie glanced up to see Charlie in the corridor, bed-ready in T-shirt and boxer shorts, rumpled and weary. There was a new dash of salt and pepper in his hair, she noticed, but he looked as boyish as ever. When he saw her appear, he beamed and strode toward her.

"Effie—" He took her arm just below the elbow and bent his dark head to look deep into her eyes.

A swirling of memories dormant for so long. For years. Silt in water stirred up again. But rather than dredging up any sort of romantic feelings for Charlie, Effie simply felt a throb of guilt and fear course through her. Guilt that she might have ruined what she had with Ben; fear that he might find out.

"Effie." Charlie's voice was hoarse, an urgent whisper, and she suddenly knew how it would have played the previous night between two people so drunk it seemed the right thing to do. Guilt-edged desire, all the more charged and less rational for its secrecy, its swiftness. Its unexpectedness.

Charlie's breath was warm on her cheek, and she cringed from his closeness, squeezing her eyes shut.

"Sorry I was so drunk last night," he said hurriedly, checking the corridor anxiously in case anybody else appeared. "Hardly my usual suave self, eh? Thanks for a fun time though, Eff. G'night."

He walked away from her before she had time to even open her eyes again, and closed the door to his room—*his and Iso's room*—before she could even register what he meant. Disappeared before she knew quite what had happened. Again.

The scream was so short and so sudden Effie wondered whether it had come from her.

Immediately, Charlie was replaced in the corridor by another shape. Steve in a dressing gown, ejected from a nearby room on the left as forcefully as if he had been shoved out from someone on the other side of its door. When he was joined by Anna seconds later, Effie realized he had been.

His expression was stricken, his wife's eyes wide with fear.

The scream had come from the kitchen. Suddenly the landing was full of people again.

By the time Effie—rooted in place—had hurtled down the stairs and reached the others, they had done the gruesome work of discovery for her. She looked at the scene in the scullery through eyes that had deliberately lost their focus, sparing her the details of it. Ben pulled her to him as she entered the room.

"I—I—I was just looking for some ice," Iso stammered.

Charlie wrapped her in his arms, eyes fixed in wide consternation on the spot in front of them, the open freezer chest. Next to them, Steve reeled backward when he saw what was inside it.

Some way off, Anna pressed her fingers over her mouth. Her eyes made an inquiry of her husband. Effie tiptoed forward.

Inside the freezer, the pale pink of flesh, wrinkles of skin.

"What the f—" Charlie swallowed the contents of an unbidden gag.

Two cloudy, lifeless eyes looked back at them from the head lying on a pillow of ice. A gaping mouth and teeth bared in a limp, dark, silent scream, matched by a savage slit and empty cavity in the abdomen.

The body was eerily bloodless, drained of its life force before it had been dumped.

Delivered, Effie corrected herself, *not dumped.*

Bertie staggered in to join them, and then Lizzie pushed wildly through the crowd they had formed, a specter in a white night-gown with a blanched, frightened complexion to match.

"Oh," she said in a dull monotone, her fear turning to a tired grimace. "The hog roast did turn up."

TWO
DAYS
AFTER

23.

Anna

"Shall we go out today?" Lizzie asked that morning, spacey despite having woken up well after the rest of them. *Sleeping pills again*. She dug her hand into the brown paper bag of croissants Steve had brought back from the village for their breakfast.

They had assembled slowly at the outdoor table again, fetching china and cutlery, glasses of orange juice and pastry crumbs now scattered where they had sat over dinner only twelve hours before. Steve sipped from a short mug of black coffee, standing on the lip of the hill overlooking the plain below. Iso, freshly showered after having gone for a run when she woke up, had wet hair and an enviable sheen.

"Only half a croissant for me," she protested, loading up a bowl with berries and freshly cut peaches.

Effie seemed distracted, if less twitchy; she and Ben had come down to breakfast together—sheepish but quite sweet, Anna thought.

Charlie arrived downstairs still bleary with sleep; Bertie had been the second to last to join them, rumpled but nevertheless in smart chinos and shirtsleeves, pleading jet lag; but Anna felt alert. After the night's adrenaline shot, she had lain awake into the small hours trying to riddle out what she had seen on the wedding night.

Who she had seen.

She was also trying to reason with her emotions, to figure out how she felt about the man asleep next to her. Deep, deep resentment matched by an equally profound and fierce sense that they were two parts of the same person, she and Steve. Pushing him away felt like pressing a hand on her own chest and heaving herself out of the frame too. This was why she had come away and left Sonny behind: to remember who she was in her own right.

Anna felt in her bones that what Steve had told her—that nothing had happened with Iso—was true, and she believed the other woman's explanation. She thought briefly of Celia, of the hours Steve spent at home during the day while Anna was in court, at the office, meeting clients, and she wondered whether he had in fact ever spent them as she had feared: groping their Welsh neighbor's staggeringly svelte post-toddler body. Or was it all in her imagination?

If it was, that made their situation even harder to face up to honestly: the fault for the fissure between them would lie squarely with Anna herself. With her stress, her job, her inability to govern their unruly son. She had turned onto her side and pushed her left hand—and its ring finger—under the pillow, and had fallen asleep just as light began to crack around the edges of the wooden panel shutters.

"Should we try calling the wedding-planner woman again?" Iso asked across the breakfast table.

"I wonder whether we really need to," mused Ben. "We've cleared most of it away—as long as you and Dan don't get charged for anything, Lizzie. But you can sort that out when you get back, I'm sure. No need to stress over it now."

Lizzie set her lips together in a line, and left her croissant uneaten. They were so buttery and fresh, nobody else had managed to resist one.

Fifteen minutes later, they were in the town nearest to the Oratoire, back to what they had begun, in their state of slightly nervy isolation at the château, to think of as civilization. It was a three-horse sort of place at best, although there were enough artisan bakeries to sustain an entire team. With sidewalks had also come phone reception, at least—around the table, a semicircle of heads bent over work emails and text messages.

Behind the cat eyes of her sunglasses, Anna stared across the town square, beyond the squirting arcs of the fountain at its center to the ornately carved neoclassical buildings on the other side. They wibbled in the heat as the spray danced in front of them.

A scientist—an old one Anna remembered learning about at school—had once tried burning things and bottling the wibbling vapor they gave off before attempting to reconstitute them from the contents of his flasks. From cold wibble. Anna felt like she and Steve were repairing their marriage from much the same. The heat given off during their passionate years, whether in adoration or in anger, had turned out to be an insubstantial ether they seemed doomed to chase for the rest of their days. Perhaps that was just what marriage was after a while.

She sipped her Perrier Menthe through a striped straw that no one had demanded from her when the drink had arrived on its silver platter, that nobody had slurped on or chewed to a blocked pulp, that had caused no arguments, brought forth no tears. Anna missed her little boy with a piercing sharpness.

She ground the soles of her sandals into the grit under the table in her resolve not to check her own in-box. She had received—and pored over—a few pictures of Sonny sent by Steve's mother: wearing a crown and waving a piece of paper around; watching television (*television!*) with his sippy cup; head back and laughing on the swings near their house. She needed no more contact from the world beyond the plane trees that lined the *pétanque* pitch they were sitting by. That Steve was spending his time in the bright sunshine reading reviews of gigs in dingy

London basements on his magazine's website had begun to prickle her skin in irritation, so Anna cast her gaze around for something to distract from it.

People-watching—that was what these tables on the square were for. *So why does it feel like so many of them are watching us?*

As the group had walked around the tents and canopies of the market that morning, Iso had nodded in greeting to a teenage girl who had stopped in her tracks at the mere sight of them, as though the brunette in a ribbed crop top and high-waisted shorts in their midst was some kind of celebrity. The girl immediately raised her phone to Iso and snapped a picture: a follower.

They made a spectacle here, this huddle of long-limbed folk on their phones, pale bodies unlocked from starchy tailoring for a week, ill at ease (except for Iso) in clothes that showed so much skin. The locals pecked around them like birds, edging closer to take a look but fluttering back again whenever any of them shifted in their seats.

Across the square, standing behind the fountain, a man in wraparound sunglasses was staring at them. Strong brows and a Roman nose.

Dan?

Anna sat up quickly and angled her head to better make him out between the plumes of water. He had the same build as Lizzie's former fiancé, the same coloring, even.

But the man moved off too quickly for Anna to get a good look; he was probably, she figured, just another local out for a morning stroll. Whoever he was, he had been scanning the group at the table from left to right with some intent—though then again, Anna noticed, so too was the little old lady on one of the wooden chairs next to them.

24.

Effie

Effie was oblivious to it all as she composed a reply to James's message. There had been nothing more from him since the last salvo, and she could hold out no longer against responding.

A room—but not a bed—shared with Ben had thrown her already jumbled thoughts and feelings for her ex back into play, tumbled her regrets about the past and her hopes for the future together like a salad. They had slept chastely in their twin beds, too exhausted, in the end, after a day's hangover and the fuss over the freezer before lights-out to even push the frames together, let alone try anything more vigorous. Waking at such a polite distance from the man she had spent so many nights entwined with had left Effie jittery with all the many unknowns in her life.

She didn't want to speak to her ex. They had met up for a coffee six weeks or so ago, and even that contact had cost Effie in regression. Her frail, feigned nonchalance had spattered up the walls of her flat along with the muffin they had shared after she'd spent the subsequent three hours of the afternoon in a bar, trying to drink away the very sight of him.

She decided to text him: "I'm on holiday. What do you need to say?"

Effie clicked Send and watched for the ticks to turn blue.

When they didn't immediately, she put her phone facedown on the table. Then she lifted it, unlocked it, and checked again. Still gray. She thrust it deep into the straw bag she had brought out with her.

"Did anyone get through to this Marie woman about collecting all the wedding furniture?" asked Bertie, and Lizzie shook her head quickly, almost violently.

"I'll text Dan," said Ben. "See if he knows anything about it."

Effie saw Anna's attention snap back from observing the scene around them. "Let us know what he says," she said, simply, from across the table.

Effie watched as, next to her, Ben tapped out a message to his oldest friend: "Mate, some of the wedding stuff arrived after all. Thought everything canceled? Give us a ring when you can."

Effie noticed the awkward phrasing as soon as he wrote it. Dan had given Lizzie a ring six months ago and—Effie saw it now, still sparkling on her friend's finger across the table—she had yet to give it back. There were two more that had gone astray in the château up the hill behind them, too.

Ben ended his message with a single telephone emoji—the black Bakelite handset of an obsolete desk phone—and clicked his screen dark again.

Why do we still think of phones that way when they've looked totally different for more than a decade?

She reached into her bag and flipped the smooth, thin brick of her iPhone over in her hand: a lifeless slab to be stabbed at clinically in bird's-eye view rather than caressed close up or laughed into. Effie's contained within its hard drive a hotline to the most intimate details of her existence—diary, several dating apps, even a period tracker and fertility monitor—but she couldn't remember the last time she had used it to listen to another person's voice.

Instead, Effie messaged friends and family almost constantly on her phone, and refreshed the headlines on it several times a day to stay in the loop. But the immediacy the device offered—the connections and relationships it fostered—was a thing apart from the warm-blooded reality of living. Rather than joining people up as the old ones had—stringing love and friendship between homes like bunting, along the lines that still hung in near obsolescence from poles on each side of the square they were sitting in—these new phones had untethered them from their surroundings and the people they existed alongside. She and James had spent so much time scrolling through theirs on the sofa next to each other, she hadn't noticed what should have been obvious: that they shared a flat but not a future.

What else had she missed?

Thinking again of the cartoon phone, Effie let her mind unfurl itself further. Why did they, the oldest friends she had, all still think of one another—their dynamic and what drove each of them—in exactly the same terms as they had at university when, clearly, they were all so different now? They had experienced that change alongside one another, but how much had they ever really acknowledged it?

Anna had always been the responsible one—that had crystallized into her being a reliable sort of fixer, her former brilliant steadfastness morphed into a mundane alarm clock–like dependency. Lizzie, at times impulsive but always considerate, still hadn't even told them why she had taken the most important decision of her life. What had happened between her and Dan, why they were all here. Not even in private to Effie, as though the secret they had held close between the two of them for so long counted for nothing.

Effie had once been lively and witty—the silly one—but she had felt her brand of humor wither to sarcasm these past months. Any vivacity she had was turning to bitterness as she stewed and steeped herself in sadness. And Charlie. Louche, caddish Charlie, despite his puppyish affection for them, was flighty with the many other women who had flitted through his life in the years they'd known him. It had been easy to laugh at his clownishness, because the hearts being broken were not theirs.

Effie's own felt a little heavier in her chest again. Once Ben had closed their bedroom door last night, he had yawned and stretched extravagantly, climbed into the tiny bed opposite hers, and turned his back on her. If it had come as a surprise, her reaction had even more so: Effie had realized she was quite relieved. She'd been so flustered by it that she had forgotten Charlie's attempt to prune back whatever might have budded between them on the wedding night.

She had always wondered—dispassionately, really—whether the way they had tessellated in their first year—so perfectly matched in both interests and intellect that they could have passed for an old married couple—could ever rear its head again between them. Now, as she remembered the heat of him next to her, and the gruffness of his voice in her ear during those grasped moments on the landing, Effie felt less objective about the possibility. In fact, she felt rather wistful.

Stop it. This is exactly what he does. What he has always done. You used to laugh at the girls who fell for it; don't become one of them.

Effie had no physical evidence of something happening between her and Charlie. She knew from having pored over her goose-pimpled skin under the bare bulb of one of the house's bathrooms that the fading bruises that dappled her legs had all been self-inflicted during collisions of a more tangible nature—with her coffee table, say, or her wooden bed frame.

"I've never felt like this about anybody before."
She heard his voice from the deep well of her memory.

Had he really said those words, or was she simply spinning what she wanted to hear? Charlie had apologized to her on the landing, but for what? Effie felt herself anxiously disassociating from the scene as her mind whirred on. The thinking part of her brain levitated like a drone high above the slatted table they were gathered around.

It's just Charlie.

There he was, sitting two people along, spinning beer mats with Bertie as if they were a pair of teenagers, the low-key aggression he had displayed toward the other man yesterday as he had tried to reconstruct the wedding night now apparently neutered.

Stop being so silly.

A warm hand on the side of her neck brought Effie back to the square, the laughing of children playing near the plashing droplets from the fountain. She refocused her eyes from reverie to short distance and turned to look at Ben's warm and smiling face, the hint of a golden tan already collecting on his strong cheekbones. His pink lips hovered near hers, and she leaned in to brush them.

He had been Lizzie's best man. But he was hers now.

They crisscrossed their way back through the tents of the market to the cars, which they had parked in a dappled grove in front of a squat-towered medieval church.

"Shall we take a look inside?" asked Bertie.

Its heavy, studded doors—not unlike those of the Oratoire— swung open noiselessly when he pushed before anyone had time to dissent. Inside, sunlight scored the darkness with dusty shafts across the aisle and between the rows of plain wooden pews. The faintest trace of incense still hung in the air, left over from that morning's service like motes of prayer.

In the old days, Effie thought, Charlie would have petulantly sparked up a cigarette and sat outside to deliberately avoid anything vaguely educational, but he had mellowed in recent years— and given up smoking, just like the rest of them. *What a cliché we all are.* She watched the curve of his dark, already tanned neck as he bent his head to read one of the information boards detailing the age of the bell tower, the provenance of the stones, the names of the saints who decked each pillar.

People came here to search the divine countenance, but as Bertie slid into a pew on the far side of the nave, it was clear he was looking for somewhere to sit and make a phone call. Leaving Ben to look at a marble effigy—a reclining knight no doubt versed in chivalry and ladies fair—Effie stole across the aisle and sat down next to Bertie, a question on her lips.

He mimed to shush her, then showed her as he tapped the foreign mobile number of Marie the wedding planner, scavenged from the dog-eared and now void invitation he had packed in his suitcase, into his screen.

She answered on the third ring. *"Oui, allô?"*

"Bonjour, Marie!" Bertie attempted in French, before stalling and diverting to his mother tongue. His hushed tones joined the general murmur of the others as they bent to look at the baptismal font, meandered through the side chapels. Effie always felt that old churches echoed with centuries' worth of whispers even when empty.

He continued: "I'm calling on behalf of Lizzie Berkeley, whose wedding was supposed to happen on Saturday at the Oratoire?"

He waited while the woman within his phone pulled up the details, and he crooked the phone out away from his face so Effie could hear her voice.

"Ah yes!" Marie trilled. "How could I forget? On, off, on—the course of true love is never straight, am I right?"

Bertie made a general noise in agreement. "Err yes, perhaps," he said. "But it was in fact supposed to be off, just plain off. The bride thought she had canceled everything. Then the setup, when we arrived was, er . . . on?"

"Oui," singsonged the tinny voice in his ear. "That's right. She canceled my services just over a week ago. *Oh là!* I told her it was too late to get most of the money back, far too late."

Bertie tutted appreciatively.

"But then," the voice continued. "Then—and I was delighted, you know, because they seemed such a lovely couple—the groom emailed me to say they had changed their minds."

"Aha," said Bertie. He turned slightly to make eye contact with

Effie, and she felt her insides plummeting with the knowledge that it wasn't simply the administrative error they had all hoped for. The thought of having to break this news to Lizzie made her stomach contract with dread. "I see."

"They had changed their minds," Marie continued apace, "but wanted it smaller, more private. So just set up and go. *Et voilà*—I do!"

Bertie was silently contemplative.

"There is a problem?" Marie said tetchily down the line.

"No, no, nothing that you can help with, Marie," Bertie replied quickly. "Just checking you'll be picking up the furniture . . ."

"At the end of the week, as arranged, *oui*. Anything else?"

"No, thank you, Marie. Goodbye."

Bertie braced himself with one palm on the cool wood of the pew in front of him. He had begun this trail of clues with all the enthusiasm of an amateur orienteer, but Effie could see that his disappointment welled not so much at the search being over but at what it might cost his cousin when she found out. He had wanted to be able to soothe some of the anxiety he had recognized in her—as Effie knew he had done all those years ago—but the news that Lizzie's spurned groom had reinstated the ceremony she had canceled would hardly be easy for her to take.

"I think we have to tell her," Effie muttered to Bertie's contorted expression, noting how his cheeks were mottled with angst. He nodded sadly.

As Bertie explained the call to Lizzie, with her braced in the car's middle seat between him and Effie, the former bride's face closed in on itself.

"I see," she said brusquely, as though hearing bad news from the office. "Well, as long as they're coming to collect it all, I suppose."

"I just wish I could get through to him." Behind Effie, having dutifully taken his turn in one of the car's cramped rear seats, Ben's voice was flat. He removed his hand from her shoulder, where he had been gently tickling her neck, to anxiously rake it through his short hair, seemingly the most stunned of them all.

The text he had sent Dan had still not been delivered. "I've never known him like this," he said, his eyebrows slanted with worry. "I just hope . . ."

"What?" asked Effie, staring up into his face anxiously.

Ben breathed out, an "Eeeesh" of air escaping through his teeth. "Dan can be a bit . . . sensitive about stuff not going his way, that's all."

25.

Anna

As the chunky rental car crested the stony driveway, the figures of Charlie and Iso were visible outside the Oratoire, but their expressions of confusion—*no, worry?*—came into focus only as Steve parked up by the open front door, around which they loitered.

"There's someone inside," said Iso, as Ben unfolded his tall frame from the back of the car.

"Great!" he exclaimed, and Anna heard a wobbling bravado in his usually smooth voice. "Let's go and ask them what's going on."

Rounding the dark corner of the Hall after him, Effie and Anna heard the banging of pots and scraping of chairs in the kitchen. Whoever was in there was taking no pains to hide his or her presence, and this punctured some of their fears. Holiday homes, especially big houses, always had several sets of keys distributed between several sets of people, a cast of thousands who roved like the staff of some great estate in eras gone by. There were cleaners and pool boys, gardeners and maintenance men. Whoever it was might even have more information about the wedding setup.

Beyond the door to the kitchen, an elderly woman was attempting to navigate the remaining detritus of the Big Day. Short and kindly-looking, she had wrapped her doughty physique in a floral tabard that made Effie think of the faded wallpaper in her mother's sitting room. The woman looked at them all with dark, inquisitive eyes that peered like currants out of a bun.

"How am I supposed to clean with all this in the way?" she lamented.

Her southern, agricultural dialect was one that Anna could barely understand, let alone reply to the way she had to the clear, bourgeois voices that had floated out of Madame Wynn's giant cassette player at school. The housekeeper fumed esoterically in words Anna wasn't meant to know, and Anna attempted, with British awkwardness, to calm her down.

She hadn't been expecting the wedding to take place either, they gleaned from her exasperated demeanor and extensive repertoire of mime. Clearly, they were not the first visitors not to be able to chat away with her in the vernacular. *Non*, her orders had simply been to check that all was well with the Oratoire's guests this week.

Anna used her thumb and little finger to make telephone gestures at the housekeeper as she removed her apron, finished with her rounds for the day. "Marie?" she asked, nodding hopefully.

"*Non, non,*" the old woman tutted, mirroring the gesture. "Matthieu. I tell."

She picked up a string bag of peaches from the kitchen table and shuffled on thick legs out of the Hall, back into the sunshine.

As they watched her leave, Charlie's voice rang across the stone floor toward them, high and with the slightest tremor to it. Anna, Effie, and Lizzie all jerked to attention when they heard it—noticeable for the fact that it betrayed something they had never heard from him before: shock. Iso seemed surprised too.

Charlie was as unflappable as he was unembarrassable, but it was clear that something had penetrated that world-weary facade.

"Guys!" he shouted back to them.

Please, not another dead animal. Anna felt sick in advance.

"Come and see this!" Not a cry but a bark. From someone who didn't want to deal with something alone.

But when they reached the terrace, Charlie wasn't alone—Ben stood with him. Despairing of the monoglot dumb show in the kitchen, they must have opened the doors onto the terrace with the intention of hurling themselves, in dusty clothes, straight into the pool to freshen up.

As Anna bounded across the terrace toward the two men, she lifted her head to see the table, still with the scattering of crumbs they had left after breakfast, and next to it Bertie's notepad—*that bloody thing again*—with its pages fluttering slightly in the very lazy breeze.

But it was not as they had left it.

Iso ran out to Charlie first, worried by the expressions she had seen on the other women's faces. They weren't far behind her. Then Bertie and Steve. They made an unconscious semicircle behind Charlie and Ben, taking in the open notepad like a group of student doctors taking instructions from a consultant.

The top page—where the night before Bertie had detailed their memories—had been ripped off. Quickly and savagely, leaving a jagged overhang onto the page below. It wilted, upside down, in the sun-bleached grass a few paces away, where, every so often, the warm, lazy air stirred it slightly. Several more pages had been torn out too, as if in a sort of frenzy, and had scattered in the slow air around the terrace and lawn.

The next fresh page of the pad had been written on. With the same black marker pen that Bertie had used but in bigger, bolder letters and with more force. The paper had ripped in places under the pressure of the angry scrawl; the scratchy block capitals— different from the ones in the wedding book—looked as violent as they felt to read.

When the huddle around the pad digested the message, each person felt it had been left there for them.

"TELL THEM THE TRUTH."

26.

Six Months Earlier: Lizzie

When I think about the woman who got ready for her engagement party and the one who returned home from it, I can hardly believe we are the same person.

The first one—blond hair freshly blow-dried in a salon that was deliberately slightly too expensive for my pay packet, with green plants trailing beadlike leaves from the ceiling—didn't have a scintilla of doubt in her mind. She applied her makeup with a showgirl's rigor around a beaming smile so broad it was difficult to even blot her lipstick.

The other one, anxious and uncertain, cried it all off once her fiancé had fallen asleep.

Dan had bought me a dress for the party, one that I absolutely loved. I have it still, an albatross in a designer garment bag hanging at the back of my wardrobe. It breaks my heart to look at that dress now, because my fiancé zipped me into a straitjacket when he fastened it that evening and dropped a kiss on the back of my neck where I held my hair out of the way of the metal teeth.

When I took it off again at the end of the night, I half-wondered whether there would be bruises underneath. There weren't, of course—not on the surface.

The dress was black with a swirling gold pattern, short and frilly, but with a high collar and long sleeves that ended in a spray of ruffles. I felt like a Christmas cracker. There was frost on the pavement outside our flat when we left and twinkling lights in the shops by then, so I fit right in. Comfort and joy: that was what my future with Dan looked like.

We still couldn't believe we'd found each other. Who meets their soulmate on a dating app? Plenty of people, as it happens, but we were still reveling in the fortuitousness, the serendipity, the kismet of having both logged on at just the right moment. We were pinching ourselves; it had felt right from the get-go, and we knew how lucky that made us.

We skittered, head-to-toe wobbly with anticipation—me in velvet platforms, him in a pair of tan leather brogues his father had bought him to break in ahead of the wedding day—into the bar Dan had hired to hold our nearest and our dearest in celebration of the much bigger party yet to come.

May. That was all we had decided so far, but I'd just that morning booked us flights to visit a couple of venues in the south of France. After all those years crossing the globe following Guy around on that bloody boat, I could hardly believe I was drawing up my own itinerary, on my own terms, for the pursuit of happily ever after. It felt wonderful.

I hadn't expected so many people to be there. They had balloons and streamers for us when we arrived, party tooters and glitter strewn across the tabletops between the cocktails—all gold, to match me. I was a gleaming statuette, Dan's prize, and proud of it.

I saw Effie and Anna leap from the edge of a crowd that roared its appreciation as we walked in; they bundled me into a hug with congratulations all of their own. A constant at the center of a busy, changeable world—and, often, near a dance floor: my two best women, and the ones who knew me through and through.

We popped corks and clinked glasses, we smiled until it felt like our cheeks were spasming. I had more conversations that night about lace than I've had before or since, more questions about flowers, more unsolicited opinions on matters that were really nobody else's business. A friend of Dan's mother's pressed me on the subject of birth control; from behind the table he was deejaying at, Steve wanted me to name our first dance, our favorite song. These are the stitches that make up the tapestry of every wedding—the dress, the guests, and the photos are just the yarn.

Steve played smoochy songs and stylish songs, some for the oldies and some for the girls; we went to the bar when the air guitars came out. Tottering slightly in my heels, I lurched around my clutch bag—gold, of course—with Effie and Anna the way we had done five nights a week at university, and perhaps now did only five times a year.

It was the way we had celebrated success when we triumphed, the way we lifted each other's spirits whenever one of us needed it. It was on one of those nights out that I had met the man who could have been the father of my child—*blood on water*—but I wasn't going to dwell on that at my engagement party.

Ten years on, we howled along to the greats like wolves baying at the moon, with more girth and gray hairs now but more strength, more power, more self-knowledge too. *Or so I thought.*

Effie was a little glitchier than Anna and me—we couldn't keep up with her at the bar, but that was nothing out of the ordinary. Wedding stuff was tough on her, given James's resistance to it but, she assured us, it wasn't a commitment issue; he just wasn't into paperwork. She was right about that: he spent all night watching us from the bar, his face as joyless as an in-tray on a Monday morning.

He could have at least pretended to be happy for me.

Anna, meanwhile, was positively effervescent. A night out, her first in some time since Sonny had commandeered the space previously occupied by indulgent and hungover lie-ins. I worried for her head the next morning, but she didn't seem that drunk—just hopped up on life. And love, I suppose. There was so much of it in that room.

I took a breather at one point: didn't want my makeup sliding too far down my face, and I needed some water. My throat was parched from the heat of the disco lights and accepting everybody's expressions of goodwill. From the great surprise that Dan had orchestrated.

If only it could have lasted. Sometimes I wish I'd never left the dance floor and my best friends, never let myself be cornered like that—kept the memories of that night purely light and joyous, rather than sullying them in the dark.

My marriage was finished even before the engagement party was.

27.

Effie

"But who . . . ?" Steve was the first to speak as the loose pages from Bertie's pad billowed lazily around their ankles, like seaweed caught in the shallows.

Next to him, Effie's brain was connecting the frozen look of fear on Lizzie's face with the invasion of the château's centuries-old serenity—not just this morning but the day they had arrived—and the re-installing of a wedding canceled, a relationship broken off.

"It has to be Dan, doesn't it?" Anna murmured quietly next to her.

"Ach, guys . . ." Ben rubbed the back of his neck with one hand, swung the other in a limp fist through the air beside him in an arc. A loose punch with no target, but it was charged with exasperation and emotion. "I hoped it wouldn't come to this . . ."

To his right, Lizzie simply closed her eyes.

"But I'm worried he's gone off the deep end, yeah," he finished, his hand now coming to rest across Effie's shoulders, drawing her to him.

Before he could finish speaking, Lizzie turned silently and walked back into the house. Effie followed her up the stairs to her bedroom, desperate to comfort her, but the door was locked and she couldn't even make her voice heard above the noisy sobs coming from the other side of its oak panels.

Suspicious and shaken after taking in the angry message, the group scattered to various corners of the house and its grounds. Like characters in a murder mystery, they found themselves suddenly mistrustful of their holiday companions, as though there might be strychnine in the tea, a revolver behind the shower curtain. A muffled thump and one fewer in the party by morning.

Don't be stupid.

Anna, too, had looked pained and taken herself to the cool of the library; Steve went after her. Charlie and Iso retreated upstairs to exchange their own truth—one of very few things that girl wouldn't put on social media, Effie thought spitefully. As Iso had moaned to them several times, the lack of Wi-Fi was severely compromising her output.

Effie retired to a lounger by the pool, where Bertie lay dozing nearby. Next to her, Ben read a magazine—a political one that asked big questions—and laced his fingers into hers as they held hands between the two sunbeds.

Despite the atmosphere, she had to admit the scene was perfect: he had reached for her almost unconsciously as soon as she had sat down, whereas she had practically had to chase James down for the briefest of embraces toward the end. But Ben's apparent contentedness only served to increase Effie's anxiety that she had somehow compromised what they had together: her mind continued guiltily to whirr over the events of their first night at the château and the possibilities it still contained.

Laughter. A shriek. A man's voice.

Whispers and tears.

And then a blackness so empty Effie worried she would collapse in on herself if she got too close to it. She was scared of atomizing in the great void of her memory; there was simply nothing there at all. Nothing, until there had been whiteness again. Whiteness and that bed. Those petals.

Effie scrolled through the grainy footage in her head. So much for all her plans to luxuriate in the sun and zone out from her fears, to allow the lapping of water nearby to lay the internal ghosts to rest. Her mind was working in overdrive, and the flapping, guzzling filters in the swimming pool provided an infernal drumbeat as her thoughts spun over and over.

What did I do? (*Thunk.*)

What did I say? (*Thunk.*)

Who was I with? (*Thunk.*)

What the fuck happened? (*Thunk. Thunk. Thunk.*)

The thought Effie had not yet allowed herself to approach directly but that kept creeping into her head, uninvited, was at which point all of her clothes had been removed.

"You're ready to be happy again."

Had he really said that?

She flinched involuntarily at the sound of Charlie's voice inside her head and gave a short, cringing moan that made Ben lift his head to look at her. *Still not ready to dwell on that one.*

This was all she had within her to build a picture of that night, those lost hours. What had she given away during the darkness? No more than she had willingly—drunkenly—offered too many others in recent months: her loneliness and her dignity.

Hooking up was supposed to be fun, wasn't it?

It hadn't been at university, but back then Effie assumed she'd been too green, too inexperienced. Too full of self-loathing to make it work for her, this universally acknowledged fun thing that some young people (men) liked to do and other young people (women) pretended to. At nineteen, she was not well versed enough in her own body to find pleasure in other people throwing it around for her.

Now a grown-up—she had a career and a mortgage; what more would it take to convince her she was one?—Effie was too self-possessed to find much pleasure in giving it away either. That was what had been such a revelation with Ben: the confidence she had found being with someone so enthusiastic for her; the way he touched her like a precious jewel rather than flipping her like a steak on a barbecue; his presence, eyes tracking hers rather than scrunched closed to make it go quicker. Such dedication to being in the moment, in fact, that he wanted to linger over it, to remember, to record for posterity. . . . Effie had never felt herself so hungrily pored over as she did with Ben, and she found that it thrilled her.

Before they'd met, she had downloaded several dating apps to make sure she didn't end up on the shelf, but they had instead brought her, several times, to an uncomfortable precipice with men she had barely begun to get to know, nor was sure she really wanted to.

Drinking was supposed to be fun too, wasn't it?

She noticed how the younger teachers at school had a steely grip on their vices, how they matched late nights in the pubs with early mornings at the gym. How, when they could be persuaded to swap their evening Mandarin or pottery classes for the sticky crush at the bar, they drip-fed themselves wine interspersed with plenty of water, while Effie drained glass after honeyed glass.

Where, she often wondered, had they learned this restraint? Effie found it suspicious and vaguely censorious. Didn't they need to cut loose? Didn't they find their tongue, their spark, their chutzpah in the easy confidence bestowed by the second-cheapest option on the wine list? There was only one explanation: they were bores, these kids. Moralistic losers saving for a house deposit. And watching them nurse their wine spritzers, Effie would order herself another sauv blanc out of sheer exasperation.

She had come of age during a time when your personality was but the slice of lemon to whatever was in the glass you were holding, had bolstered herself by knocking back whatever at hand was least warm and least bitter. They all had—at university, where friendships were formed through weights and measures, optics and ring pulls, reinforced by each "Cheers" and "Bottoms up." Salty hands and citrus grimaces. This was how she, Anna, Lizzie, and Charlie had socialized, not exercise or ceramics! Their favorite story was how they had once found Charlie asleep in a phone box; Iso's generation didn't even know what one was.

And hadn't it been fun? Hadn't drinking helped Effie forget her every care? The shyness, the awkwardness, the clanging sense of her own imperfections and devastating lack of things to say— all alleviated with the warm flush and sugary finish, the red faces and shouty slurred words. What was the worst that could happen? They'd stumble home, wake up in time for lunch, and do it again the next night, awarding each other different badges of honor each time. They continued to do it once they had jobs too, adjusting their hours slightly around the office.

Effie hadn't felt a moment of regret until her late twenties, when hangovers began to announce themselves in nausea and a dread so existential it deserved an -ism all of its own.

More recently, however, she had realized that she did in fact have some regrets during that time. The fact of having hurt feelings, of saying rather more than was politic, of not being taken seriously. The fact of having shared her body with people that, in the cold light of day, she'd rather not have done. Effie had always thought of these facts as things that could be shrugged off, like the sluggishness that followed any night on the sauce, but when she watched the junior teachers she worked with, she understood that they were things that could have been avoided instead.

She had been careless with herself for most of her life, careless of her friends, careless of James. Now she had been so careless that she literally didn't know what she had done or who she was anymore.

Effie thought again of the message in the notepad. She didn't know her own story, let alone whatever truth it was she had to tell. How could she when so many of the details in her life remained beyond her reach?

Beside her, Ben stirred and put his magazine down. "I'm going to try calling Dan," he said with a resigned expression, and set off some way down the drive, phone aloft in one hand—as if that might help locate his friend, the man they were all coming to suspect was behind the strange campaign of terror in the château.

"Do you think he's here?" Effie asked Bertie, simply, after a few minutes. Lizzie's cousin was the only other person by the pool with her while Ben roamed the perimeter.

Lizzie's cousin hadn't tried to insert himself into her thoughts the way most men did. Effie found herself enjoying both the proximity and the distance he so instinctively seemed to gauge. Bertie tucked a corner of the page of the book he was reading down into a point to save his place.

"He seems to be," he said carefully. "But I think we're safe. This . . . intrusion is unsettling, but we haven't been threatened. There's no sign of forced entry or violence."

Effie raised her eyebrows over her sunglasses.

"None of us know what happened between Lizzie and Dan," Bertie continued. "The most likely explanation is that the person trying to unnerve us is the groom. The groom who un-canceled the wedding and isn't picking up his phone."

"But the note," she pressed. "Do you think he's coming for her?" Effie felt her gaze mist over at the ballsy Hollywood gesture. She had always liked Dan. Then came clarity as her default cynicism restored: "Isn't it all a bit creepy?"

"The intersection between romantic and creepy has always been a difficult line for some men to tread," answered Bertie. "Especially now that women have realized that they're often one and the same."

Effie laughed and looked out over the turquoise pool, her spirits lifting once more with some mental space from her own problems. How inviting it looked was directly proportional to her mood, and she began rummaging in her bag for sun cream.

She was climbing out of the bath when she noticed it—just a trickle at first.

Effie had retreated to the bath when her skin had begun to feel tight with sun exposure and the rime of lotion and salty sweat on it had hardened into a gritty layer. She, Ben, and Bertie had spent all afternoon by the pool, exchanging a few words now and then but otherwise simply enjoying the mutually comfortable silence that came from reading and staring out across the plain beneath them.

She and Ben had regained some of the ease that had eluded them the previous night; some awkwardness, she rationalized, was only to be expected, given the strange atmosphere at the house, the fact that he didn't really know anyone other than Lizzie. The fact that he and Effie had only really been together for, what was it, a month? She didn't think of herself as schoolmarmish, but she was certainly not the type of person to go on holiday with someone after only four weeks. Then again, did this rather fraught trip still count as a holiday?

Gradually they'd been joined around the water by some of the others: Charlie, who had left Iso sleeping; Steve, recruiting for a game of cards that Bertie and Ben signed up for; Anna too, eventually, blinking the guilty day-sleep of a child-free woman out of her eyes with a self-conscious grin. Spirits, it seemed, had improved—although Lizzie remained behind her closed door.

On her way along the corridor to the bathroom, Effie had tapped on Lizzie's door—once, then twice—and tried the handle. Still locked, but with sleep-heavy breathing audible behind it. She'd left her friend to nap unmolested. Effie would question her later about Bertie's theory.

Dan. Quiet, unassuming Dan, with his gentle face and his gentle ways. Was he really the sort of man to turn up, uninvited, on a quest to get the girl? It all seemed so Byronesque, and Dan was . . . well, Dan was an accountant.

Then again, he hadn't seemed the sort of guy to let the girl slip through his fingers either. He had been a devoted boyfriend, excelling at everything Guy had failed at: good at remembering birthdays, making himself useful, simply being present. Effie had been thinking that he and Lizzie should get back together—the relationship had been a great fit for them both. But Dan was only making himself look scary with all these grand—*or were they angry?*—gestures.

Effie shifted her weight in the milky water and bent her bony knees up, so that their knobbles pointed to the ceiling of the steamy room. Built to keep the sun out, the ancient building retained its cool from thick walls and small windows. However, the very same principles conspired to make a small Mediterranean bathroom in which someone had run an out-of-context British bath—deep and unflinchingly hot—a swirling steamy box of condensation. The thick, damp air rolled above her, and Effie let her sweat mingle with the water.

She rested her head against the edge of the bathtub, scrolling internally through the ever-lengthening list of self-improvements she would make as soon as she got home again.

No drinking, no carbs, no more drunk-smoking (not much), some yoga, less TV.

She remembered how she had sometimes felt trapped in someone else's lifestyle when she was with James—not unpleasantly so, but with the inevitable decreasing of space one took up when there was always somebody to tell when you were going to be late, always somebody whose dinner might be delayed, who might wait up, who had asked you to pick up some milk on your way home.

Effie had tried to enjoy expanding again in the wake of his departure, but she'd all too quickly felt remote, like a helium balloon that slips a babyish hand and bobs farther and farther away into infinity. Sometimes she wondered when and how she would stop bobbing, saw her old life in retreat as though she were an astronaut blasting clear of Earth. All she was looking for—in those strangers' arms, those backs she hadn't recognized—was an anchor, although she knew enough about life and truisms and motivational quotes from the self-help books she couldn't quite bring herself to make a start on to realize that she had to be her own. But then there was Ben.

He had proved a grounding force already; still, there was something she couldn't quite put her finger on about him. Handsome, attentive, charming . . . but somehow not quite on her wavelength. Their humor clashed at times, or missed the mark entirely. The references she had shared with James had ranged vastly from politics to pop music; Ben, it seemed, didn't have much to offer in the way of culture beyond the pop-economics books he liked. *My God,* she thought, *listen to me reasoning myself out of a perfectly good relationship with a gorgeous man who genuinely seems to enjoy my company.*

And yet, in the dripping tap, she heard: *Don't settle, don't settle.* She had gone along with so many of James's whims; perhaps some time alone would show her that life was more comfortable when she wasn't bending to fit someone else's tastes.

Effie closed her eyes and listened beyond the tap, to the cicadas outside and the fitful hum of the bathroom fan above her head. She saw in her mind a bedroom and shivered away a memory of retrieving her belongings while a man whose face she didn't recognize pretended to sleep on until she left. She had drifted too far that time.

And what of this time? What of two nights ago?

I've never felt like this about anybody before.

There had been a moment at the market that morning, while Iso was taking pictures of glistening seafood laid out on ice and buxom tomatoes cascading from wooden crates, when Effie had stolen silently up to Charlie's side as he perused a trestle table full of cheeses. She wanted to ask him what was going on, but her voice failed her. "Are we okay?" sounded too much like they were a couple; "Are we good?" was something two passive-aggressive colleagues might exchange. Before she had been able to formulate anything satisfactory, Charlie had noticed her hovering.

"That one's got his eye on you, Eff," he'd drawled, pointing at a particularly baleful-looking fish, its sharp teeth bared in a downward grimace, before winking at her and strolling away toward Iso.

Since their strange, whispered interaction on the landing, Effie felt she and Charlie had orbited each other like vague acquaintances at a cocktail party, neither of whom could remember the other's name. Embarrassed at each other's existence because it served only to highlight their own failings, their own unreliable memories.

Effie took a deep, calming breath and hauled herself upright in the bath, releasing the plug to drain the water as she did so. Dripping onto the already slick tiled floor, she reached for a towel from the hooks on the wall. As she leaned out of the tub and into the line of the reflection in the mirror, which hung above the sink, steam billowed loosely around her body like a diaphanous sheer gown.

That was when she saw what was on the mirror—scanning upward from a trickle that her eyes followed like a delta to its source.

The rectangular mirror had fogged in the warm, damp room. In the obscuring clouds, Effie could see herself in pinkish outline but no longer make out her face. Except in the rivulets that crisscrossed its surface like cracks in dry earth.

The steam had resurfaced a message there, like a cry from the past, memories bubbling upward in the brain. The blaring capitals reminded Effie of those others they had found on Bertie's pad, which were now etched into the heart of the group. These spoke to her every bit as directly, as though yelled into her face at close range—so much so that she let out a blurt of fright. Not quite Iso's bloodcurdling scream the night before, but enough to draw footsteps from a group that was already on high alert.

The others padded swiftly from nearby rooms and congregated outside the door.

"You okay, Eff?" Anna's voice called through its wooden panels, as loud in the small room as if she had burst right in.

"Did you slip?" Lizzie asked anxiously. *So she's awake again.*

"I—I—I'm fine," Effie stuttered, wrapping a towel around herself and wondering whether to wipe the mirror clean.

As she swung the door open and two more sets of eyes alighted on the words, Effie's heart sank to watch two more faces—Lizzie's and then Anna's—visibly blanch at the force of them.

"YOU'RE MINE."

The letters were warped and streaked in the condensation as though they were melting.

No, that wasn't quite right, Effie thought: it was as though they were bleeding.

28.

Anna

As she walked quickly down the hill away from the house, Anna nervously tied and retied the belt of her green jersey dress in a jerky knot. Her hands shook and her heart was still thumping from the message in the mirror, summoned in the steam like a spirit during a séance.

Anna did not know for sure who had left it there, angry prodding fingers squeaking against the glass as they scrawled, but she had an idea.

Anna didn't want any of this in her head. She'd never asked for it.

How she wished she hadn't seen what she had on the wedding night.

How she wished they would just admit what they had done.

When she had walked far enough down the field to be out of sight of the rest of the house, Anna sat heavily and stared at the countryside spread out like a blanket in front of her. She felt Sonny's absence in her empty arms and wrapped them around her knees. The almond-shaped face of her antique gold watch told her it was six P.M. at home.

He would be in his high chair—an ergonomic Danish variety

that had come with enough promises of health benefits that she half-expected it to raise him for her. By this point in the meal, he would no doubt be covered in whatever he had nodded regal acquiescence to for dinner that night. He had this haughty expression sometimes, one that made her either laugh indulgently at the little prince she had created or want to scream, depending on her mood and his.

Anna recognized the total confidence of the well-cared-for child—the unquestioning knowledge that whatever he wanted he would get—in some of the male partners in her office. Then she worried she was raising another of them.

Nobody had taught her how to be a mother; Anna had simply found herself approximating one, as she had done in the playhouse her parents had given her on her sixth birthday. Back then, the power of make-believe had given her a sense of purpose: sweeping and dusting, stocking imaginary cupboards, cooking invisible meals. Now, as she did it all for real, she ran purely on fear and guilt. Fear that she was doing it wrong; guilt that she wasn't doing enough. (These days, she outsourced the sweeping and dusting to another woman, and felt dreadful about that too.)

Her and Steve's fridge had gone from empty but for beer, wine, milk, and a piece of cheese to one that was filled with fresh fruit and vegetables. Their bedtime had crept forward from midnight to nine P.M. They worked, ate, and slept, and in between they absorbed Sonny's love like essential nutrients when he was happy so that they might better bear the drudgery when he was not.

Anna used Tupperware now. She cooked things and froze them in portions that were perfectly calibrated to line Sonny's tiny stomach, so small they stacked in the freezer like plastic matchboxes. She had a laundry day—several actually, spread out across the week like some protracted purgatorial punishment—when she separated and folded like an old-fashioned washerwoman. She was grateful not to have had to master a mangle or a washboard or strong lye soap, but she reflected that, for those women, this had been their actual job, as opposed to something they did in their supposed leisure time.

They didn't have any leisure time; be more grateful.

This last was a constant refrain. Grateful for Sonny but also for the chance—the opportunity!—to work. Grateful for her salary, two-thirds of which went to the house and the rest to childcare she was unable to provide in person while she was earning it. And grateful to Steve—always, and reminded of it constantly by her friends—for the simple fact that he helped her at all.

Sometimes Anna felt so grateful she wanted to scream.

She had bought a sewing kit online recently, after she found a hole in one of Sonny's jumpers—a soft, luxurious garment bought as a present at such expense the giver could not possibly have had children of their own yet and known how swiftly and remorselessly it would be ruined. When the kit arrived, clinically arranged in neat spools and packets, it was so far from the organic mess of haberdashery that lived inside the well-used tin her own mother—who had never worked but had raised four children instead—kept in a drawer at home that it made Anna want to cry. Nobody had ever taught her to sew either.

She darned the hole inexpertly; when she was finished, it made a lumpy scar across the flawless cashmere, as if transplanted from a pirate's cheek. It reminded her of what she was: a Frankenmum reanimated from the corpse of who she used to be and stitched together with a barrister skin, improvising at everything because there was no one to show her how to do it. Her other friends were either childless or similarly struggling, trying to have it all without drowning in it.

Anna had a degree and a pupilage in law; her only qualification for being a mother had been her biology and her age.

Nobody had taught her what to say to her son or how to play with him. When they were alone together, there were sometimes great stretches of silence in which she felt Sonny's little brain atrophying. The days she came home late and found him and Steve together, wrestling in the sitting room or lining up all his model animals on the kitchen table, she wanted to ask them what the rules were—not just for their game but for this life they were all feeling their way through.

She rubbed a stalk of lavender between her fingers where it sprouted in the scrubby grass of the hillside. What exactly was she complaining about?

Anna had lost track. A vague sense of being taken for granted, of being dreary with tasks and haggard with other people's expectations. Of the sensation that life was one long to-do list and then, when she did manage to tick everything off, there was always another swing to push or story book to read. She was mourning time that was purely hers. On the rare occasions when she and Steve made it out for dinner, there was the knowledge that any wine consumed or late night embarked on—even at the weekend—they would be punished for the next morning, the inevitable headache even more pronounced now that Sonny had learned to climb into their bed and pry her eyelids open.

How had they spent their Saturdays and Sundays before him? Mostly drunk and asleep. It had been wonderful.

Now, though . . . Anna shuddered at the memory of the last night she'd spent drinking.

After they had found the second message—the one on Bertie's pad—Steve had followed her to the château's library, with its book-lined walls and low beamed ceiling, the long sofas where he and Iso had spent the wedding night.

"Are you okay?"

It was a question they asked each other regularly, except Anna's queries were laced with varying degrees of passive-aggressiveness. "Are you okay?" was no longer an inquiry but a signal: too sharp, too stressed, too brimming with silent fury—with work, with how tired they were, how messy and dissatisfied they felt. "Are you okay?" meant *Pull yourself together* or *Don't take it out on me;*

it meant *Snap out of it* and *If you don't like it, do something about it.*

When Steve said it now his face was soft, the lines either side of his mouth—deeper in the past few years—relaxed while his brow creased with care. "Are you okay?" was the question she'd been so desperate for him to ask her for so long that she didn't know where to start with her answer, so instead she simply cried.

"I'm so sorry, love," her husband breathed into her hair as she snuffled against his chest. He smelled of sun cream. "It was so stupid of me, so disrespectful. But nothing happened, you know. It never would."

"I know," Anna sobbed into his T-shirt—because she did. But his kindness made the secret she was keeping even more piercing, more shameful.

She'd got herself so caught up, it was no longer hers to tell.

But there were other truths she could share with her husband, ones that had been born with Sonny and hatched into spiky little creatures that had pecked at them ever since.

Sonny's nursery school still always called Anna when he was sick, despite knowing that Steve worked from home five minutes down the road. The senior partners at Anna's firm regularly remarked on her "real job" as a mother despite her working something like sixty hours for them most weeks and regularly missing her child's waking up and going to sleep. She didn't often make evening plans, but on the few occasions when she managed to get home before 8 P.M., Steve would arrange to meet one of his friends for a rare pint.

Why shouldn't he, simply because I can't?

Why should his life change, just because mine has?

Because they were supposed to be a team.

Between Anna's desk and her duty of care, there was little time for anything else. She saw Steve still able to visit his record shops, go to his gigs, even—*for fuck's fucking sake*—play his bloody computer games, although he had recognized that to do this in front of her anymore was petrol on a fire. The things Anna did in her spare time—her so-called *spare time*—were yet more chores: the leg waxes, dental appointments, and haircuts that kept her feeling (and looking, she hoped, although she had begun to doubt) like the person she used to be, rather than one growing gray hairs in neglected places.

Some women can't afford that; be more grateful.

Anna had felt so betrayed by Steve's larking around with Iso because, in her fast-paced and hectic but nevertheless very organized existence, the hurt pinpointed the very things she knew she was not on top of: her body and her husband.

The care they used to take with each other had dulled. The pleasure they found in each other had settled into cozy jollity rather than a sharp urge. Anna had expected the wonder to abate, but not the need. She slept in a T-shirt that had come free with their house insurance in order to guard against her husband's interest, but she'd found that his eyes, his lips, his hands no longer even bothered to frame the question.

Celia.

Anna subconsciously gripped the spare tire of fat around her middle, tweaked the fleshy drape under her chin. She still got a surprise every time she saw herself in photographs—bigger and looser now, recognizably her but wider, as though she'd been steamrollered. *No, Steve, it isn't a problem with the lens.*

"What are your best tips for having a family in this profession?" she'd asked one of the older women at the firm when she and Steve had started thinking about babies.

"Get to your target weight before you get pregnant," the brittle blonde, immaculate and trim in corporate suiting, had answered. "Or you'll never reach it again."

Now, at work, she was surrounded by sinewy women in their forties whose bodies belied having ever reached puberty but had produced two or more children; Anna—early thirties, mother of one—looked like she'd had five.

She told Steve a simplified version of this in the library that afternoon, much of which he struggled to hear through her strangle of indignation, snot, and tears.

"Is there anything going on between you and Celia?" she asked, aiming for calm but barking the words out regardless.

"Celia!" Steve looked baffled, and Anna's blood pressure slowed again. "Christ, no. She's nice enough, sure, and I do really feel for her sometimes, but she's . . . well, she's pretty annoying, really. Always texting and stuff, always needs a favor."

Anna began to laugh. "She is *really* annoying!" Then she began to cry. "She's *always* texting you!"

Not Celia.

"Never," Steve solemnly told her. "I could never."

As they spoke, Anna began to enjoy the feelings her words seemed to drag out of her. In the early days with Steve, Anna had felt her emotions like a dusting of glitter on her skin—easily swirled, disturbed, aroused with the slightest touch, the most gentle breeze. The longer the two of them had been together, the deeper the love and intimacy had sunk in—like moisturizer or wood oil, to keep things supple. Despite those feelings having long since reached Anna's core and become a part of her, stirring them up again seemed difficult. No: impossible.

But as they talked in the library, Steve in soft, calming tones and she still with the irregular breathlessness of upset, the ripple effects of the wedding night could finally be felt—in anger, disappointment, and sadness, but also in tenderness and mutual need. Anna felt the wasting away and near destruction of their relationship like a horror, and her skin burned in a way it hadn't since her son had been born. Steve's remorse was even more urgent.

They rejoined the others at the poolside, slaked. Never had Anna felt so strongly for her husband.

She just wished she could forget about everything else.

Furry bees droned on mechanically between the bobbly purple heads of lavender now swaying in a light evening breeze. The sun was a smashed egg yolk on the horizon. Up on the terrace, Anna heard the clink of cutlery and food being brought out to the table for dinner. She closed her eyes and sniffed to savor an act of domesticity that she hadn't been required for. Perhaps she was discovering herself anew after all.

When Anna opened her eyes, the landscape looked darker. Night was closing in—not hurriedly and impatiently as it did in London, as though evening had somewhere else to be, but languidly and louchely, an arm draped across a shoulder tentatively, a hand reached for instinctively.

Tell them the truth.

Anna's deep out-breath landed in her stomach like a fistful of guilt.

She looked down at her wedding ring, remembering the day when Steve had—with nervous, clammy hands—pushed it onto his new wife's finger and grinned down at her.

She looked down at her wedding ring, remembering the day—a week before Sonny's birth—when she'd had to take it off because her pregnant hands resembled a chain of uncooked sausages. It had been six weeks before it fit again afterward—the same amount of time before she could walk without pain, and she had wondered whether there was a link. Whether as soon as they could move again, mothers needed to be identity tagged, like sheep and cattle, in case they were tempted to wander off in search of greener pastures.

She looked down at her wedding ring, remembering the night earlier that week when she had removed it and placed it in a Nile-green color-washed pine drawer next to the bed she had ended up sleeping in alone.

Where it still was.

Anna's wedding ring had the word "STEVO" engraved inside it like a secret she kept nestled against the cosseted skin underneath it.

The one on her finger had two.

"YOU'RE MINE."

THREE
DAYS
AFTER

29.

Effie

"Somebody slept well!"

It was a statement rather than a question, lobbed by Charlie across the table to Lizzie, who'd appeared among them that morning, bright and smiling, dressed in a white broderie smock to show off the intensifying brownness of her skin underneath.

"I did!" She beamed and helped herself to a croissant from the baker's paper bag, this time fetched from the village by Charlie.

"I think we need to start treating this more like a holiday," she continued, spooning apricot jam onto her plate and reaching for the *cafetière*, which had already powered the rest of them into conversational mode. "And less like a murder mystery."

Across their end of the table—the farthest from Lizzie's—Effie and Anna briefly met each other's eyes.

"I'd like to go on one of the day trips we had planned for after the . . . as part of the guest itinerary," Lizzie explained through a buttery mouthful. "There's a set of caves not far from here, where they project art onto the walls. It's supposed to be amazing."

"Great idea!" exclaimed Bertie. "Mum mentioned it too—I'd love to go, if anyone else is up for it?"

He leaned back to better look around the table: a full house of nodding heads. Nobody mentioned how stifling the château had seemingly become, but they were packed into their two cars within half an hour.

The landscape flicked past them like a showreel of greenery and bauxite, jutting cliffs and the odd crumbling tower above the canopy. They drove with the windows slightly down to take in the aroma of cypress bark warming in the sunshine. Effie almost purred.

The day was so glorious it was easy to shake off the strangeness that had enveloped them at the house, to leave their unanswered questions behind its stolid wooden doors.

They came to the caves—an old quarry, in fact—at the foot of a steep hill, on top of which a village perched in readiness for lunch. The gray cliff face rose impassively above the entrance to the caves, although it was the void at its base—a gaping maw with a queue snaking out—that seemed more impressive somehow: a proscenium arch of only blackness. Effie felt her insides constrict a little at the fullness of that emptiness.

At the head of the queue, Lizzie negotiated tickets for the group, just as she and Dan would have done had things turned out differently. One by one, they filed through a narrow metal turnstile and stepped into the blackness.

"They highlight a few different artists every month," Lizzie declaimed, tour guide–style. "This month is"—she checked the leaflet she had been handed with her receipt—"Bosch and Brueghel."

"Oh, very cheery," said Effie, a slow, cold sweep of dread washing over her in the dark. She reached for Ben's hand, but he had shifted beyond her in the queue on a wave of other people.

She could make out little other than the faces of her friends in the dim light of the tiny bulbs dotted along the ragged walls of the cave. They downlit a path from the entrance into the body of the deserted quarry, deep beneath the sunny hillside. Effie felt sweat spring out on her top lip, and she tried to breathe more deeply, to use all her techniques.

Count things, be aware of sensations, list colors—but the only shade here was black, the only touch emptiness. Effie's hands were wet with nerves, and her fingers trembled.

The group moved almost in tortoise formation along a gritty corridor, straining their eyes at indeterminate shapes—another visitor, a bat—until they emerged into a cavern. The subterranean chamber was as tall as a cathedral's nave and lit on every side with projections of paintings that spanned and slid across the uneven walls to a choral soundtrack every bit as atmospheric as the scenes they contained.

Skulls, evil eyes, and devils. Writhing masses of bodies piled high by hell's worker demons and directed by an army of the dead. Mouths pulled downward in pain and cadavers spilling putrefaction. A woman, expensively dressed in fur-trimmed gown and hennin, tried to hold back a phalanx of skeletons intent on picking her clean enough to join their number. Lurid creatures squatted and shat out sinners, whose earthly delights were followed by eternal agony.

Effie missed her footing in the dark and turned on her ankle. The jolt and jarring pain, distracting her from the many calming techniques she had attempted to use to quell the panic, was enough to send her spiraling mentally too: her breath became short, and the paintings surrounding her, already rotating slowly around the space the visitors were standing in, began to spin as though she were trapped on a merry-go-round.

Twisted faces of villagers and hunters, goblins and knights whizzed by, some pained and some angry. Malevolent grins and dripping chins, sucking on devils' teats or hoisting pitchforks full of hay. Shouting, dancing, laughing, carousing. An imp that looked like Charlie, a lady in ermine that could have been Iso. Anna and Steve arm in arm. Skeletons clashing with swords and shields; peasants toiling with the harvest; villagers skating; and Lizzie shaking. Shaking her head at someone in the dark, and jabbing a finger, her lips round with a shout and her face as pale as any of the subterranean creatures on the walls.

Effie had had panic attacks before, but that detached and logi-cal information never helped in the moment when she felt herself whizzing around and around, smaller and smaller, disappearing down the plughole of her existence to be flushed away on a tide of terror. There had been more of them since James had left, times when she had truly believed herself to have been con-stricted in the pinhole of the world ending. Times when she had tried to fight it and then finally surrendered to the horror, only to find her breathing slow once again and the world carrying on around her, despite the blood in her veins pumping at full speed around her body, hurtling through her arteries like an emergency vehicle to a crash.

This time, however, there was Bertie. He noticed when she tripped and then crouched, so he lifted her gently to her feet, murmuring and calming her in words she could barely hear, let alone make sense of, as everything swirled around her. Gradually the whooshing stopped and the dark stabilized. Effie stabilized too, and she raised her chin weakly to Bertie in thanks. As she did so, her phone buzzed in her pocket and she pulled it out.

A message on the screen. James: "Don't worry—it's nothing. Speak when you get back."

She thrust it away again before she could feel either disap-pointment or elation. *Not now*.

"No wonder they call Bosch the Hangover Artist, eh?" Bertie murmured behind her, and she moved her head to swing her gaze around. The horrific visions displayed on the walls seemed to sum up exactly how Effie had felt for the past few months, give or take a few specifically medieval torments.

"Do they really?" She was surprised at this string of empathy that linked her own travails to a fifteenth-century Dutchman who had battled through similar circumstances without even the pros-pect of an aspirin to ease the pain.

"No," laughed Bertie, apologetically. "But they should."

She swatted his arm and walked farther in, feeling a little sturdier already for the—*rather Daddish*—joke. There were benches set among the spindling natural columns that held up the ceiling of the vast chamber, and she took a seat in front of the widest wall of the cavern. On it, a thirty-foot-high dystopian Judgment Day scene faded out into Brueghel's *Fight Between Carnival and Lent*.

Effie scanned the lumpen face of the Carnival clown, drunkenly riding his barrel of mead as, in the background, village maidens danced in a circle, and wondered if his was the role she had been cast in on this trip. Then a fading and a dimming of what low light there was, as the next image—another Bosch—appeared on the rocks, in which a demon held a flagon of beer up to a man's lips and another pinned him down forever.

On the wall to her left, grisly phantoms peeled back a curtain to watch a pair of heedless lovers fresh from bathing in a vat of wine. *What was that stupid internet phrase?*

"I feel seen," she said simply to Bertie.

He knew not to laugh, as Anna and Lizzie might, and Charlie definitely would have. She couldn't have said it to Ben either, she realized: he didn't seem to know where to put negative emotions, and instead focused only on being upbeat and positive.

Instead Bertie nodded slowly. "I think that's exactly how they wanted you to feel."

"Dirty and guilty and—"

"And utterly, totally, downright, disgustingly, inevitably human." Bertie turned to her in the dark, and now that Effie could see all the demons from around the room reflected in his good, wholesome—*yes, a bit nerdy*—eyes, they didn't seem to be closing in on her anymore.

"Are you okay, Effie?" he continued.

She played with the buckle on her bag where it rested in her lap. "I don't know."

Effie told Bertie about how she had woken up after the wedding night—the real, unedited version. About the dent in the pillow, the short, dark hairs, and the other glass on the nightstand. About the lost parts of her memory and her clothes on the floor, the snatches of things that might have happened: laughter, a shriek, a man's voice, and tears. About how Charlie had behaved around her ever since, and about what she thought that might mean. About how it could ruin things with Ben, when he'd been just what she needed after James.

The devils continued their waltz around them, peasants feasted and farmed, and the cavern began to fill up with people as the day wore on toward lunchtime. Their group—the bridal party, as Effie still thought of them—had been among the first to enter the cave, and though it was not uncomfortably full yet, there was the sense of a crowd forming. As the newcomers scrutinized the wall to fathom the deeper meanings of early modern life, nobody noticed the two figures on the bench trying to riddle out what had happened only a few days ago.

Bertie was quick to grasp the situation and—most importantly for Effie—judgment-free. He agreed that Charlie seemed the likeliest candidate for having shared the honeymoon suite, but not Effie's sense that it was a catastrophe if he had.

"There might still be another explanation," he said, awkwardly patting her shoulder.

"Yes, you're right," she said, blinking dry her eyes, which had become wet with relief and gratitude during the course of their conversation. "I've been trying to hold on to that. It's just, Ben and I were having such fun in London, and this has made me overthink it all. . . . I just don't know what I—"

Effie's thoughts ran out as she peered into the gloom at a painting on the other side of the vast cavern. A head, a nose, a stance that all seemed familiar. A face in a crowd, realistic and expressive like one of Brueghel's burghers, only sleek and modern, trim and handsome. Effie closed her eyes to refresh them and squinted again, incredulous at the trick her mind was playing on her.

Then movement. Not a part of the painted scene but standing in front of it. Looking right at her, gesturing wildly.

What?

Effie stood up abruptly, and Ben darted toward her from within the depths of the crowd.

"Come now," he said urgently. "We need to leave."

30.

Lizzie

I couldn't let him win.

I had done as he asked, played my part, thought that was an end to it—that was what we had agreed back in London.

But then I realized he was making up the rules as we went along. The way he'd just turned up out of the blue and was raising the stakes, changing the script, demanding more, even though I'd already given everything I had.

Given everything up, more like.

So this time, I refused. Refused to go along with it, refused to let him ruin my "wedding"—if that was what he still insisted on calling this trip.

He had pushed me so far already; I wasn't willing to go over the edge.

So I clung on. I was stubborn—at times, cheerful even. I didn't want him to see what he was doing to me.

That was a mistake: trying to beat him. It just made him even more determined that I should be the one to lose.

31.

Anna

As they waited outside the cave for the others to emerge, Charlie took pictures of Iso, who had come out that morning dressed in a long blue-and-white striped kaftan embroidered with a hot pink Aztec design and strappy leather sandals with golden wings at the heels.

She had an endless supply of the sorts of things Anna never seemed to see in the shops—not that Anna had any interest in wasting her weekends trawling round the high street. That, Anna pondered bitterly, was what people needed "content creators" for.

She remembered first following Iso's sun-drenched account by the half-light of her dimmed reading lamp during one bleary, predawn feed with baby Sonny, and her stomach clenched with bitterness. Anna would have preferred her insecurities remain within the pixels of her phone screen, rather than following her on holiday. If she hadn't met Iso—if Iso hadn't met her husband—would Anna have clicked through on Instagram to buy that kaftan in the hope of resembling this limby burnished girl? Anna checked with her fingertips that her permanently pink face was still slick with factor 50 sunblock. *Probably*. Although it would have looked like a traveling circus's big top on her.

Anna's relationship with her Instagram account was a Mobius strip of envy and self-loathing. She tried not to use it—had taken it off her phone twice—but regularly found herself scrolling before dawn when she woke up airless and anxious about the day ahead. For every hundred or so posts she saw that made her feel terrible—*fat, old, left out, joyless*—she'd pop a shot of Sonny up there—cute in a raincoat, foamy and adorable with an oat-milk babyccino (*ugh*)—and bask in the warm glow of likes from people she barely knew.

From her spot in the queue she watched Iso contort herself so she looked even thinner in the already roomy dress. Here she was leaning back against the cliff, one arm extended beyond her head, eyes closed in sunlit ecstasy; there laughingly "balancing" a distant outcrop of rock on the end of one finger. Anna knew that these shots would go up with captions like "Be true to yourself" or "So summery RN" or maybe just a little row of peace-out finger emojis.

And then there were the posts Anna thrived on, both for their earnestness and for their ridiculousness: the most elaborately staged, waspishly-waisted, sucked-in cheekbones, and carefully angled, waifishly skinny arm-legs would be accompanied with a blurb about how insecure the influencer was feeling within herself, how thorny a subject self-esteem could be, how Instagram wasn't real life and they should all be kinder to each other. It would be sponsored by a brand of muesli, and Anna would "like" it as though clicking the little heart was a means of expelling some of the poison that had built up inside her.

More like squeezing a pimple with dirty fingers.

After the improvised shoot, Iso took her phone back from Charlie and began busily paging around its screen, lightening, filtering, framing, composing.

Behind them, from the mouth of the cave, Effie plunged through the crowd and out into the daylight.

The shift into daylight took its toll on her pupils, and she staggered slightly as she met a midday sun made even brighter as it reflected off the white-gray stones of the cliffs on all sides. As her gaze adjusted—to the primary-colored tourist T-shirts, the azure blue of the sky overhead, the navy-gray asphalt of the tarmac— the people closest to her came into focus.

"We were wondering where you'd got to!" cried Anna, breaking off from the circle and stepping toward her friend.

"And what you and Ben might be getting up to in the dark, eh, Eff?" Charlie gave his finest imaginary mustache-twisting leer from behind expensive sunglasses.

Effie scowled reflexively and spun around. "Where's Ben?" she panted.

A few yards away, Lizzie was standing just beyond Anna, laughing about something with Steve, who was pointing toward the village on the cliffs above. Her face was creased in a smile and was pretty in the sunlight, less drawn than it had been, more alive than they'd seen her for what felt like many months. Her short white dress clung to her brown thighs in the languid heat.

Behind Effie, Bertie appeared in the cave's empty and light-absorbing mouth.

"You're here," he said, shielding his own unaccustomed eyes from the glare of daylight. "You and Ben ran off so quickly! What happened in there?"

Anna switched off her smile and saw the rest of the group's eyes swivel toward her friend curiously. Expectantly. "Effie? Are you okay?"

"Errr," she began.

But before she could say more, she heard her name behind her, on the path from the cave's mouth. *Ben*. He walked briskly toward them, eyes darting from the road below to the group and back again. When he reached them, he bent and braced his hands against his knees, drawing hot breath from the even hotter air.

"We need to go back to the house," he said. Smoothly, but in a way that would brook no dissent.

"Ben . . . ?" Effie started toward him, one hand outstretched to lay on his broad back.

"Now," he said, his smile fixed and tight. "I think Dan is here. I think I saw him in there."

Lizzie's smirk faded. Her expression changed as abruptly as a channel on a television, zapped from life into standby. Closed, quiet, numb. Her dark eyes went black with shock.

"Let's go," she said, turning and beginning a brisk march in the direction of their cars.

None of them moved, not quite sure what was going on. The shift had been so swift, so immediate that Steve's face was still caught in an uncertain grin.

Striding down the driveway, a hundred yards ahead of them, Lizzie spun on her heel. Her face was streaked with tears and red with rage as she spat back a shout at them:

"Now!"

32.

The Wedding Night: Lizzie

It's what every girl dreams of, isn't it? A man so devoted that he'll follow her to a foreign land to prove it and win her heart?

What sounds romantic during the years we while away in teen-age bedrooms longing for a knight to find us turns out to be something very different when you're old enough to realize women aren't Rapunzel, they're Joan of Arc. And that the men who pitch up at the foot of the tower are more likely to burn you as a witch than want you for a wife.

I realized, too late, that it wasn't even about the wedding. The fact that this hadn't ended when the relationship did was proof that there was a bigger axe to grind. A debt to settle beyond the bargain I thought I'd agreed to.

I'd ended things so that everyone involved might move on, but clearly he wasn't planning to. In some twisted way, he still wanted the wedding to go ahead, so that he could play his final, terrible card.

It was the sounds of the first dance that woke me, even though I'd taken enough of my pills to knock out the whole party. At first, I wasn't surprised—we'd listened to that song, me and Dan, so many times in the past six months that I practically heard it in my sleep anyway. We had been trying to perfect our moves for the evening of our big day: he focused obsessively on his footwork, and I practiced keeping a smile on my face while, inside, my pulse raced in anxiety rather than excitement.

Those horns, that Motown beat, the high hat. "Happiness condensed to three minutes, joy transliterated on a stave." Steve wrote that about the song in an article of his I'd found on Google. The soaring strings wormed their way into the blank space where my dreams should have been and crowbarred me back into reality. The place I least wanted to be, the place where the photographs existed.

Then I realized groggily: they were celebrating my wedding. My friends, enjoying my wedding without me. I almost threw the tooth mug of water I had filled and put by my bed at the chimney breast opposite, but I didn't want them to know I was awake.

I lay up there in the dark, disinvited from my own party, simmering with silent and heartbroken resentment as they tucked into the wine I had chosen, the food I had tasted, ummed and aahed over, *paid for*. I had felt abused for so long now, I hadn't thought it possible to hurt more than I already did—but there is nothing more painful than an injury inflicted by your closest friends. In their cups, their rowdy partying, they had forgotten all about me—even Effie, after everything we'd gone through. That's what really stung as I lay upstairs listening to them like some madwoman in the attic.

Vengeful Medea on the roof, more like. I wanted nothing more than to set light to the bonfire I'd built underneath us all—I'd already saved Effie from the flames once, though she didn't know it, and she'd paid me back by bringing the spark to the tinderbox.

If we'd just got married quietly at home—been clapped through the lych-gate of St. Swithun's and trundled back to Mum and Dad's garden for cucumber sandwiches—none of this would have happened.

None of the setup, I mean. None of the drama. The mistake

had been made—I could never go back and undo that. But what I hadn't realized was that I'd also provided the stage for it to be unveiled to my friends like a comedy of fucking errors. Scene one, Bangkok. Scene two, a hotel room. Scene three, a bar. Scene four: France, a big house, a big wedding. The bigger the day got, the more there was to spoil. The more collateral damage.

I had canceled every last vol-au-vent and champagne flute, as soon as I sent the email. He must have rebooked everything to torment me when he realized I was still planning to come.

It was beautiful, all of it. Everything I'd asked for, right down to the shade of the ribbons around the flowers to match the ones I'd planned to wear in my hair. Hair I had instead taken to pulling out in desperate fistfuls as the intimidation, the threats reached their peak.

Hearing my wedding taking place downstairs without me as Charlie popped cork after cork and Effie and Iso whooped was devastating, but what I feared most was a knock on the door behind which I was cowering.

When the music died down and I heard the tread of feet to bedrooms along the tiles outside my room, I waited until everything in the house was still and then I got up. I didn't know what I'd find, but I understood that the silence was the signal. My summons.

Now that the rest of them had passed out, there was a chance to resolve things. As if I hadn't tried that several times already.

I walked through the debris of my wedding like a ghost bride moving backward through time. I'd give anything to go back and undo it all, rebalance my life, take control of it again—for Effie's sake, too. I was overwhelmed by a wave of melancholy. This was really happening to me. This had been my chance at happiness. Now it was gone.

Since the engagement party, I'd been observing it all from a distance, as though I were floating high in the air as the circus tent collapsed beneath me. Disassociation—it's an anxiety thing.

Perhaps helped along by all the Valium I'd been taking and the wine I'd been drinking to keep everything at bay.

And so I sat, despairing and disheveled in my long white cotton nightgown—excessively bridal and bought for this very night—at the head of the table I had expected to preside over in ivory silk.

A noise, and my head flew up like a deer's in the road, looking first toward the door, then to the stairs. The Oratoire creaked almost constantly with the weight of the centuries it had witnessed, but this had come from outside—beyond the double doors, left open when the others had retired in their varying states of incapacity.

The disarrayed furniture out there looked as drunk as my friends had sounded.

It was only a small rasp—quieter than a cough—but it caught my attention in the otherwise still and silent room.

Then he was there, standing in the doorway, and still—despite everything, despite what he had done and the things he had said—I felt the echo of that thrill in my chest, the hardness behind my solar plexus again. I had been infatuated with him, and those feelings had been so strong. But time and terror had snuffed them out like the long-gone flames in the sconces on the château walls.

"Finally," he said, stepping through the doors and reaching for a switch on the decks. He put the music back on, softly this time, not loud enough to wake anybody but enough for me to hear those horns, that Motown beat, the high hat. "I've got you to myself."

Every word of those cancellation emails had felt like a knife to the heart, every keystroke a punch in the face. The first to all of our guests, the next to our nearest and dearest who we had planned to have stay with us at the château. Dan didn't even know I was sending either of them until I'd done it; I couldn't face his attempts to persuade me not to. I'll never be able to forget his expression once he'd seen them.

I knew when I arrived at the château—saw the tables, the napkins, the candles, the bouquet—that I would never be free of him. He had a psychopath's taste for precision—either that or a bride's.

"Did you think you could win," he sneered, "after you humiliated me like that? Do you know how it feels to be dumped for your best mate? Because Effie soon will."

It was Ben.

The man I spent a night with in Bangkok before I came home and met Dan on a dating app.

33.

Effie

"This can't be happening, let me out!"

As Ben climbed into the car and clunked the door shut behind him, Lizzie, previously desperate to leave the caves—and Dan—behind, began to thrash against her seatbelt, trying to undo it.

Next to her, Effie tried to soothe the bride. "Lizbet, calm down. Let's just get back and figure out what to do when we get there."

"You don't get it—ugh!" Lizzie railed, still scrabbling for the door handle, bucking against the embrace. "None of you get it! He's a fucking lunatic!"

"That's why we need to go back, Lizzie," Anna said gently from the front seat. "It'll be easier to sort out at the house."

The passion seemed to leave her as quickly as it had taken over, and Lizzie quieted. From the driver's seat, Ben contemplated the bride in the mirror: she had one hand over her face, eyes covered as she regained her composure.

"Are we ready now?" he asked, key in the ignition and almost impatient, like a parent dealing with a tantrum. But when he caught Effie's eye in the reflection, they exchanged a sad, wearied smile.

Ben eased the car back out onto the road, following the route that wound toward the Oratoire.

It was intoxicating, Effie thought, the way he so smoothly took over. As though someone had charged Ben with the welfare of them all. Perhaps that was what a certain type of schooling provides you with, she reflected: the ability to stay cool under pressure.

Barring a couple of student PE teachers and an ancient maths tutor, Effie's colleagues were mainly women; she had limited experience with meeting men beyond her friendship group and James's. Beyond the depressing handful of dates she'd recently gone on.

Tall and rangy, with a swimmer's triangular torso and a well-defined Head Boy chin, Ben was nothing like any of the men Effie's apps had coyly suggested to her. Nor was he like the ones she had met from James's office. There, masculinity was skinny and frugal, protected via a shibboleth of obscure websites and cool-related humor that was neither interesting nor funny. Where their manliness had been distributed sparingly, as though it were rationed, Ben so overflowed with it that he made even Charlie look a little smaller by comparison.

That was what had attracted her in the first place, back when he hadn't seemed to show any particular interest in her. Then, his quiet solidity and calm had seemed like arrogance; now, despite being shaken by the prospect of what Dan was there to do, he was no less solid, no less calm, but had moved into a staccato safety-first mode, and Effie found his natural authority reassuring.

Charlie and Iso raced ahead in their sports car, and Ben drove the others quickly but precisely in near silence. Silence but for the former bride, now crumpled and crying softly in the backseat.

Perhaps she wanted to tell them what exactly it was that she seemed so terrified of, reasoned Effie, who rode alongside her friend and proffered a tissue—accepted and subsequently soaked with tears into a soggy pulp.

Perhaps Lizzie had wanted to explain why the prospect of Dan had struck such fear into her, to get it all off her chest—*finally*—so they might help her. Perhaps she was desperate to share it—only the racking sobs that emanated not so much from her chest as from her gut would barely let her draw breath, let alone get the words out.

As Ben drove, Lizzie curled away, blond head pressed up against the window, the knuckles of her fists clenched white against the tanned skin on her legs.

Now, after they pulled up to the Oratoire's entrance, she drew back as Ben climbed out of the front and ran round to open the door for her. Pushing herself upright, Effie did the same.

"Lizzie, I'm so sorry." He spoke softly but sternly, and leaned into the car where she sat, still belted into her seat, as though he were a roller-coaster operative checking a safety harness before sending her off on the ride of her life. "I didn't mean to give you such a shock."

Lizzie's breathing was still ragged. Effie felt both the warmth of Ben's care as he offered it and the stillness that had descended on Lizzie, trembling exchanged for an absolute rigid tension. Their friend was like a wild animal cornered, gaze unblinking where she met Ben's, breath shallow as she seemed to gauge whether he was friend or foe.

Poor Lizzie, her nerves are shot.

Effie had once thought Ben was haughty, but she could see the strain on him now; his every sinew was taut as he carefully attempted to talk Lizzie down: "I think we know what this means."

Lizzie shook her head minutely. Her eyes had not left Ben's face since he'd started talking. They lingered there still, reading him like a map, and as he formed his next words, they filled once more with tears.

"I don't think you have a choice. We need to go inside," Ben said gravely. "And then we need to explain to everybody what has been going on."

Lizzie's expression was one of frightened pleading. *Make this not be real, please.* She was still strapped into the car, as though the release button on her seatbelt was the timer on a bomb.

No reply to our messages, no ringing even, and now . . . here? Is accountant Dan on the lam?

Effie's lips perked inappropriately in a half-smile just at the thought: the prospect of mild-mannered Dan in the ill-fitting guise of hot-blooded lover. The notion was so out of character it was comic: quiet old meat-and-two-veg Dan slipping his London life in pursuit of love thrown off, determined to unjilt himself by sheer force of will. What would he do, rend his corduroy blazer and beat his pale, hairless chest? It would be like watching City men in expensive suits attempt an orderly fistfight at closing time.

Effie flicked her eyes to meet Anna's and saw that her face was drawn, her skin ashen, the tip of one white tooth visibly biting her bloodless bottom lip.

"Come on, Lizbet," she murmured, shifting on her feet to gaze back at the spot on the horizon at the end of the track, as though they might suddenly see him—*Dan*—framed at the bottom of the cypress avenue.

Effie remembered the wedding figurines with their heads sawn off, the lucid, floating letters in the guest book. Words scrawled into the steam on the mirror, the torn page of the notebook as another message had been stabbingly etched onto the paper there. Surely they were safe, like Bertie had said?

"Do you really think we have anything to worry about?" she started to say to Ben, doubtfully. "It's just D—"

But he spoke across her like a blanket smothering flames: "There's a lot you don't know about Dan, Effie."

He stood and stretched out a hand to Lizzie. Mute, the former bride finally unfastened her seatbelt, tipped herself like a ragdoll into Ben's open arms, and let him half-lead, half-drag her into the cool of the château.

Behind them—Bertie's gentle face full of concern, Charlie's a mask of confusion, Iso puzzled and curious—the others fell in and followed, just like a wedding procession.

34.

Anna

Inside, Ben led Lizzie through the Hall and back out to one of the sunbeds around the pool, where the rest of the group gathered.

If Slim Aarons did sob stories. Anna tutted herself for the sarcasm; she had never seen Lizzie like this.

"There's a lot you don't know about Dan," Ben repeated, after he'd helped the former bride—as creased and pale as her white dress—to a lounger. There was something almost triumphant in his demeanor as he played hero of the hour; Anna realized he was reveling in it slightly.

"He's . . . a great guy," he continued, and Lizzie bit her lip. "I've known him since boarding school, and he's always been a really loyal friend. Someone you knew would always look out for you, always stand up for you. It's a kind of code-of-honor thing with him, you know?"

At this, Lizzie snarled a half-laugh.

"Let me tell them, Lizzie," Ben said quietly. He turned to face the others. "But recently he's become, well, more than protective of Lizzie. More like her keeper, really." He paused and wiped a hand over his face. "Look, I didn't know any of this until Lizzie told me—last week, when she canceled the wedding."

A ripple moved through the people assembled as the wind sent a flurry across the surface of the pool: the reveal.

"She called me last week," he said. "Dan had taken her purse with all her cards—she had no money, couldn't leave the flat. So she asked me over, and told me what had been going on. I couldn't . . . when I got there, I couldn't believe how scared she was."

Anna watched as her friend's eyes rolled back in her pale face and she let Ben do the talking: Lizzie was the last woman Anna had expected to let a man narrate her life like this for her.

"It started with comments about her staying out too late, drinking too much," Ben said. "Hanging out with her friends when she could have been with Dan, him worrying when she didn't tell him what time she'd be home."

Anna knew immediately how welcome those comments, that clucking, must have at first seemed to Lizzie, more used to Guy's remote apathy and laissez-faire style of boyfriending. She watched helplessly, with a stomachful of foreboding, as her friend's head sank forward to her knees, bent in front of her on the sunbed.

Ben continued: "That was when she began to find Dan a bit intense."

"It *was* intense—we'd just moved in together," Lizzie broke in with a weak moan, barely lifting her head up. "You go out way less, you stay in together. . . . Everyone does! It was nice!"

"That's right." Ben's voice was kindly, but he seemed irked by Lizzie's lingering instinct to excuse her former fiancé. "But then he wanted to know where she was all the time, so he could 'keep her safe,' he told her. And then Dan started putting you down, didn't he? Saying you were stupid, weak, confused. He told Lizzie she was pathetic—that she'd done well to snare him, that her life was empty beyond him. Even though it was his campaign that had shut down her social life."

Anna thought of those sad six months between the engagement party and the week planned for the wedding when she had known—instinctively, like language—that there was something Lizzie wasn't telling her. She felt ashamed for not trying harder; she had been so wrapped up in her own busy life that she hadn't even noticed her friend walking wounded beside her.

Anna was outraged on Lizzie's behalf, but something in Ben's demeanor stopped her from speaking out—there was more. He was managing the story just as he'd managed Lizzie by the car. Even though the bride had hardly been in the same room as him since they'd all arrived at the château, there was a bond between the two of them. Anna looked across to Effie, who was—*as ever*—hanging on Ben's every word, and she felt a stab of worry for this friend too. For how she now suspected Effie's hopes with Ben might end.

"Dan read your phone, didn't he, Lizzie?" Ben said. "He had the password to your emails?"

"That was just once," Lizzie said bleakly. "Because he was worried—"

"So worried he began to insist on collecting you from work every night too," Ben added, finishing the sentence, and it was Effie's turn to moan. Poor, poor Lizzie—trapped in her life, trapped in plain sight, and the rest of them cheering her on to get married to the man who had boxed her in.

"Who bought the dress you wore to the engagement party?" Ben asked Lizzie carefully, and she burst into fresh tears.

"It was a gift! He knew I liked it! He was doing something nice!" she cried.

"He chose every outfit after that, didn't he?"

Lizzie's shaking shoulders seemed to nod an affirmative, even as she shook her head miserably.

"Oh, Lizzie!" Anna cried, her own voice rent with emotion, and Ben met her appalled eyes with the saddest expression in his own.

"I just wish I'd known sooner," he said quietly. "I told her I thought she should cancel the wedding." He spread his palms at his sides. "What else was there to do? Lizzie didn't want to go to the police, so I helped her get Dan out of her life. We changed the locks, began boxing up his stuff."

"Lizbet?" Effie, stirred from her horror, rushed to share the sunbed her friend lay supine on as the events of her life washed over them all. But Lizzie could only sob and splutter, heaving in one breath and then another, her grief assaulting her again and again.

"Why didn't you tell us?" Effie looked up at Ben, her voice cracking as she asked him the inevitable question. The question Anna had been waiting for.

This man Effie had been so close with had understood, for the past week at least, what their friend had been suffering and not told her. Anna wondered why exactly that might be and felt her heart begin to race.

"I hoped that canceling the wedding would be the end of it," Ben answered, hanging his head and setting his mouth in an apologetic line of self-recrimination—*or was it a failed attempt to hide a smirk?* "I guess I didn't want you to think of Dan that way. I'm sorry. I said he could move in with me while he sorts himself out. . . . He doesn't know my role in helping Lizzie, of course."

Lizzie sniffed and wiped her streaked face with the palm of one hand. "Yet," she said emphatically. "Doesn't know *yet*."

Ben cleared his throat purposefully. "It took me too long to find out what Dan was capable of. When I didn't hear from him for a few days, I thought he was just angry with me, annoyed that I was siding too much with Lizzie. But his phone's been dead for so long now, I'm wondering whether he's actually changed his number. And if he has, why?"

He ran a hand through his hair, and it bristled upward where it was damp with sweat.

"We know Dan ordered the wedding to be set up again," offered Bertie. He was sitting a few yards away in a deck chair, his usual warmth swapped for sadness like a portrait covered in mourning.

"And the messages," Iso said. "Sneaking in and leaving us

those messages—and the one in the book the morning after the wedding! That must have been him too!"

You deserve each other. Anna couldn't fault Iso's logic.

"The wedding stuff I thought was an honest mistake," Ben acknowledged, nodding, "but then Bertie found out from Marie. . . . Then the pad, the mirror. And then, this morning, in the caves—that's when I knew for sure."

He paused, clenched a fist, and banged it against his knee as if to flagellate himself. "Dan's not going to let Lizzie go."

35.

Effie

She watched as Ben pulled one strong hand over his face as if rearranging his features might lift his mood. As if, when he took his hand away, the scene would somehow have changed to one of happiness.

"Oh, mate," he said sorrowfully to himself. "What have you done?"

"I'm not marrying him," Lizzie said to Ben tersely from the sunbed. "Shouldn't this be over now?"

Effie felt she was following the proceedings from under a thick glass dome. Every line Ben spoke seemed distorted: This monster we were talking about was Dan. And his victim was Lizzie. *Our* Lizzie.

Since James had left, Effie hadn't watched any of the scary movies her ex-boyfriend had so enjoyed—clicking the light on in the middle of the night to discover that she was still alone matched any dread the supernatural could offer. But she felt like a character from one now. In those films, the least credulous were always the first to go. Even though Effie knew there was no such thing as ghosts, she would find herself urging the on-screen skeptics to wake up to the fact of them so they might escape in time. She felt herself doing something similar now: there is a new Dan to believe in, and you must believe in him before he comes for Lizzie and it's too late.

But why hadn't Lizzie told her? Even more bizarrely, Ben—whom Effie had spent the past month languidly enjoying, moving with hungrily, claiming ecstasy—had not thought to mention the sad story he had just shared. She felt somehow embarrassed at having been left out, faintly—*pathetically*—jealous of the secret bond that had developed between him and her best friend.

"So Dan has been here since the wedding night?" Effie asked slowly.

"I think there's every chance he has been," Bertie replied.

As she staggered to the kitchen to get . . . something that might take the edge off the revelations, Effie felt sick, but vindicated.

She had long had the smallest shred of niggle in her mind—after a throwaway comment Ben had made at his best friend's engagement party all those months ago. It had seeded and bloomed in that time, as they'd watched Lizzie grow pale and stop communicating with those closest to her—and it had now been proved correct.

The comment had been muttered in a silky undertone onto her earlobe, one eyebrow cocked for the punch line, as Effie hooted along in merriment to a twisting story of teenage misdemeanors and boarding school ribbing—as James stood back, looking grumpy—of how the two men had become such firm friends.

"Then again," Ben had laughed beerily, "Dan's always been the possessive one."

Gazing at the happy couple across the dance floor, where they were attempting a shimmy to some obscure seventies disco track—despite Anna's plea to Steve to play only things people knew the words to—Effie had shivered off the words that gave a different color to the hand on Lizzie's waist, the palm cupping her ecstatic face. As the sequins of light from the glitterball faded from blue to pink, so Effie chose to see what she wanted to, not what Ben had implied.

Now that she knew the whole of it, Effie was devastated not only for Lizzie but by her own failure to examine the pulsing of instinct in her own heart. A cup of tea and a snuggly quilt wouldn't cut it in eighty-five-degree heat, so she reached instead for yet another cool green bottle from one of the scullery's bottomless fridges and arranged enough glasses on a tray for the whole group to swig from as they sat around Lizzie in watchful pity until a time when she wanted to speak to them of it.

A campaign, Ben had said. *A campaign.* Effie thought first of all of the very billboards and TV spots that Lizzie herself dealt in at work: the strategically planned, guided, and gradual doling out of selective information until such a point when those lapping it up were indisputably hooked, loyal, willing consumers. But as Ben talked, her mind had turned to the military sort—to the pushes, the clashes, the falling backs, and the sieges. The wearing down of defenses and cutting off of resources until the stronger party could set a flag in this newly won territory, declaring that it now belonged, wholly and entirely, to them. It had been that sort of campaign.

She reappeared on the terrace with the tray of glasses and a chrome cooler but missed a step as she began descending to the poolside—as her foot landed awkwardly, one of the stems wobbled and fell, then smashed on the pale flagstones.

"Mind your bare feet!" she called out as Bertie and Charlie flew to recover the bigger shards and Steve scanned for the tinier, more insistent pieces, which could lie in wait and pierce unexpectedly, long after the accident had been forgotten.

"Are you okay?" Effie asked, lowering the tray onto one of the side tables and sitting on an adjacent sunbed next to her tear-stained friend.

Quieter now, Lizzie sniffed and smiled gratefully when, from her other side, Iso passed a tissue from within her pretty wicker basket bag. Effie put a hand on the nearest part of her friend she could find—despite beginning its freckling of new suntan, Lizzie's foot felt like a block of ice. She looked at the toes crooked in her palm, their nails painted in the bridal blush of a shade called Sweetness & Light. Though Effie had been there like a good best friend when Lizzie chose it at the nail bar, she had not been a good enough one to know that life behind the facade had been anything but.

"Did he . . . hurt you?" Anna asked, hardly believing the Dan they knew to be capable of it. Lizzie had joked often that it was she, not he, who stamped a foot, raised a voice. Dan had always seemed so easygoing, so passive. Clearly there had been a strong current under those still waters.

"No, never." Lizzie shook her head vehemently, still protective of his reputation, like a doting captive.

"Well, that's something," said Ben, standing and clearing his throat. "I know it came close a few times—"

"I can't do this anymore, I need to go and lie down, I'm sorry." Lizzie got to her feet and swayed a little, pale-faced beneath her tan.

Effie stood and made to support her at the elbow. "Let me come with you, Lizbet."

But Lizzie insisted: she would go inside alone. She needed space. Time to think about what to do next, but also to sleep. The grief and worry that had clung to her like an illness these past months had made her weak, like an invalid.

"But we still don't know where Dan is." Anna's angst was palpable. "Someone should be with you."

"I'll go," Ben said, smiling at Lizzie reassuringly. Kindly, brotherly. "I feel like this is all my fault. If only I'd known what he was really like, I might have stopped all this."

Lizzie hung her head in acquiescence. Then to nobody in particular, but to all of them—to Charlie, who was pouring himself a glass of wine, and Steve, still sweeping up the broken glass; to Iso and Effie on the loungers; to Bertie, Anna, and Ben, who were closest to her—and with the weary look of someone who has had to do it before: "I'll lock my door."

36.

Lizzie

Prickled skin, big eyes, a jumping heartbeat—they have the same effect on your body, love and fear. I tried to defend Dan against what Ben was telling them, but I couldn't: I was too afraid. My body trembled with it—with fear and with outrage. I didn't have the new script he seemed to be working from; in my draft, the story ended back in London.

I'd asked him to leave while we were in the caves—the only place I could talk to him bluntly without anybody else overhearing. Despite the sensation of him breathing down my neck every second I was under the same roof as him, in reality we had shared very little air, barely exchanged any words directly, since arriving at the château. In the dark, with all those hellscapes whizzing round us on the walls, I told him I'd done everything he'd asked; now it was his turn to follow the rules of the game he'd set up. If he didn't, I'd have to reveal the truth to everybody—my final, desperate out.

That was what made him switch to this new tack, this Dan angle. He was incensed that I'd tried to fight back and he wanted to show me who was in charge.

I'd learned over the past months how slippery Ben was, how

persuasive, how insistent. Like a tide that starts by filling up your shoe, then chases you up the beach, intent on covering the top of your head, too.

I felt myself drowning now—not only in his lies but in my own fury. Here I was, cooped up in my bedroom, with my jailor pretending to be my guardian, my closest friends steps away but unable to help. It was all I could do not to rip the curtains down from where they festooned the four-poster bed or smash the place up; I was crying still but the tears were now of hot and stupid, frustrated rage rather than sorrow. My whole chest burned with it, and my fingers became fists.

When I'd slammed the door and breathed out properly for what felt like the first time in the past hour, I'd sounded more like a snarling dog than a person. And when I looked at myself in the vast glass that hung on one wall—having briefly contemplated hurling a chair into it to relieve some of the tension—I saw a mask of pure hatred staring back.

I'd had to just sit there as I'd watched it dawn on each person's face—each beloved face of someone I'd known my entire adult life—that the man they thought I had once been in love with was a monster. The loveliest, kindest man I'd ever met, who accepted me and adored me for all my flaws, twisted beyond all recognition. Dan told me he had always been in awe of Ben at school for his confidence and his cheekiness—his ability to grapple with life where meek teenage Dan had allowed events to wash over him—but Ben's destructive streak was as vast and infinite as Dan's capacity for love. Just how much hurt, how much pain, would be enough for him? Was his plan to ruin Dan's life—Dan's reputation—as well as mine?

Now that he was changing the rules again, I was scared Ben wouldn't stop until he had destroyed something even more sacred: my friendship with Effie. What if he persuaded her that he and I had been seeing each other behind her back, the way he'd planned to persuade Dan? Or worse, what if he made her believe that we had enlisted her in some kind of bizarre game to take the heat off us around the time of my wedding? Would she see through it?

I leaned my head back on the door I had just locked against him, shuddering at the fact he was right there on the other side of it.

Was he laughing? Smiling that complacent smirk? I knew then that if the door hadn't been between us, my inner schoolgirl would have lashed out at him: I wanted to scratch, bite, pull, kick. I wanted him to feel the same frenzy of wounds he had inflicted on me, on my life and my friends.

But I knew the real wound had already been dealt. The blow to his pride when I had chosen Dan. If that first cut really had been the deepest, then the way to deal the final blow would be to fight back. Not with fingernails and slaps, not chaotically but cautiously.

I knew then that I'd do anything not to let him get away with ruining my life, or Dan's, or Effie's.

But I still didn't know the answer to the most crucial question: Would my best friend choose Ben over me?

FOUR
DAYS
AFTER

37

Effie

As Lizzie slept behind a locked door and Ben guarded the stairs, Effie and Bertie sat out on the terrace as the night made dark, hulking lumps of the mountains at the edge of the skyline, and the moon frosted over the plain below like ice. The heat of the day had dissipated but they were warm enough still, caped in blankets lifted from a chest in the Hall.

"They think of everything, our hosts," Bertie said absentmindedly, as he wrapped himself more tightly. "Every comfort catered to."

Effie snorted. "Rather overzealous, if you ask me—setting up a wedding that had been canceled and all that . . ."

"Touché. Except that it had been uncanceled, after all." Bertie sipped his glass of red wine. "Poor Lizzie. Awful to think of anybody treating her like that."

He paused, and Effie knew they were both thinking of the same thing in that moment. The pale sprigged curtains of Lizzie's teenage bedroom, bleached because she had taken to keeping them closed during the day. He had sat with her for days on end when she came home from university for the final time. The aftermath had been so much longer than the incident itself.

"Thank you, by the way," he said. "For what you did back then. I've never had the chance to say it to you."

Effie had first heard Bertie's name in connection with what had happened that summer after graduation; he knew what Effie and Lizzie had gone through together, and Effie, living back with her own parents, had been glad that Lizzie had someone she could turn to. Keeping a secret like that was hard enough, especially once it had sapped you of the strength to even get out of bed in the mornings.

Lizzie had returned home that summer, changed and chastened but even then still full of the light that seemed to have more recently gone out of her. Back then, Lizzie had been determined to do better—never to make such a demand of a loved one again, nor to forget what she owed her best friend. And to respect herself, her body: not to let a repeat carelessness happen again.

Lizzie had always been the golden child in her and Bertie's family: blond where the rest of them were strawberry, bordering on carrot. Clever and bookish as they all were, but irrepressibly sociable where they were not; beautiful and proud of it, where her cousins all tended to hunch away from scrutiny. Lizzie had achieved the impossible at school—been both clever and cool, and Bertie's rep (or, at least, his standing among the boys who might otherwise have tripped him and called him gay) had benefited from it immensely.

Effie knew the old story well. "Men don't make passes at girls who wear glasses," Lizzie had said to Bertie after Sunday lunch one weekend as they hung around in her bedroom listening to music—around seventeen, they must have been. She'd gone to the optician's the next day and become the first person in their family's lineage of blinkers to get a pair of contact lenses.

It was only once she'd gone to Cambridge, left the village in the wold—now a golden, hay-scented sort of place in Bertie's memory, even though it rained there as much as it did in the rest of England—that the cleverness and the cool had collided. She'd gone off the rails, to use a phrase of her mother's. Not, of course, that Lizzie's mum had known the half of what had gone on in those sunlit quads. Lizzie had always had secrets.

Effie stirred awkwardly at the memory. "What are friends for?" she said. "I only wish I could have been there for her this time."

Bertie nodded. "Me too. What's your view on Dan? I only met him once—he seemed . . . completely fine."

It was hardly a ringing endorsement, but Dan had appeared completely fine to Effie, too. More than that: really quite pleasant. Mild and funny, supportive and caring—if a little on the neurotic side perhaps. *But who wasn't?*

"He didn't like being late," she said after a few moments' thought. "He always apologized profusely if they were ever late—which, given Lizzie's respect for punctuality, was always. He practically dragged her out of the pub once when they were expected at some friend's house for dinner."

Bertie's eyes widened. "Dragged . . . ?"

"No, look, it wasn't really like that," began Effie. "I just meant . . ."

But maybe it was. Maybe it had been like that. It had to have been, hadn't it, because although Lizzie had protested at various parts of the whole, sorry tale, she hadn't denied it outright, and Ben had seemed on edge, all day. And Dan—the fact that he was here, watching them and leaving them notes. Even according to Effie's currently rather skewed, chaotic barometer, this was not how normal people behaved.

"What do we do when he turns up?" she asked. "Anna's convinced there'll be a showdown. It feels . . . sinister, that he might be lurking about here somewhere. I'm not scared of him, but I'm scared for Lizzie. We don't know what he might do."

"No, we don't. We just have to keep an eye on her," Bertie said.

To that end, Ben had offered to move his single mattress to outside her door and sleep there overnight. Lizzie had accepted reluctantly, and they'd once again heard the turning of the key in her door when she retired to bed—early, and having barely eaten—as they'd finished clearing dinner away. Not long after Effie and Bertie had settled into a pair of chairs outside, the rest of the party had climbed the stairs, tired from the day's events, punch-drunk at the unraveling of a story they thought they knew and one whose new ending they could not yet predict.

"I suppose," Bertie said, "we'll need to get the police involved once we're home again if things don't settle down. I don't envy her that." He narrowed his eyes and squinted across the valley floor before he started speaking again. "One of my lawyer friends just prosecuted a policeman who actually fined a woman who came in complaining about an ex-boyfriend who'd turned stalker. Thought she was a time-waster, apparently."

"Oh?" Effie asked, sipping her wine, eyes searching his face even as he avoided her gaze. "What happened?"

"The guy killed her." Bertie's features were grim in the moonlight. "Some men can't be trusted with love. It's more than they can handle."

She had no idea how to respond to Bertie's quiet anger, so she drained her glass and ignored the urge to refill it. When, eventually, after a few minutes' silence, she stood, a gentle smile uncreased the furrow in his brow and he wished her a good night's sleep. Effie hurried to her room, stepping over the sleeping form of Ben where he lay like Lizzie's guard dog in the corridor.

It would mean another night alone in a single bed, but she could hardly resent Lizzie for that.

What was that? That noise?

Confused with the fug and bleariness just two glasses of wine had veiled her with after a couple of nights off, Effie struggled to the surface of her thoughts, kicking her legs like a swimmer against the tide, only to find them tangled in cotton sheets.

She rolled over in the sunshine that had begun to pool on her where she lay. The first thing she saw as her eyes opened was the empty blue wooden bed frame that stood parallel to the one she was in, the bed now divested of its mattress and the dust on its slats exposed to the air.

Had it really only been three days since we all arrived to find that wedding scene laid out?

Effie shuddered at the thought of the message in the guest book. *Congratulations—you deserve each other.*

After Iso's assumption, the others had agreed that this note had been the first of Dan's threatening messages but, for Effie, something jarred with that interpretation. Who was Dan talking about, for one thing? And for another, the writing had been different—less full of vitriol, less menacing. More benign some-how, even if the meaning could be skewed unpleasantly. Why would Dan have written that?

Effie didn't think it had been a message for the original happy couple; she was convinced that it was, instead, intended for a new pairing, a match born, awkwardly and unwisely, in a champagne haze.

The letters had been plaintive in their simplicity, hurt almost. That was why Effie still wondered—with an intense feeling of guilt toward Ben—whether they had been written by someone who might have seen her and Charlie together. Before they had retired upstairs to the honeymoon suite. Effie grimaced; would the whole day be this bad? She hadn't even sat up yet.

The noise came again—a soft tapping at the door, her door.

"Come in," she gargled through her last mouthful of sleep.

Anna squeezed herself into the room, curling her body around the door's wooden plane so as not to open it too far and risk it scraping against the tiles again, waking the others. "Morning." She smiled, sitting down on the edge of the bed and smoothing out over her legs the light patchwork-print skirt she had on.

Effie stretched her arms over her head and thumped them down onto the bed on either side of where her narrow body lay beneath the thin sheet. She pushed herself upward and shifted the pillows behind to support her back.

"What's the latest?" she asked Anna, rubbing her eyes. "How's Lizzie?"

When Anna failed to answer immediately, Effie jerked to another level of awake, stirring her legs to get up. "What? What is it?"

"Shhhh," her friend said quietly, stopping her where she had moved with a soft but firm palm against her chest. "She's fine. Nothing has happened. I just—I need to tell you something."

Effie raised her eyebrows.

"I saw them together—Lizzie and Ben—on the wedding night," she said apologetically. "I think there might be more going on than they've told us."

"More how?" Effie said, her gorge rising.

Anna sighed, quietly devastated for her friend and for herself, for having to be the person to deliver the bad news. "I think . . . I think with everything Ben helped her through last week, they might have fallen for each other."

38.

The Wedding Night: Anna

The ungainliness and discomfort of having fallen asleep fully clothed, with the lights on and her mouth open, was something Anna hadn't experienced since university. Moving in with Effie, Charlie, and Lizzie again, even if only temporarily, was all it had taken to fall back into old habits.

The ability to drink rapaciously, and capaciously, had returned, along with a headache that threatened to fork like lightning from her left temple right down the side of her neck and into a fully fledged migraine if she didn't take something for it soon.

She pushed two pills out of a blister pack and picked up a glass to wash them down with. Motherhood 101: Drink water as though you have just returned from a forty-day sojourn in the desert whenever even a drop of alcohol passes your lips.

Anna had followed her own good advice to the letter before she'd passed out and had gulped several refills of water from a small glass tumbler that had, in a previous incarnation, been a little mustard jar or a Nutella pot, but the hardworking little receptacle was now empty. And her headache was getting worse.

What time was it? She could hear music below her, though not as loud as it had been when she'd taken herself off to bed. When Effie had tossed the bouquet, which she'd been using as a microphone, out onto the patio with a manic glint in her eye, Anna had known it was time to turn in: things would only get messier from here.

A stream of bubbles moved from her stomach to her chest in protest as she stretched, and she rummaged in her bag once more for the milky indigestion fix she had become semi-addicted to during her pregnancy.

I need to get some more water.

Lucky she was still wearing all her clothes. Quite practical, really.

Oh God. I am shit-faced.

The corridor beyond her room was dark, the door of the bathroom nearest to her locked; a slew of snores came in response when she knocked. Down the hallway, light from downstairs bled up to the landing along with the music. Slower now, less frantic. Almost beguiling.

Anna had cared about music once. Never quite as much as Steve, but then it was his job to know the new and the edgy, the cult classics and all the lore that came with them. He'd introduced her to so many bands to love, so many songs that spoke to her soul, just like he had when they first met.

Where was he?

Passed out somewhere probably, and she caught the habitual snarl of contempt before it spread across her lips with the memory that she too had just woken up facedown with the lights on. She hiccuped.

Did I really just wake up a few minutes ago? Or was it more like an hour?

It was late, but it might also have been early. The sky was dark, but somebody was still up, partying. Over the music she could hear voices downstairs. Which was where she supposed she'd have to go for some water now.

Don't accept any more shots from Ben. Do not engage with Charlie.

Where is Steve?

They were good at being codependent, she and Steve; neither of them was too needy. Not like some couples, where the wife was always hectoring, the husband a frustrated sex pest.

No, their lives intertwined nicely, like two climbing plants growing around each other. Steve was the fragrant perennial, dependable and nice-looking. She was the one with thorns. And quite a thick trunk. Why was she so cross with him all the time when actually the person she was most angry with was herself?

Angry with her own anger, her own short fuse, her quick-to-temper lack of resilience at home with a toddler who didn't want the food she had cooked, told her he loved Daddy the most, put his shoes on the wrong feet first to make her laugh but then to make her cry. Anna spent her days at work dry-eyed being bellowed at by some of the worst people in London; by night, she fought back tears and scraped mashed potato off an expensive polished concrete floor she had insisted on and then realized was utterly impractical in a home that also contained a child.

Anna had reached, on the landing, a large, deep-set window ledge that looked out over where the cars were parked outside. She jumped up onto the ledge and sat, her feet dangling in the dark. As she settled into the nook, she heard a crisp metallic scratching noise, felt something move on the stone beneath her right hand. A ring. Golden, like hers, but shinier and newer. Less tarnished.

Anna thought cringingly of the tone of voice she had used with Steve when they'd discovered the wedding all laid out. She remembered how she had instructed him to pack Sonny's suitcase, as though he were a certified cretin, when actually he had a first-class degree in philosophy, just not from the university she, Effie, and Charlie had gone to. A cooler one, she grudgingly admitted.

She remembered trying to look through his phone in the dark for evidence that Celia had gone further than simply offering Sonny a lift to nursery school and that Steve had accepted. She laid her cheek against the cool stone wall of the window seat's nook and cringed again.

That tone, the exasperation and suspicion, the latent scorn—these were the things that had made their own wedding rings sparkle a little less surely, taken the dazzle off how they saw each other now, snuffed out the mystique.

It wasn't all her fault, though. He had nose hair now—soon there would be more there than on his head—and she could tell he quite often thought that she was silly and shrill, when really she was just worried about their son. The streetwise, jivey music journo words she'd thrilled to hear on his lips when they were young now had the ring of someone's dad still trying to keep up. *But Steve actually was someone's dad!* And he was by far the best-looking of the ones who also suffered to push the little waterproof bundles on the swings in the park near their home on Sunday mornings.

She thought of the way he had looked at her when he thought she'd tell them to put the wine and antipasti back where they'd found it, and the love that had then suffused onto his features when she hadn't. This was the expression she wanted to recapture: adoration pure and simple. The thrill of surprising each other, as well as the delight in what they both already knew.

Anna twisted her own ring off her fourth finger, whimpering in pain as it seemed to pare skin and bone from around the knuckle. Anna had lost a lot of weight ahead of her and Steve's wedding and then proceeded to pile it all back on—and more!—afterward. The ring Steve had shakily pushed onto her hand still correlated to those girlish fingers, and the throbbing, naked *chipolata* in front of her had a dent where it had sat and the flesh had started growing around the metal.

In its place, Anna pushed the new ring on—quite tight—and pocketed the old. She vowed to be kinder to Steve in the morning, when she was less thirsty.

Oh yes! Water!

Anna jumped back down from the ledge and continued along the landing, down the first set of stairs toward the kitchen.

If she hadn't been quite so drunk, there was every chance she might have taken those steps and the next segment where the staircase crooked a turn two at a time to speed up what had now become an intolerably inefficient journey to refill her very small glass.

As it was, however, she was so aware of where she was putting her feet, of how cold and hard the stone stairs looked and how much she didn't want any of them to collide with her head, that she took the descent gingerly and cautiously. Slowly.

Because of this, she edged her creaking joints timidly down the stairs and into the Hall. Anna's eyes were now showing her a few shots of the scene all at once, as though she were trapped in the end of a kaleidoscope, but they caught a flicker of movement at the end of the terrace.

The outside was dark but illuminated by both the lightening sky and the several stocky candles they had lit in glass lanterns as they'd sat by the pool earlier, working their way through bottle after bottle.

Two figures were talking earnestly, his head bowed over hers, their bodies in a proximity only lovers would allow. Anna was struck dumb with surprise.

What was Ben doing over there with Lizzie?

All this time she had been worrying about an infidelity inside her head—Celia and her bloody messages—but the actual betrayal had been happening out here all along. In real life. In front of her own eyes, except she had been too dim to notice it.

She was suddenly filled with silent fury. Anna winced with a preemptive hurt for everyone involved; the fallout from this would not be pretty at all.

She went to dash her empty glass against the wall, but then she saw, on the table in front of her, something pure, white, and inviting. She could spoil things too.

CONGRATULATIONS, she scrawled in unsteady block capitals. YOU DESERVE EACH OTHER.

Anna stole clumsily back up the stairs, sick with her own naïveté, and along the landing, grateful for the fact that whoever had been in the bathroom was now not. She filled her little glass up at least seventeen times before climbing back into bed.

This time, she put her nightie on and turned the light off, and the questions already forming in her mind were smothered by the sort of dense and insulating sleep for which Anna so often envied both her husband and her son.

39.

Six Months Earlier: Lizzie

I was regaling a group of Dan's colleagues with the story of how we met when he first introduced me to Ben at our engagement party.

The three women crowding around me in an eager semicircle were all single, and as they listened, they each wore the anxious, strained look I'd seen most recently on Effie's face—as though they had a train to catch but none of them knew which station it was leaving from. Perhaps that's cruel; I know the feeling too. The sensation of seconds passing and everybody else's glass being topped up with happiness. The notion that it might run out before the waiter got to me, my glass, at the other end of the table. Perhaps that feeling was the reason I rushed in so quickly when I got the chance.

I was describing to the women my surprise at Dan and I having matched with such ease after my rather depressing experience of the other profiles on most dating apps—I tended to ham up this part in my telling of it, obnoxious in my own happiness, reveling in my delight at having scooped the prize—when I felt a tap on my shoulder. *My fiancé.*

"Do excuse me," I simpered to the women, and spun around to look at the face of my forever.

Both versions of it.

There was a moment inside me like a fuse had blown. Even thinking about it brings back the sensation, weaker now, like ripples fading but reverberating still from those few seconds of intensity—the power outage in my brain—and what had caused them.

The lights, the music, the buzz of chatter—all dimmed, it seemed to me, for a few seconds before returning, even brighter, even louder. My whole body throbbed with it. I felt like static on a television screen; white noise coursed through me.

Ben. That face, his slow smile. My stomach churned. I felt in those seconds the weight of every year he and Dan had known each other, every second they had spent in each other's company, every laugh shared, every secret. Their life together—some twenty years or so—was a marriage in itself.

Was this how I would feel every day, every time my husband mentioned his oldest friend? How would it be when Ben came round for dinner, played with our children? Would this infatuated churn be there still? Would it last another forty years?

"Allow me to introduce you to—" Dan was talking, but I heard his voice as if he were behind several panes of glass. He was chatting as though I were still standing next to him at a party—*our party*—when really I was underwater, out of air and sinking fast.

When Ben cut in and interrupted the man I was going to marry, his voice—a well-formed baritone that made my skin vibrate and the hairs on the back of my neck stand up—was as clear as a clarion, the only thing I had heard properly for hours. Days. Years. As though I had woken up from a coma and his was the first voice carried on the air to me.

His eyes laughed at me, but warmly and with affection. In my turmoil I could hardly bear to accept their beam; I thought my every emotion must be visible on the surface, running across my flesh like a news ticker carrying the headlines. The dimples where his smile carved into his cheeks pricked the solid muscle walls of my heart like a pair of lethal arrows.

Ben reached his hand out to me and—taking it, shaking it—I wondered whether he was simply going to whisk me out of there and into the night.

Dan—my love and my faith, my anchor and my port in a storm—looked on merrily, delighted that the two most important parts of his life had slotted together at last.

He wasn't to know that we had done so before, and found that we fitted almost perfectly.

Ben shook my hand, which was clammy with shock but also desire. His was warm and smooth.

Another jolt of electricity and a message carried between our roving, wonder-struck eyes like a flare shooting up from a ship's deck: Not right now.

"Lovely to meet you, Lizzie," he said with a grin.

40.

Effie

Lizzie and Ben?

Effie skittered on flip-flopped feet in her pajamas to the door her friend had shut herself behind and Ben had slept in front of. Inside her chest, her heart pounded with the knowledge of Anna's words, its pulse thumping in her ears and resonating through her body.

The door was open, the window too, the white voile curtains around the bed lifting gently in the warm breeze and stirring the currents in the empty room. More voices came from downstairs; behind her, Anna had caught up, her face twisted with worry. *With pity*. They took the last few strides along the landing toward the stairs together.

The others were standing in the Great Hall, a grouping not unlike one of Brueghel's from the cave, only Steve carried a *cafetière* rather than a flagon of mead. Next to him with a stack of bowls, a tub of yogurt, and a glass jug of orange juice was Bertie. In Charlie's hands, the usual bulging bag from the *boulangerie* in the village—there was no crisis serious enough, apparently, to distract either from the breakfast order or the ritualistic way in which they had all begun to congregate for it, as though they had been living here together for years.

A few paces away, Lizzie, wearing an unzipped gray hoodie over her white nightgown, pressed both palms to her forehead. Her long fingers splayed, taut and white, over her loose blond hair. Next to her, Ben reached out an arm, as if he could help stop her panicked and rushing thoughts, but she barely seemed to notice him.

"It's okay," he was saying, to her but as much to the assembled group, too. "It wasn't him."

His eyes flicked upward to where the two women stood. "False alarm!" he called.

"What was a false alarm?" asked Effie, walking toward him warily.

"Iso thought she saw Dan this morning," Bertie explained. "She went out for a run and saw a car pull up at the house—"

"Here?" Anna interrupted incredulously. "This morning?"

"Sorry," mumbled Iso. "I panicked, assumed it was him."

"—but Ben's just been out there, driven around a bit," Bertie finished. "Looks like it was just somebody who'd got lost and needed directions."

"Not that I knew the way either!" Ben shrugged, holding his hands out at his sides: nothing to see here. Effie looked at the thickness of his forearms, the very breadth of him, and felt her stomach crease.

Farther off, she saw Iso braced, feet wide and slightly hunched, in front of the double doors, still cooling down. She was wearing a pair of fluorescent snake-print leggings and a matching bra top that Effie recognized from a nosy, listless scroll through her Instagram feed, courtesy of the local café's Wi-Fi the other day. Part of a paid partnership with an exercise brand keen to empower those with low confidence by enlisting very thin, very beautiful women who wore makeup even to go running.

"You've never even met Dan, have you, Iso?" she said, closing the distance between them. "How would you have known it was him?"

Iso shrugged, her thick brown ponytail slipping from one

shoulder to hang down the middle of her back, and dabbed at her face with the back of one hand.

"I wasn't sure," she admitted, suddenly bashful. "I suppose I'm just on edge, like everyone else."

Effie spun around to meet Anna's gaze, and they rolled their eyes in sync. She looked to Lizzie, but the other woman was still standing nervously to one side, worrying a loose thread on the sleeve of her hooded top.

Wait. Anna mouthed the word to Effie: they needed Lizzie alone before they could ask her anything about Ben. Alone, and calm.

The group moved outside to the table on the terrace and took their seats around the morning spread, reaching for bread, picking at fruit. But Lizzie sat motionless. Her hard stare traveled into the azure distance, taking in scenery not of the local *paysage* but from months gone by. Action played out in the home she had shared with Dan, their kitchen, their bedroom. Scenes of love and scenes of pain.

"Why don't I just try calling him again?" Ben suggested.

Whatever it was that Lizzie seemed anxiously trying to mouth wouldn't come out properly.

Scraping his chair back on the stone and walking toward the pool, Ben held his phone high in the morning sunshine, swiveling this way and that as a water diviner uses his rods.

Charlie smirked and rolled his eyes. "Seriously mate, there's no—"

But Ben's face lit up as the screen in his hand did. "Found it!" he called, rooted to the spot, the backdrop of the valley behind him. The others gaped; Iso rummaged excitedly in her runner's belt for her own phone.

"Not much, but . . ." Ben swiped to call. "It's ringing!"

They sat expectantly back in their chairs and watched him.

"Dan, mate," Ben said, and Lizzie gave a start. But as he talked, silhouetted against the landscape with the sun behind him, it was clear that the erstwhile best man was leaving a voicemail rather than speaking to his friend.

"Bit worried about you, old man," he continued. "Are you in France, mate? Thought I saw you yesterday. Just give me a text, let me know you're okay. Always here, buddy. Bye."

Ben clicked the phone into darkness once more and returned to the table, where he picked up a plate and surveyed the food.

As though the call he'd just made had been a routine inquiry with his bank.

Effie—nursing a cup of black coffee and nothing else—knew that Bertie would strike up a conversation to take the pressure off the rather strained breakfast gathering even before he had opened his mouth.

"You said the other night you used to work abroad, Ben," he began. "Did you enjoy it?"

"Oh yeah, mate, expat life's the best," Ben replied, dropping a napkin onto his lap and breaking the end off a baguette. "Never quite feels like real life, even when you're working like a dog."

"You're right about that," agreed Bertie, "but I think that's what I miss most—reality."

"Where were you based, Ben?" Anna asked, a table's length away. "You'd only just come back when I first met you at the en—" At this Lizzie's eyes flew up, but Anna stopped herself just in time. "At the party."

"That's right, yeah." Ben nodded and swallowed a swig of water. "I'd been away for a couple of years by then, but I was in Bangkok. Loved every minute."

In the shade of the table's parasol and from a habit honed over a decade spent in each other's company, Effie's and Anna's eyes met and they exchanged the same thought: *Oh.*

When they looked to Lizzie, her eyes were already fastened, glintingly, on their faces.

Anna stood and wrapped one hand tightly around the bride's wrist. A little too tightly.

"Lizzie, I think you need to come with us," she said briskly, gesturing back toward the Hall—adding, when Ben made to move to accompany them: "Not you, thanks, not just now. Effie—come on."

They left the others to their croissants.

41.

Lizzie

I knew as soon as they'd heard the word what they were thinking. The one-night stand in Bangkok had become the stuff of folklore between the three of us—a puerile joke involving the city's name meant the details had lodged in the memory well enough to raise red flags in both of their heads as soon as Ben answered the question.

I never told them the name of the man I had spent my layover with in Thailand. In fact, I actually quite regretted even furnishing my best friends with the scantest details when their first reaction had been to list the many safety precautions I'd thrown out of the window by climbing straight into bed with him.

He could have been a murderer!

He could have been a rapist!

He could have been . . . your future husband's oldest friend?

Just kidding. Nobody saw that coming.

When I'd caught my plane home from Bangkok eighteen months ago, lovestruck after that night in Ben's company, I'd felt more desolate over the loss of him than of the boyfriend of four years I'd left behind on the yacht.

I'd felt like mine and Ben's future was waiting to start, for us to press Play. Instead, I'd clicked Stop and left. Waved goodbye to it as I had to him where he stood in the doorway of the hotel room we'd shared for a few hours only. He leaned on its frame, wrapped in a sheet, as I walked away down the corridor as slowly as I possibly could, turning every so often to get one last look at him. He'd stayed there smiling back until I was finally out of sight.

After I picked up my suitcase from that wretched hostel—resenting every minute of the journey there as ones I might have spent still entwined with him—I sobbed all the way to the airport as though I were bereaved.

My dreams on the plane were of him sailing along the sullen brown water of the Thames in Guy's boat, straining from its prow as he tried to find me.

As the wheels touched down on the damp tarmac in London and the familiar gray rain began to spatter on the porthole windows, I switched my phone back on and it lit up immediately with a message. Messages. Ignoring the ones from my mum, I went straight to those from the newest number in my phone, the one I'd typed in there as he'd dictated it over cocktails in the sky. Had it really only been yesterday? Did we kiss goodbye only that morning? I didn't even know his surname.

The flight had muddled me and shaken up my emotions like snow in a paperweight, but the sight of his name on the screen pulled me right back down to earth. I was several thousand miles away, but he was still thinking of me.

"Missing you already," the first one said. "Are you home yet?"

We messaged each other for as long as it took me to collect my suitcase and get a cab home. By the time I unlocked the door to my shared house, I was even more besotted than I had been when the plane took off.

I booked a flight back to Bangkok in three months' time to go and visit him again.

For three weeks afterward, Ben and I called each other, and we texted like gossipy schoolgirls—on and off but regularly. I gamified the time between each communication so as to draw out the exquisite rush of having replied or having received a reply, before the lull as I waited for the next. He told me he was coming home at the end of the year. I would simply wait; I had met my man.

I told Effie and Anna about him in abridged form. I didn't want their cynicism to take the shine off the diamond that was mine only, to polish up with hope and longing. I knew that if I told the full story, the happy ending I was superstitiously hoping for would become make-believe.

Both of them—Anna an anxious new mother, Effie with her school rules, rape alarms, and Take Back the Night marches— high-fived me initially but then told me how dangerous it had been to go on a date with a man I'd never met in a city I didn't know without telling anyone where I was—even though that is precisely what those apps have been designed to facilitate. "Promise us you won't do it again," they said over cocktails that night.

How right they were.

They tried to jolly me along and on to the next, set me up on blind dates with single men they knew peripherally. These were no longer the friends of friends they had been in our twenties but now, in our thirties, the friends of friends of friends, the relatives of colleagues, the in-laws of someone they had once worked with but hadn't spoken to for a while. Such were the tenuous tangles I found myself sitting opposite and, let me tell you, those men weren't rendered any more interesting or attractive by the contortions people I didn't even know had gone through to get them in front of me.

It had been a long week at work and an even longer Friday night with some of the girls from the office when they encouraged me to set up a profile on another app. One less frisky that promised Sunday afternoons as well as Saturday nights. I gave in, I did it, figuring it couldn't hurt just to have a look after all. Ben and I were still texting, still chatting at least once a week, but the frequency of contact—the urgency—had slowed.

Four days later, I met Dan in a bare-bricked, bare-bulbed

wine bar of the sort people less jaded than me enjoy going to and taking selfies in, and I loved him right from the off.

He made the familiar seem cozy rather than mundane, showed me in his own quiet way that there didn't need to be some breathtakingly dramatic backdrop, some out-of-the-ordinary set of circumstances. Real life was enough if what was at the heart of it was sturdy and good.

That was when I should have sent the message. The next time Ben got in touch to ask what I was doing, where I was—invariably in bed as I caught up on messages after another weekend spent with Dan—and whether I'd like to send him another picture. But I didn't.

I enjoyed chatting with him. He was clever, he made me laugh and squirm and feel like that girl in the sky instead of the one back behind a desk in Soho. I thought Dan was wonderful, but we were two weeks, three weeks, four weeks in—I'd been on enough dates before to know that, after any night out with Dan, there was still a high chance that he would simply drift off the radar, never text me back, blank my attempts to get in touch with him. With Ben, though, there had been what some people (not me: too jaded) might have called "a connection."

I knew I had a propensity to breathlessness over this sort of thing—God knows I had learned that much along with literature and rhetoric at Cambridge—but, over the month or so since I'd been back, my brain had started referring to Ben as the One. I was counting the days, the hours, until my plane took off and I would see him again.

Until I wasn't. Ben and I celebrated a month since we'd met with a meal over FaceTime—lunch for me and dinner for him—but a week later, he stopped responding to my texts. It didn't seem like a big deal at first—he was busy at work, he'd told me—but then I didn't hear from him for full weekends at a time. Weekends I was now spending mostly with Dan.

When I'd check in with Ben the following Monday, he either

couldn't take my calls or seemed distracted. Then five weeks, six weeks, seven weeks with Dan—finally I sent the message when, after two months of being together most days and most nights, Dan told me that he loved me.

"Ben, I'm so sorry but I've met someone and I think he might be the real deal."

It was two days before my plane took off, and I knew then that I wouldn't be on it when it did.

At first he was jocular, mock indignant down the line: "There aren't any skyscrapers as tall as mine in London."

Then a little hurt, and almost persuasive. But, when I didn't budge, he was short. Terse and sharp.

"Fine then, have a great life."

I felt bad letting him down, but he clearly had a busy schedule out there and I'd been clinging to him through my phone the way I had with Guy before him. With Dan I was out in the world, smelling and tasting it like a whole, present person. A happy person. Someone with a future.

That, I thought, was the end of our story—until, of course, I turned the page on the most exciting chapter of the new one I was telling.

42.

Effie

The library was still dark and cool, the night air not yet chased away. After Anna pulled Lizzie into the room, Effie closed the solid door carefully and stood, sad to feel awkward among her closest companions and unsure how to interact with either of them.

Anna seemed so cold, and Lizzie . . . Lizzie seemed as though she were on another planet, either with fear or the sheer unrecognizable, unreachable remoteness that so often veiled her features these days. They had barely spent any time alone together as a three so far this trip, and even now as they stood together, Lizzie still seemed to be somewhere else, far, far away behind features so closed they might as well have been the château's studded and impregnable front door.

If Ben was the man she had come home from Thailand so hung up on, what Anna had seen made even more sense. Perhaps it was his arrival, and the revelation of what had gone on between him and Lizzie, that had tipped Dan from supportive fiancé to jealous, coercive bully.

"Right." Effie felt a pulse behind her eye begin to flicker like a faulty connection. "Lizzie, you need to explain yourself. Is Ben Bangkok?"

Lizzie slumped as if the air had been drawn out of her with bellows. "Yes," she said simply.

Effie knew her friend's talent for self-justification, but her skin had grown thick to it over the years. Lapses in judgment, moments of thoughtlessness—these were forgivable along the bumpy and uneven road female friendships often take, but all-out betrayal would be hard to bounce back from.

"Anna saw you, Lizzie," Effie continued. "On the wedding night. With Ben."

No space for ambiguity: time for answers.

"We had to discuss something," Lizzie replied quickly. "It was to do with the wedding and all the stuff that arrived. I thought he had canceled lots of it, I wanted to know what happened . . ."

But the words tumbled into the vacuum like snow onto a wet pavement; there was nothing for them to stick to, nothing to keep them solid or real, and they melted away.

When Effie spoke again, her voice splintered just as her throat did under the crushing realization of what Lizzie's next answer might mean for their friendship.

"You have got to tell me what's going on, Lizzie," Effie demanded, almost breathless with the weight of tears held back. "Are you and he . . . Are you . . . Have you been cheating on Dan with Ben? Are you two together?"

The air Lizzie hadn't been able to breathe in moments ago whooshed out of her now instead, and as her frame sagged, Anna's grip seemed to be the only thing holding her up on the thin legs beneath her nightgown.

"Yes," she said, not without difficulty. "That's right."

Effie staggered backward and leaned her weight against a sturdy wooden writing desk; she felt shame all over her, an extra layer she was now forced to wear despite the heat. She had either been Ben's means of making the bride-to-be jealous or a fig leaf for the two of them to hide their illicit relationship for as long as it took Lizzie and Dan to say their vows.

"I look . . . I look . . . like such a fool," she whispered, and then louder, as if the words had been ripped from her: "How could you do this to me?"

Lizzie threw her a look like a plea. She began to vibrate where she stood in a teeth-chattering tremble from head to foot so intense she could barely stand still. It was the first time Effie could remember not rushing to Lizzie's aid when her friend needed her to, and she felt the beginnings of a fissure in her heart that she didn't know how to stop.

I don't owe you anything anymore.

Anna's face, too, had closed like shutters on a shop; she looked pained. The air seemed to gain in density, harder and thicker to breathe in, as though it were curling around their ankles like mist instead, and there was a collective shifting of weight in the room as the women braced themselves for the impact of whatever came next.

"After everything we've been through," Effie said quietly, though her voice began to rise like a plane readying its engines for takeoff. "After everything I did for you!"

Then a noise, behind them. The heavy door opening. A sweep of rubber sole on tile, the clearing of a throat.

Ben stepped into the library. "I think I know what you're talking about," he began earnestly. "And we owe it to Effie to come clean—about us."

He lingered on the end of the last word like a snake with its hiss, and Lizzie's mouth formed a straight line of pearly teeth and anger in response.

"Fine!" she choked. "Fine, let's have it all out in the open."

Ben approached her, hands outstretched and tenderness in his eyes—directed at Lizzie, Effie thought bitterly. *Only at Lizzie.*

"Do you want to tell it," he asked gallantly, "or shall I?"

43.

Lizzie

Trapped again. Boxed in by lies—only this time, they were mine. I'd had to lie to Effie to stay one step ahead; I knew I needed to be on the front foot from now on if I were to have any chance of stopping Ben.

But, my God, with the two women who knew me best staring at me like we'd never met before—and the knowledge that, soon enough, he'd have me cornered again—I couldn't see how I'd ever manage to pull it off. I had to install one more roadblock between me and Effie—for the simple purpose of protecting her from herself.

From the truth, really. If that came out—if the photos did—that was the end of everything. Not for me, but for Effie.

So I walled us in further, bricked us up in Ben's tangled story to protect us a little while longer—until I could work out what else I could do. I couldn't risk the chance of Effie forcing him into the revenge he really wanted: a showdown in which the truth was revealed, and the pictures were too.

My mind grasped for a way to convey to Effie and to Anna that whatever words might be coming out of my mouth, they should be reading the silent scream behind my eyes instead. But the yarn Ben had spun was horribly, deliberately believable, and my behavior for the last six months so bizarre and aloof, I had given them no reason to doubt it.

"Ben and I met in Bangkok," I said sullenly. "You probably remember me telling you about the date I went on there. And when I got home, I met Dan and I thought that was that."

"But then—fate!" said Ben, eagerly picking up the thread, some grotesque happy-go-lucky look on his face. "Fate brought us together again at the engagement party. We had no idea of the link—and neither did Dan—but, when he found out . . . Well, you remember what I told you—this was the reason he became the way he did. I'm afraid me and Lizzie were the trigger."

Effie shook her head and laughed bitterly, looking from his face to mine. Perhaps she was thinking he owed her nothing, but me . . . I owed her almost everything. My job, my happiness: the life I had woven for myself would never have happened without her help all those years ago. Now Ben was unpicking every last stitch of it.

When she spoke, her lip curled and the ugly contempt looked foreign on her usually mild features. "Then why, *why*, bring me into it? Why start something up with me, if you two were going to get back together?"

I closed my eyes and answered for him. "Because he didn't know, Eff. I didn't tell him about Dan's behavior until last week, when I canceled the wedding. And I didn't know about you two until a few days after that. Otherwise . . . Of course. I would never have knowingly let you get tangled up in all this."

This much, at least, was true.

I saw Ben give a small nod at my performance—if it worked, Effie would at least be free of him by the end of tomorrow, when we all got home. Whether I would or not, I still had no idea—but I could tell that my best friend wouldn't be around when I found out. I had seeded too much doubt along with the story Ben wanted me to tell her; the trust—that incredible, rare alchemy we had nurtured between us over the years—was gone.

"Right," Effie said, pinching the bridge of her nose between her thumb and forefinger. "Right."

Anna swooped to embrace her with arms that I desperately wanted to feel around my shoulders, pressing me in toward the two of them, where I belonged. But the gesture spoke so loudly, she might as well have pushed me away with her other hand.

"I've always known you could be selfish, Lizzie," Effie said. "And thoughtless in pursuit of your own happiness, your own gain. But I really thought I deserved more from you than this. After everything."

The words would have been a slap in the face had they been true, but the fact that they so neatly cut across precisely the contortions I'd put myself through to spare Effie far worse— sacrificing my future, sending Dan away, boxing myself into a cor- ner precisely because of what I owed her . . . Well, I felt as though I'd been skinned.

It emptied my final reservoirs of self-control not to scream it all out at her then. It might have felt good for a moment— righteously soaking up their sympathy and their horror, watching them direct it at the person responsible for all this, rather than his hapless victim—but what after that? Only the grinding and inevitable conclusion my brain had already reached at least a thousand times when I'd tried to riddle out my options before: Effie splashed across the internet, the end of her career, of all her dreams.

She and Anna swept out of the library, leaving me trapped in the center of Ben's web. I wanted to stretch out a hand and beg their retreating backs to save me.

"Well done," Ben said as the door swung closed behind them. "Very convincing."

I could see that me having been out of his sight, even briefly beyond his control, had made him nervous. He needn't have wor- ried. The threat was still there, the sword over Effie's head.

"She hates me," I said.

Ben's eyes shone with relief—and something else: triumph. "Good," he said.

He had cut me off from everything—everybody—I held dear. He was all I had left, and now he was standing so close to me that I couldn't see anything other than him.

44.

Effie

Effie lay in the bedroom she had shared for only one night of the holiday—and even then in separate single beds—with the new boyfriend she had been so excited to introduce to her friends. Utterly humiliated, she consoled herself with the fact that he had ever looked twice at her at all, and it made her feel even more pathetic.

Stupid, really, to think that a man like that might be interested in a woman like her. The past month had all been a game, something to make Lizzie jealous. To bring her back to him, make her see what she was missing.

Of course.

Effie hadn't cried when Anna had told her, carefully and gently laying out what she had seen on the wedding night as though she were dressing a wound. Her friend's soothing voice had acted like a balm. But she cried now, after Lizzie had confirmed it—after everything they had been through together. Even after what Effie had done for her at university.

She thought of Ben downstairs with Lizzie. Ben, Dan's best man, and Lizzie, her best friend, who deserved each other for the hurt their relationship had caused those on the periphery. Those who stood a chance of being hit by the shrapnel, burned by the heat given off when two people finally give in to the sexy, clandestine urges they have tried and failed to suppress.

Of course Dan was angry and very much on the warpath—he must have found out. Despite everything Ben had told them about the former groom, Effie struggled not to feel some kind of sympathetic kinship with him: he too had lost out to his closest friend.

"I saw them, I remember now—" Through the tears, Effie's mind flicked fitfully back to the whirling of her panic attack in the cave, and her pulse followed suit.

"When?" Anna asked from where she sat on the bed, stroking Effie's tear-soaked hair. "Where?"

"In the caves," she replied. Amid the terror, Effie had seen, among the gruesome faces in the paintings spinning about her, Lizzie's—white, accusatory—and her pointed finger stabbing at Ben's chest. "They were fighting in there."

"No wonder she was so keen to go," said Anna. "It meant they could finally have a private chat without worrying the rest of us might overhear."

Without his girlfriend noticing.

But no, Effie realized now: she had never been a girlfriend. Ben had never allowed her that far in. She'd never even been round to his flat—they had always been at hers, and he'd never left so much as a phone charger behind.

Effie cringed at the way she'd clung to Ben over the past few weeks, the way she'd hung so many of her sorrows and grievances on him, as though he were a coat stand, to relieve herself of them for a while. She was grateful, at least, that none of her friends had been there to witness her at her most lovestruck—in the pub, on Hampstead Heath, in bed. *Oh God, in bed.* Where he had made her feel more confident, more desirable, more extroverted than anyone ever had before.

She swallowed grimly and blinked away the visions of herself—

laughing, beckoning, arranged—and with it some of the humilia-tion she felt accruing in her chest. What she was unable to shrug off was the sense of betrayal: Lizzie had neither told her anything about her and Ben, nor stopped Effie from going any further with him. But then Effie had not told Lizzie either, had she? Was it really possible Lizzie hadn't known?

All of this made Ben the first secret they had had between them, the only secret. The bond they had forged playing dilet-tante during those fairy-tale days at Cambridge had been strength-ened by what had happened in exam term. After that, Effie had never anticipated anyone or anything coming between her and Lizzie again.

It had been a Thursday, a weekly slice of disposable R&B at one of the many terrible student clubs, when Lizzie had disap-peared from the dance floor. When the lights came up on the clinches and the debris, she simply wasn't there anymore. Anna and Effie, first curious, then worried, had checked their phones and each found a message waiting from her: "Got very lucky, see you tomorrow."

But they didn't see her tomorrow, or the next day, or the one after that. Effie's lecture-free days were spent alone, but for the ebb and flow of other course-mates through the college gates, at lunchtime, in the library. When she met up with Anna every eve-ning, they went to the weekly film night as a twosome or shared a bottle of wine, then went to bed. The following day brought still no Lizzie.

They were not worried so much as intrigued. Lizzie texted them constantly with updates: the man she had met was not gown, a student, but town, a—as Lizzie described him—"real person." He was older than them, had a job, lived by himself in a small cottage on the outskirts of the city. She tackled our course's reading list in his garden, having gotten the prescribed books out of a suburban library. She wrote up her study notes at his kitchen table, between cooking meals in an actual oven. In the student halls, their rooms had only two electric burners; on day four, Lizzie roasted a chicken.

On day five, the man's girlfriend came back early from a work trip. The weather broke and Lizzie walked all the way back to college in the rain, wearing the tight and rather brief minidress she'd been out clubbing in almost a week before. Her blond hair hung in wet streamers around her face; her eyes were red and swollen. Effie and Anna never even found out the man's name: he was known as Shithead forever more.

Lizzie took it badly, stopped eating and barely got dressed. She had seen a life she wanted and she mourned it, even though it had been a mirage—an escape to ordinary as her finals loomed. The exams were two months away, dissertations due in one.

They took turns looking after her, Anna spooning soup into Lizzie's mouth as she stared at the walls, Effie dragging her to the showers and persuading her to wash her lank hair. But as time passed, Lizzie grew more lethargic, not less. What little food she forced down settled about her jawline and her waist like an extra layer of bulky clothing. She had agonizing, temple-splitting headaches, and her gums began to bleed. It was only when she theatrically puked on the wall tiles of hers and Effie's shared kitchen that they recognized the symptoms from TV.

Effie made the appointment and went with her, stroked her hair and brought her hot water bottles for the days afterward as Lizzie lay, cramping, in bed. Anna brought noodles through from her room down the hall, encouraged them to eat vegetables, tried to remind them both to study when they could. Exams were three weeks away, dissertations due in one, and Lizzie had barely started hers.

Effie blinked a tear out of her eye and it rolled over the bridge of her nose, where she lay on her side, and dripped onto the French linen.

She couldn't help feeling that Lizzie had used her, again.

45.

Anna

"Did you put the ring on because you were so unhappy with the one I gave you?"

Steve's lovely, lined faced was careworn with drying tears. The pain Anna had experienced trying to soap the fucking thing off was nothing compared to this.

After she had left Effie to sleep, Anna had found her husband and told him what she had seen on the wedding night. He had gone very quiet.

She'd thought he would be angry with her for not telling him about the scene she had stumbled across, hazy as her recollection of it was, but his upset at the fact of her having put on the alien wedding ring was far stronger. His tears reminded her of the stormy emotions she often had to contend with during one of Sonny's tantrums—the little tyrant with Steve's face could rage for what felt like hours on end if he felt particularly hard done by.

Steve was far better than she was at remaining calm until the storm had passed and Sonny had been put successfully to bed; Steve would wait until he had a cold beer in his hand before blowing the stress away with one heavy out-breath. Now, in the library, his sadness was as noisy and abundant as that of the tiny person they had made together, who Anna was beginning to ache for.

"No, Stevo, I just . . . I was drunk. I felt like I needed a change." She spread her hands where she sat, opposite him on a sofa that either he or Iso had slept on and that the two of them had reclaimed in grand style only a couple of days ago.

"A change?" Steve's eyebrows and Adam's apple shot up like a fairground high striker. "Is there somebody else?"

"God, no! No, no—that's not what I meant at all," Anna sighed and rubbed her face.

She thought of how much she had enjoyed Lizzie's engagement party, how when she had sat at the bar while Steve packed away his records, she had wondered—briefly—what it might feel like to be going home with someone else. The thought had gone no further; it could never have happened—and yet she had felt guilty for months afterward about what she might have meant in her mind.

Somebody else. She almost laughed at the notion, but stopped herself just in time. She appreciated Steve's faith in her ability to have met somebody else, but the logistics were hardly stacked in her favor. Her working hours, for one. The fact that when she wasn't at her desk she was usually with Sonny, for another. She wore funereal suits and a gown for her nine to five; away from work, she haunted supermarkets and soft-play cafés rather than bars.

Christ, Steve is far more likely to meet someone else than I am.

That no man had even glanced at Anna since she'd given birth was one unassailable hurdle to her having an affair—and one she despised herself for even using as a metric for her own sense of self-worth. That the very idea of revealing her deflated, puckered, and battle-scarred body to anyone who wasn't Steve made her want to cry was the final, incontrovertible reason why, no, there was categorically no one else. Not that she wanted there to be. She remembered watching Effie enviously at the airport, giggly and flirtatious with Ben—and just look what he had been up to behind everyone's backs.

The memory of the wedding night and of Effie's tears rose in her throat; she was finding Lizzie and Ben's dishonesty hard to stomach.

Anna knew women who were raising children by themselves. There was Celia, for one, but many more at the local playgroups and libraries, and she marveled at the reserves of inner strength they must have to care for a child alone, when both she and Steve were regularly punch-drunk by the end of a day spent doing so between them.

She listened, over coffee and the heads of their adored children, to their hooted tales when they resumed dating again while thinking she would rather pull out her own teeth than make sexy small talk with a man she didn't know, would happily set herself alight instead of offering up to someone new the wasteland she hid under her ever-baggier clothes.

Perhaps this was where she had been going wrong with Steve. Reveling in their familiarity even as it bred contempt between them. Forgetting that her husband was not, in fact, an extension of herself and Sonny but another person who might enjoy sexy small talk, who might want to visit the wasteland every so often.

She wrapped Steve—tall, thin, lovely Steve—in her arms what felt two or three times over. She wanted to bind him to her, to make them both one person. Anna felt like she was sewing a limb back on that she had temporarily lost.

"I think we need to change some stuff," she said. "Well, *I* do really. I need to stop being so tense and so impatient with you."

She breathed out. "And with Son."

Steve took her hand, the red, raw one that had been held under the tap for the past half-hour as they'd both tried to remove a wedding ring that wasn't her own. It had eventually squeaked off and clinked into the bottom of the vast porcelain sink in the kitchen. They reunited it with its pair—the other Bertie had found, rolled away under a chair in the Hall.

"You are a wonderful mother," Steve told her, holding her eyes with his.

Anna started to cry again then, because it was the constant and wearying suspicion that this was not the case that lay at the heart of why she was so stressed, why she disliked herself so much, why she medicated with so many cookies.

"And I'm sorry for being so crap." Steve rubbed his eyes so hard it made the carefully moisturized skin around her own smart in sympathy. "I'm really, really sorry for letting you down."

"You're not crap," she said, soothing him, and she knew then that he wasn't really. Whatever the wedding night's high jinks might have looked like the next morning, it was nowhere near what her mind had turned it into. Steve was not that man; he never would be.

After Sonny's birth, Anna had spent her maternity leave feeding and weaning, soothing and routine-ing. When she returned to work to sit at her vast desk, and to take difficult clients to lunch in dimly lit but keenly priced dim sum restaurants and City-boy steakhouses, then fight for them in court, Steve swapped in. Tapping away on his laptop at their kitchen table on one of their dilapidated dining chairs while Sonny was at nursery school, then persuading him—a trickier customer even than many of Anna's—to eat his fish fingers and beans every evening. This was as close to equality as parenting came, except Steve was more likely than her to end up covered in tomato sauce.

Hers was a better deal than the ones most of the mothers she knew had struck with their partners. Some of them didn't work and saw the lights go out behind their husbands' eyes as soon as they started talking about their day at home. Some of them did and were expected to do the bulk of everything else anyway. Others relied on a complex patchwork of help from grandparents and neighbors and cleaning ladies and office juniors that cost them

more in gratitude and resentment than even the most extortion-
ate nursery fees.

Women from each of those categories exclaimed over Steve,
and this, Anna thought, was really the thing she found annoying—
not him. The fact that he wasn't doing anything another woman
hadn't, and yet praise was heaped upon him for it just as surely as
nobody seemed to remark on how hard *she* was working, how
stretched thin *she* was.

Anna knew men—worked with men—who would talk about
the mothers of their children as though they were sainted mar-
tyrs, broken on the wheel of nappy rash and BuggyFit, a zealot's
glint in their eyes at the hardships their wives faced and the sac-
rifices those beneficent, long-suffering women had made. Those
men bought them designer handbags for Christmas and diamond
rings for their VBAC—billable gestures with a value that offset
how little help they actually offered at home and that Steve would
never lavish on her but Anna sometimes thought she might want.
But how many of those men would help clean actual worms from
their child's bumhole as he had? Steve had even sung "One Wink
at a Time" by the Replacements as he'd done it.

When those men's baby daughters got overlooked for an award
or a first-class degree, started working and didn't get the same
pay or promotions, had a baby and found themselves unofficially
demoted in the office—would they realize they'd had a hand in
it? Probably not.

And none of this, Anna reiterated inside her own head, was
Steve's fault.

So why take it out on him?

"I'm sorry for being a cow, Stevo," she whispered.

"You're not a cow," he smiled, pink-eyed, and persuaded her
horizontal once more.

46.

Lizzie

At first I wondered whether it was my fault—and then I understood. Men like Ben make you question your own behavior so that you won't see that it's theirs that is problematic.

I thought at first that perhaps if I had just been a little kinder, a little more sensitive, taken more care with his feelings, not led him on, it might not have happened. I was so caught up in those early days with Dan, I didn't realize what Ben was at first. I know now what a fragile, dangerous thing the male ego is: like a plant that needs watering and constant attention or it withers and poisons the water supply for everything else in the vicinity.

We are taught to nurture it in ways we don't even realize. Lower your voice. Laugh at his jokes. Giggle your way through this encounter, because it's easier than taking issue with how he just spoke to you. Pretend you can't manage by yourself so you don't seem like a threat—whether it's a photocopier, a car, or a condom.

Anything to avoid triggering the nail bomb they all wear just beneath their clothes. Even the ones in plaid shirts and nice suits. Especially the ones in nice suits.

I had my first taste of it at Cambridge—the lost week, Anna and Effie called it. The lost six months, it became, after I graduated and couldn't get out of bed for the rest of the year.

I hated myself for having let down another woman—the one who let herself into her boyfriend's home to find me, practically a child still, sitting in his armchair wearing one of his T-shirts and reading *Tess of the d'Urbervilles*. Her mouth in an O, her eyebrows raised in surprise—but her face soon closed up that shocked expression like a blind rolling down on a window.

"Oh, another one," she sighed, as I rushed to grab my belongings and leave.

She must have been around the same age I am now.

I hated myself for having been so naïve. By the time I got back to college I was so catatonic with self-loathing, I couldn't write the dissertation I'd been avoiding even if I'd wanted to.

So Effie wrote it for me.

She started it as soon as we got back from the clinic where I'd taken the tablets. Where as I'd left, a homely woman around my mother's age and wearing a bonnet wreathed with flowers had pressed gory literature into my hands and told me I was eternally damned.

As I shivered and heaved in my bed, racked with pains I thought would break my back and my hips—would empty me until I was hollow—Effie tapped away on her computer next door. She authored seven thousand extra words in addition to her own paper on Emily Dickinson about how modernity is the corrupting force at the heart of the male-female dynamic in Thomas Hardy. He wasn't wrong: just imagine how Alec d'Urberville would have treated women if he'd had an iPhone, or sanctimonious Angel Clare with a righteous Twitter account.

Effie quoted from reams of books she had read and I hadn't bothered to; she gave me her eloquence, her breadth of knowledge. She loaned it to me for the future, so I could leave university and start my life again.

Blood on water. My baby was a raspberry in a bowl. I flushed it away in the girls' loos of our student block.

What is it Hardy says? "Women do as a rule live through such humiliations, and regain their spirits, and again look about them with an interested eye."

And I did eventually. But clearly, I learned nothing from it.

The night we met—or re-met, I should say, at the engagement party—Ben and I made innocent-sounding, awkward small talk. I was flustered, more by the context than by his presence. Surrounded by friends who had gathered to celebrate my getting married to another man, I guppy-mouthed and hedged while Ben asked increasingly banal questions. About our relationship, our engagement, my heart, he asked not a word.

It is not simple, hunting a person with your eyes when you are the focus of everybody else's in the room.

I next saw the top of his head all the way across the crowd when I was on the dance floor with Eff, attempting the self-conscious shuffle of the woman who feels herself to be under observation, intimidatingly but deliciously so.

Except I wasn't. Ben wasn't even looking my way.

When he pulled me into the cloakroom later, it was the first contact we'd had since our handshake, and it was like I'd been branded with his touch—a burning patch on my arm where he had held it and steered me toward the back of the small room, behind the rails of coats.

"God," he said, running one hand through his hair, breathing out forcefully through his mouth—*whoosh*—as though he were expelling the tension between us.

Close up for the first time in a year, those bottomless blue eyes, perfect teeth, strong jaw, and burly shoulders had almost the same effect on me as they had the first time round. I felt my stomach swoop toward my feet when I remembered how infatuated I had been with him back then.

Despite that, I saw the insecurity flash through him as he

started talking. Though he practically filled up the tiny space with his burliness, Ben seemed smaller in here than he had before. Than he had that night all those months ago.

I realized in that moment that the Ben I had fallen so hard for was a figment I'd built up into something more. Dan was the real thing, a thousand times more real than the rooftop in Bangkok.

"So, this is weird," Ben continued, laughing but without humor.

"Such a small world," I murmured. "You can't escape your demographic, I guess."

I could have prattled on with platitudes for a while longer, but he stopped me.

"Look, I wouldn't tell Dan about us if I were you. He'd find it too weird."

I nodded, grateful to him for the advice. It hadn't yet crossed my mind that my fiancé might have an opinion on a previous life of mine that had inadvertently intersected with his. Though Dan mentioned his school friend Ben regularly, he rarely used his full name; I never added the man saved in my phone as "Ben Bangkok" to my Facebook, where the link lay waiting to be discovered. We never stumbled across it—until we did. In person.

"I know what he's like about stuff like this," Ben continued in the dark of the cloakroom. "He's the kind of guy that wouldn't be able to get past it—not with me."

I knew that Dan was a thoughtful sort of guy—far more thoughtful than anybody else I'd ever been with. I knew he was a considerate sort of guy, too. If being a bit jealous was the flip side of those qualities . . . Well, we all have our flaws, I told myself.

"No, of course," I said. "I see. Let's just leave it, it was nothing."

Ben's features tightened briefly. "That's right," he said firmly. "Nothing."

Nevertheless, I felt a cold tide rising from my velvet-clad feet.

I swayed slightly where I stood, hemmed in by the dimensions of the room, of Ben in front of me, of things I had done before I had even met Dan. I'd never wanted the man who would be my husband to feel anything but admiration and love for me. I certainly didn't want to ruin what we had or the friendship he'd shared with Ben since they were both eleven.

He put a hand on my shoulder and looked deep into my eyes, so far that I felt I was standing there in front of him naked. Again.

"That's why I won't tell him," he said, with a sad, regretful smile playing around his white lips. "I won't tell him about all those texts you sent me," he added, with a doleful flourish. "Even though you two lovebirds had met by then, I think?"

Cold, cold, cold from my head to my toes.

I had spoiled the purest thing I had ever had before I'd even said, "I do."

47.

Effie

Effie felt pathetic to have pinned her hopes on him. Pathetic to have staked her happiness on another relationship. Pathetic to have handed Ben her baggage, and yet somehow relieved to know now without a doubt that he wasn't capable of carrying it for her. She was just going to have to learn to shoulder life all by herself.

That, Effie hoped, was how she might begin to feel comfortable in her own skin, relaxed in her own company. How she had reached her thirties and still didn't—when everyone else seemed innately to understand that acquiring this sort of self-reliance was a large part of becoming a grown-up—she couldn't explain. But she had the sense that Ben—and Lizzie, Effie remembered again lurchingly—had taken away her final excuse for not learning.

Effie had attached her self-esteem to so many other people over the years that it had lost its stick; now, rather than leave it lying in the dust after Ben's departure from her life, she'd pick it up and treasure it for herself. Nurture it like the girls she did at school, like the friends she had counseled round pub tables over the years—women so bright and full of potential she'd be shocked to find them staying in a relationship that wasn't good enough for them just for the sake of a bit of company. For the sake of feeling wanted.

From now on, Effie would start taking her own advice.

Her bitterness over Ben and Lizzie's affair had already begun to balance with the sense of having been handed a reprieve.

Plus, there were the niggles she had felt since he had arrived among her nearest and dearest, and the air between the two of them had changed. The growing feeling that, as pleasant a distraction as Ben had been from the everyday business of heartbreak, this might be all he ever was. Beyond the pub, beyond the bedroom, Effie never quite knew what to say to him, how to act around him—as though the self she had been with Ben was one she could not also be in front of her friends.

At least the guilt of something possibly having happened with Charlie was dissipating with every passing minute since the realization that she had meant nothing to Ben—although pain at the fact that she had meant just as little to her best friend was filling the space that guilt had vacated.

Lizzie could have Ben if she wanted him—only, who would want a man who had slept with her best friend to make a point?

One who had been victimized by the man she was supposed to marry.

Effie's anger was tempered by the revelations about Dan; that sort of constant domestic trauma—a regular pulse of fear beating out the rhythm of every single day—explained so much of her friend's behavior over the past six months and why Ben had so doggedly lingered outside Lizzie's closed door, in case the man who had waged his campaign of cruelty against her turned up to claim his prize. Effie shivered, despite the golden sunshine.

The household had disintegrated, the strain on its fabric too much to bear, and the cozy if rather disquieted ambience in the château had ripped apart. The rest of them had skulked awkwardly outdoors, where the pool stretched out, still and glassy, in blue magnificence. Just the sight of it lifted Effie's spirits; her tears had dried and sunglasses hid her inflamed red eyes, but her brain remained trained on Lizzie.

If Dan's treatment of his fiancée had been what brought his best man and his bride-to-be irrevocably closer than they had once been, why hadn't Lizzie admitted it sooner? Fear? Shame? The exhilaration of secrecy? Effie had certainly experienced the potency of the latter in the last month. If things had resumed between the two of them only in the week since Lizzie had canceled the wedding, it made the deception slightly less pointed. But she still couldn't help feeling as though something connected her and Dan: a bond of betrayal from the very closest quarters.

People fall for their best friend's partners all the time.

Effie counted silently back to the last time she and Ben had spent the night together—not just under the same roof or in single beds but really together—and came up with the date she had last visited Lizzie at the flat to persuade her to come with them all to France. Five nights after the cancellation email, and two before they had caught their plane: just over a week ago. Why had neither of them told her?

She thought guiltily about the secret she had not yet discussed with her friends—the dark hairs on the pillow, the scraps of conversation she could remember between herself and Charlie. Effie knew they must have shared something that was difficult to take back again once given—his flighty avoidance and mannered behavior since the wedding night had all but confirmed it to her. All there was left to do was finesse the details of what had actually happened between them.

Could it really be true that Charlie, in the half-light between dawn and day, had told her that he had never felt this way before?

Was there any scenario in which the words "Nobody else has even come close" might have left his lips where they had just about kissed the cotton pillowcase next to the one her face, its profile a symmetry, also lay on?

What, Effie ached to know, had she said in return to snuff out Charlie's feelings so comprehensively ever since? Her side of the partially recalled exchange was entirely missing, scrubbed from the tape like classified information. She just hoped she had been kind; a future with Charlie might have seemed one way out when drunk, but after a mostly sober week Effie knew it wasn't what she wanted—what she had ever wanted. Or, for that matter, what was good for her.

After this week, Effie resolved, she would concentrate simply on the latter.

She hoped Charlie could be happy with Iso in lieu of her—though she took it as no small compliment to have been ranked over the burnished supermodel lying on a sunbed only a few strides away along the terrace. Little had Effie realized that the candle had burned undimming since university: ten long years, six of them while she had been with James. No wonder they'd never met any of Charlie's extravagantly unserious other girl-friends: the procession that had masked his pining for the one that had got away.

She looked over at him now, and her heart burned fiercely—the sort of love refined by moments of weakness and chinks in the armor, screams of laughter and hugs of solidarity, rather than the kind that pounces before the lights come up. It was the same way she felt about Anna, about Lizzie.

As Effie looked toward the house, Anna stepped out onto the patio, walked across it, and came to sit on the sunbed next to hers. A little flushed, a little smug-faced. Behind her, Ben emerged into the sunlight too, and Effie's pulse quickened—not in excitement, but in nervousness. She was grateful when he turned to sit at the other end of the pool, over by Bertie.

"Everything sorted?" she asked Anna knowingly.

Anna nodded and looked across the shimmering water as she spoke quietly, an answer just for the two of them.

"I've thought of Steve as part of me for so long," she said. "That's what you're told to look for: a soulmate. Someone who knows you better than you know yourself."

She swallowed thickly. Cleared her throat and adjusted her sunglasses.

"I'm always angry with myself these days," she continued. "And I forgot I wasn't married to myself, but to another person who needs kindness and attention. Just like I do."

Anna gestured to the bottle of mineral water in the shade of Effie's lounger and, after a nod from her friend, picked it up, took a swig. She looked more peaceful, more resolved. Happier.

"We made a commitment to look after each other," she finished. "We haven't been doing enough of that recently."

Anna shrugged awkwardly, peroration over. "How about you, Eff? Are you okay?"

"I will be," she murmured.

Effie smiled at her dear friend, but she felt something snag on her heart as she remembered the face that was missing. Their three had never felt complete as a two—for the odd afternoon perhaps, but no longer. When Lizzie had absconded at university, when she'd gone on those endless make-or-break boat trips with Guy, Effie and Anna had always been waiting for her to come back.

This time, Effie thought sadly, Lizzie had gone too far.

48.

Lizzie

I couldn't lock myself in that beautiful bedroom forever. I couldn't shut him out indefinitely. As I paced between the four-poster bed and the window, I understood that I was running out of time and places to hide. I already knew how persistent Ben could be.

After the engagement party, weeks passed during which I didn't see or hear from him again.

"He's flat-hunting now he's back from Thailand," Dan might mention, though I was careful rarely to ask outright. "I'm seeing him for a drink after work next week."

On those evenings, I'd climb the walls, alone at home with my wedding spreadsheet open and gleaming, waiting for my fiancé to come home and kiss me so I would know I was still his golden girl. That Ben hadn't let anything slip. I organized and booked and hired and invited like an automaton, just to fill the hours. I saw Anna eyeing the new "bridezilla" me with surprise and disappointment, as though I'd let the side down, when really I was doing my utmost to remain bright and breezy.

As the weeks went by, the clench of dread in my stomach eased and some of the nagging guilt lessened too. After all, if Dan did find out, what had I really done wrong? Nothing. Who wouldn't have kept someone interesting in reserve until they knew Plan A would work out? Let me rephrase that: Who hasn't?

But it would all come flooding back when I considered the particulars. I began to wish I'd simply told Dan everything straight after I'd met Ben at the party; it would have been easier that way. I'd left it too long, and it would look weird if everything came out now. More than weird: suspicious.

So I had to trust to Ben's good nature—and I did. Until, suddenly, I knew I couldn't.

We were in the pub, the three of us—not an irregular occurrence since Ben had moved back but one that was still a fresh hobby, a new way to spend our time—when Dan got up and went to the loo. Once he had disappeared from sight, Ben gripped my wrist where it lay on the table between our three pints and a stack of the Sunday papers.

"I can't do this, Lizzie," he said urgently. "You know we had something special. Please don't throw it all away."

I was surprised but sympathetic and firm, drawing my hand away, pulling my sleeve down over my fingers as if to protect them, prevent them feeling him again. Just the touch of his hand had been a reminder of the electricity there had once been between us.

"Ben—" I struggled to grasp the right words. There was no point in being cruel, but I didn't want to soften the blow too much; I didn't want a repeat of this conversation ever again. There could be no gray area after this.

Just trying to form the sentence made me realize how often I hedged my words so as not to offend, how I'd tie myself in knots socially just to avoid saying no. How I went along with things I didn't really want to, gave consent without actually meaning to. How much easier it is to simply hurt someone's feelings and get on with it. It was a valuable lesson.

"I'm with Dan," I said eventually, simply. "I'm sorry. We had a great time, but I just know that Dan is the one for me. There isn't anything else to say."

It sounded so bald like that that I reached out and stroked the back of his hand where it still lay on the table in front of us. I wanted him to be okay.

"*You* ghosted *me*," I said softly.

Ben jumped back as though I'd pinched him, knocked one of the glasses and splashed beer on the varnished wood, across the blaring front page of the newspaper.

"And what will Dan say when he sees all your texts?" he sneered.

"Dan is a grown-up," I said firmly. "He will understand that people see other people, that there's sometimes an overlap. It isn't exclusive until it's exclusive. We had that chat. He was seeing other people when we met too."

Ben just smiled at that. "I'm not 'other people,' though, Lizzie. I'm his best friend. And Dan will never love you the same way when he knows that you were in love with me."

It felt like he'd punched me in the stomach.

When Dan got back to the table, he found us both sitting in silence staring at a puddle of craft ale, the chic weekend supplements sopping with it. Ben was looking out the window and I stared at the cuffs of my navy wool fisherman's jumper as though they might show me a way out of the mess I had made for myself.

"What have you two been nattering about then?" Dan smiled as he slipped back into his seat, onto the bench between us, and draped an arm around my shoulders.

A few days later, Ben texted me and asked me to meet him after work in a bar near my office, the sort where managers take their receptionists in order to start affairs. Busy, anonymous. Not particularly pleasant.

As soon as I saw his sandy head bent over his phone at the table in the wooden booth, I felt the ghost of an attraction now gone tug in my stomach. When I sat, he took my hand, and my heart flipped a somersault. A sharp zap of voltage ran through me.

"Please, Lizzie," he said. "Please. Don't marry him. I'm in love with you."

The response came easily, but even at this point—even after he had scared me, threatened me—I still felt like I was dragging the words out of myself. I loved Dan, but I thought I had loved Ben too. I told myself that I had spent a whole year actively loving Dan—planning a life with him, burrowing into his personality, exploring his hinterland, conjugating a whole new language with him. I had spent one night—really, only a matter of hours—loving a version of Ben that had turned out to be a figment of my infatuation.

"I'm sorry," I said huskily, awkward but decisive. "I'm really sorry. I'm going to marry Dan in a few months, and I really hope that you and I can be friends. I know how much you mean to him."

Ben dipped his head so low that all I could see was hair and the hollow of his nape. His shoulders began to shudder, and my stomach turned again—not for love of Ben but with the realization that he would always be there to remind me of this. How could I live by Dan's side for the rest of my life and avoid him?

When he looked up again though, his blue eyes shone like ice rather than with tears.

"And how much do you think you'll mean to him when he knows you've been sending me pictures of your tits?"

There had been just one picture—not long before Dan and I had met for our first date, but very much in advance, I'd believed at the time, of the thought of meeting somebody else, of me ever joining another dating app. I had been out and got home late, and drunk; the time difference meant Ben was at work. I thought it'd be funny, but I blushed when I woke up alone the next day and remembered it. Even though the picture itself had been rather chaste, it was suggestive enough.

Now that Ben was prepared to hurl that image at me in anger, in threat, I realized I had given away my privacy as though it were any other belonging that someone might borrow and return. But there is no going back once your body, your hidden self, your sense of personal space has whooshed off to somebody else's phone, somebody else's memory card.

"You wouldn't . . ." My legs began to tremble beneath the sticky table, jerking like a puppet's on strings. "If you love me . . ." I whispered.

"I do love you," he said briskly. "But you're mine. He's always taking what's mine."

My heart went cold to hear the phrase Dan and I had chosen to be engraved inside our wedding rings come out of his mouth. Ben made it sound far more sinister than I had ever realized it might.

I remembered then, dimly, the story of some girl they'd both liked at the nearby girls' school. Ben had gotten so wasted at the Christmas disco she'd come to that he passed out and woke up to find that Dan had been the one to claim a snog at the end of the night. Was I revenge for that?

As I stood up, I thought I might vomit. I had never felt so unsafe. Not in the way of physical harm but as though I had drunk bleach, some brew that would turn me inside outside, burn my secrets to the surface, rip through the identity I had created for myself and, yes, for Dan too. Everything was at stake; I was being flayed alive in that bar, only nobody else could see. The people at the other tables around me simply went on eating their bruschetta and drinking their wine.

I staggered out of there as if he had poisoned me.

Ben stepped it up a notch after that. I made plans every weekend, pleaded important wedding stuff, to ensure that I wouldn't end up in his company again, but Dan would still invite him round for dinner, or he'd stop by on the pretense of needing to collect something he'd left at our flat. I couldn't bear the way he appraised me from head to toe, like some medical specimen, while Dan wasn't looking.

"Hello, beautiful," he'd say if Dan was out of the room. Or he'd find a reason to follow me when I left a room, then push himself close and whisper in my ear.

Ben acted as if the affair he'd threatened to tell Dan about was still going on.

He sent me the first photo over email while I was at work, and I leaped back from my desk so fast I sent my chair clattering to the floor. I closed the window on my screen, righted the chair before anyone could come to help, then locked myself in a toilet cubicle to look at the message on my phone.

Me, on a bed. A bed surrounded by the brushed steel fixtures and fittings that denote five-star accommodations. I was asleep and naked in a funny pink half-light that I eventually realized was dawn. The sun rises in Bangkok, another woman makes an error of judgment with a man she barely knows.

"I have more," the accompanying message said. "And they are worse. Do you want Dan to see them? Do you want the world to?"

I went home from work early that day and lay on my and Dan's bed—squashy, soft, and comforting, unlike the clinical starched and pressed sheets on the one in the picture—until Dan arrived home. I resolved to tell him everything and beg his forgiveness. When I heard the front door open, I rushed along the corridor in my pajamas, frenzied for the relief that the truth would bring—and found he'd brought Ben with him.

"Thought I'd make a curry," my fiancé said, kissing me on the cheek and hanging his coat up on a hook in our hallway, crowded as always with his bike and my shoes.

"A nice hot one please," Ben said, mocking me with his eyes, and using the squeeze of the space as an excuse to press against me as he walked past. "Just like in Bangkok."

I told them I was ill and lay in our back bedroom with the lights off as they cooked together, ate, and drank wine, reminiscing about their school days. Their laughs erupted only a few yards away as silent tears soaked into my pillow. Even after Ben went home, the jolt I had felt at seeing him on my doorstep—inside my home—left me too sick and scared, too intimidated, to tell Dan the truth.

Ben began emailing every day, pleas and then threats. He said I was running out of time to see sense, that soon he would have no choice but to put the photos online. Dan was his friend, after all; he couldn't let him marry a woman like me.

It was Ben who began to turn up outside my office, not Dan. Lurking in a side street until I appeared, like some sneaky after-dark animal—the sort that goes through your bins while you sleep and leaves your own rubbish strewn around your garden, making a display of the things you thought you'd discarded for everybody to see.

He'd scoop me up by the crook of my arm and steer me into pubs or bars down quiet side streets, where he'd lay siege to my confidence and assault my defenses over drinks I either could hardly force down or drank far too much of to try to drown him out. When that tack didn't work, Ben launched a lunchtime campaign to bring me round to him and to being with him, showing up outside my favorite sandwich shop near the office. I loathed him more every time I saw him.

I began to change my routes to and from my workplace, and arrived home exhausted with looking over my shoulder, with trying to reason with him, with the endlessness of it. The remorseless pursuit. I could see Dan's giant heart trying to puzzle out whether he'd done anything wrong.

Ben would show me fragments of the other pictures, cropped and indistinct: the curve of a waist here, a bare thigh there. How drunk had I been that this man had arranged me like flowers in a vase and snap-snap-snapped my life away as I slept? I barely remember closing my eyes that night in Bangkok, but I must have been out for a while, because he seemed to have at least a hundred shots.

"There are more," he'd always say. "Do you want your family to see them?"

That was what had stopped me from taking a stand against him. The shame. The eyes. The pixels and the pupils of other people gazing at them—at me. Their screen-lit faces and shocked curiosity. But the more I thought about it, the less guilt I felt—if Ben shared those pictures, he would be the one at fault, not me. I would be the victim. And once they were out there, perhaps I would be free.

It would be mortifying, of course—at no point did I particularly relish the idea of my family, friends, and colleagues ever seeing them. But my parents were pretty liberal, my friends were hardly prudes—and my colleagues . . . I worked in a boozy, licentious ad agency, where hands roamed free and extramarital slip-ups were common. Nude photos of me might provoke some comments, but they'd hardly start a moral panic.

So I called him on it. One night when he cornered me as I left to get the tube. I had decided to take the direct way home, rather than skulking through backstreets and choosing roundabout bus routes to avoid him.

"Leave me alone," I said, trying to steady my wobbling voice. "If you don't, I'm going to tell Dan everything. You can do your worst—I don't care anymore."

He laughed at me, tried to style it out. He tried to mask the surprise in his eyes with mockery, but I saw what lay beneath it: failure. He had banked on me being too afraid, and now his plan had hit a wall. I mentally scrubbed his name off my guest list, my seating plan, my future. On the way home, I felt so light that I smiled at other Londoners on the train, and they looked at me as though I were mad. Perhaps I had been.

That was the evening Ben got in touch with Effie.

That was why there had to be no more useless crying now. No more cowering, knowing he was listening to my sobs from the other side of my door. I had to wrest something back, find some kind of justice before it was too late.

49.

Anna

The bride appeared at the top of the stairs that evening, pale and wan. Even though Ben was standing right behind her, Lizzie had never looked so solitary.

The others ferried plates, serving spoons, and glassware from the kitchen to the table and laid it beneath the evening's first glimmers of stars. The lavender tang that had infused their stay was at its most heightened at this time of day, and the note crept inside the Hall like an extra guest.

Anna wondered whether she would ever be able to smell it again without thinking back to this moment: their final night of the holiday and the one when a friendship had come to an end.

Ben hadn't even attempted to talk to Effie since the conversation in the library. Instead, by the time she had finished crying on Anna's shoulder—not just over him, Anna understood, but for all the other bodies she'd tried to find solace in among the rubble of her self-confidence—the door to Lizzie's room was shut once more and he was nowhere else to be found around the château. *What more was there to say?*

As Ben appeared now with Lizzie on the stairs, one hand on the small of her back as she descended, he didn't even appear embarrassed—although, Anna noted spitefully, Lizzie didn't look as happy as she should, given how things had worked out.

Would they be going on Lizzie and Dan's paid-for honeymoon next week too?

"There you are!" Charlie's bright face appeared below from the kitchen doorway, but his smiled slipped when he noticed the body language between the couple on the stairs—and Effie watching them balefully from just beyond the double doors. "We're, um, nearly ready with the food."

He ducked back through the archway, quickly replaced by Iso, whose watchful dark eyes followed Lizzie and Ben across the Hall. Anna tugged on Effie's arm and brought her back out to the bench on which she and Bertie had been folding napkins and polishing smudges from wineglasses, so she wouldn't have to see. Lizzie's cousin was sipping from a small, lurid goblet in front of him on the table.

Under her hand, Anna felt Effie's tremor of sadness at the scene, as if taken from a parallel version of this trip where happiness and camaraderie might have dominated, rather than isolation and menace. Every one of the Oratoire's inhabitants wore a now-constant expression of expectant worry—as they all had since the wedding night, as though it had been smuggled into their suitcases along with their bathing suits.

"Pastis!" Anna cried, but she refused Bertie's offer to pour her one with a mock shudder. "Too strong for me, but let's have a sniff."

The licorice scent rose from the glass he offered like fumes, and she breathed in its deceptively sweet vapor like a fin de siècle lush. Once, she might have inhaled far more of it than that, but this trip had turned out to be a lesson in moderation as well as self-discovery.

The renewal Anna had hoped for had come not, as she had supposed, in nightly boisterousness and the retreading of old drunken jokes but in her capacity to say no to all that. To enjoy the days without rushing headlong into the nights, savoring the mornings as much as the evenings. The rejuvenation she had been looking for was not to exhume her younger self but to replenish the woman she was now.

That Anna had also been sipping from a chilled glass of white wine in the kitchen ever since she'd left Effie to freshen up and help her husband cook had no doubt gone some way toward making her mellow and sentimental, but she was anticipating tomorrow's trip home with the same excitement she had left it, rather than dread at returning to reality. She couldn't wait to leave this place and the callousness and resentment it had fostered in them all.

Tomorrow Anna would see her son again. Her life's meaning was to be found in the hollow crease of his neck and behind the downy lobes of his ears, not at the bottom of a wineglass. That said, she had also enjoyed the spiritual refreshment that four mornings of waking up at her own leisure, rather than her three-year-old's, had bestowed, so perhaps the meaning of life was somewhere between the two.

There were grateful murmurs now as Steve and Charlie carried the lamb, oozing juices on a broad wooden board, out to the table. Lizzie sat at one end, next to Ben like a little doting doll—blank-looking somehow—and Anna wondered whether she'd downed a Valium or two to take the edge off this final evening. Not a bad idea, she thought, switching her glance to Effie, who sat at the other end, looking resolutely at the cutlery in front of her and worrying at the napkin in her lap.

"Our last supper!" said Charlie, raising his glass with a nervous smile that was already askew.

We won't get through dinner without a fight.

Anna wasn't sure what they were toasting other than the sheer fact of the week being over and the opportunity to return to normality. Although a version of normal in which her two best friends were no longer on speaking terms was hard to imagine.

Oh, Lizzie, what have you done?

Opposite, Iso offered her glass to clink, and Anna obliged.

It was hardly Iso's fault that her every dimpled smile reminded Anna of nighttimes spent leaking milk and smelling like a goat; the Anna that had followed Iso on Instagram a few years back was the one who'd been awake breastfeeding at four A.M. and unable to move because there was a sleeping baby on her chest.

Pretty cool to meet her, really.

"Santé!" she said. "Happy days!"

Anna tried to make eye contact with Effie as she drank, Anna suspected, through a throat constricted with anxiety.

Happy days were something to aim for, at least.

50.

Effie

Beyond the trembling in her limbs and the butterflying sensation that her life would look very different without Lizzie in it, Effie tried to seek out positives. She would carry herself with more care, greater respect in the future.

In the drama of the week, she had at least almost forgotten James, had put him down like a heavy shopping bag and then neglected to pick him back up again. Her heart, rather than her back, was grateful for the lightening of that load, among its many others.

Effie knew that returning home—clicking that lock open and finding nothing moved behind the door, no other human to welcome her—would be another rite of passage to tick off, but she felt more capable of doing so now than she had since James had left. She didn't feel strong exactly, but Lizzie and Ben's revelation had hollowed her out: there was nothing to feel and, so, nothing left to fear either.

She had a job she adored, although she had neglected it of late, at a school full of girls who idolized her. She would make them stronger than she had been. In the coming years, all being well, she would take over as the head—everyone on the staff knew the job was hers for the taking—and build generations of young women who wouldn't take anything like the sort of shit hers did.

Effie looked along the table at the woman after whose engagement party James had said goodbye to her forever, the woman who would be leaving here not with the man who had arranged that engagement party but with the one who had shown up at it as a fluke of circumstance. It was the sort of story they would tell their grandkids perhaps—with certain details omitted—and Effie's heart cracked at the thought of not knowing Lizzie's children.

She wondered whether this might be the sort of bitterness that long-term friends slough off like old skin with the changing of the seasons. But for now, she couldn't help but feel an electric-sharp gratification that Lizzie's face wore the expression of a woman not particularly happy with her lot.

The clinking of cutlery on plates as people served themselves without speaking, passed dishes without making conversation, and then chewed to the rhythm of the cicadas rather than the patter of the news about one another's days was excruciating.

Perhaps we can all just go to bed before the dessert even comes out.

"What was that?" Iso asked, as a rare swirl of wind rattled the fairy lights winking valiantly above the despondent group.

Frozen under the jovial glow, those around the table in the middle of the broad terrace felt as if they were players on a stage. The château sat in its horseshoe on three sides, holding them in the center of the action; the plain below them was the audience pit, stretching right the way to the horizon.

"I thought I saw something move by the pool," she continued, craning her neck to look down toward the bank of grass.

"Probably just an animal," said Bertie, turning to follow her gaze. "A squirrel perhaps, or a mouse. I thought I saw a polecat the other night."

"Whatever it was, it's gone now," Charlie said firmly.

Next to him, Lizzie blanched where she sat and put her cutlery down. She had hardly touched her food as it was. After a week of tragic-heroine rations, she was looking weak and drawn, sadness and worry having taken their toll on her beauty.

"No, no," said Anna, looking past Bertie's shoulder into the darkness. "I can see something, too."

The sunsets over the château were stately, bejeweled affairs, but when they were over, night thudded in with a quick and inky intensity. Besides the few lights in the valley, there was nothing much to leaven the vast emptiness beneath them.

Across the terrace from the Hall doors, just visible in front of the valley view, the pool lights were still on, which made looking beyond them or around them difficult in the dazzle, but slowly— uncertainly, and wary of upsetting the gathering—Anna made out a shape. Just to the right of the water's edge, between it and the far corner of the quad they sat in. Still some distance away but steadily approaching.

A figure. *A man.*

The silhouette was breathing heavily, it seemed, shoulders heaving in time with its steps and the effort of drawing breath.

"Oui, qu'est-ce qu'il y a?" What's going on?

Bertie's tone was new, its friendliness and natural generosity exchanged for a sharp alertness. His voice sounded thicker than usual and came from higher in his throat as the adrenaline flowed.

Lizzie leaped up from her chair and spun in the direction he was looking. Her eyes peered through the beams and strained into the blackness around them. The lights were blinding the fig- ures at the table even as they lit up the group perfectly for their guest.

Anna clutched Steve's arm in fright—even he was tense like taut elastic, humming with nervous energy.

We are in France, not a horror film; we are in France, not a horror film.

Finally, the shape detached from the beam of the pool spotlights behind it and stepped toward the group. Closer now, and closer again, the crunching gravel testified footfall by slow footfall its progress toward the table, where plates had been forgotten, wineglasses untouched, forkfuls of food en route to mouths laid down.

"Have you told them the truth yet? Have you?"

The sound of Dan's voice came hoarse and scratchy to them through the velvety night.

51.

Lizzie

He was here. The man I'd exchanged my future with in order to save my best friend.

Hearing his voice brought all the love and the hope that had been gradually leached from my life over the last few months roaring back, like when the Technicolor washes over after Dorothy lands in Oz.

My heart buoyed, then plummeted in fear. What if Dan made things worse?

He looked dusty and travel-weary—angry, too. He had every right to be; I wondered whether he was still cross with me for disappearing or whether . . . I didn't dare hope he might have worked out who should really be in the firing line for his rage.

If I canceled the wedding, Ben had told me, all the pictures he had would be gone. Once I'd clicked Send on those emails ending my and Dan's future together, Effie would be beyond his grasp, and I would be free. Heartbroken, but free.

The photos Ben had been sending me for the past few months might have made for some coarse remarks in the kitchen at work, a few choice comments in the pub. Mortifying, but then again, there aren't many virgins working in advertising.

The ones he had taken of Effie these last weeks, however . . . It would mean the end not only of her livelihood but of her professional life. One does not become headmistress of a school like Coral Hill Prep—or any other in that bracket, for that matter—if there is even a hint of a smudge on one's gleaming reputation. There would be no coming back from a dirty, permanent, internet-eternal blot like this. Those pictures would have ended her beloved career. They simply had to be destroyed—otherwise, her life would be.

If I had to suffer the loss of a man I had thought I might grow old with to save my friend, I would. Effie, the woman who had not only brought me back from the dead all those years ago but had made sure I was equipped for the rest of my life too.

The agony, though. The sheer gut-punching agony of deliberately wounding the people I loved the most: first Dan, as I pushed him away and out of my life; now Effie and, by extension, Anna too. Because of the nature of the wedge Ben had so carefully, so deliberately, with such cold efficiency, driven between us—the photos of Effie that nobody must ever see—she would never even know why I had been so cruel.

If the past six months hadn't already felt like a slow trickle of poison into my veins, that in itself would have been the death blow. I'd felt hollow and empty; I thought my own pain would finish me off. That was Ben's price for saving the best friend I'd ever had. That was the deal I had made with him.

But the moment I saw him at the airport, I realized he hadn't stuck to his end of the bargain. Now I began to wonder why on earth I should either.

52.

Anna

Disheveled and dusty, the groom stood there, his very presence a rebuke to the food they had prepared, the crisp wine they were washing it all down with. It was his hospitality they were enjoying; he had paid for everything. Anna saw Bertie look awkwardly at his feet, then scowl as he remembered the threat Dan posed to his cousin.

He had come round the corner Lizzie was supposed to, dressed in long ivory silk, hair gently tonged to perfection and a bouquet in her manicured hands, ready to walk up the aisle and take her vows in front of the Hall's French doors. Congregations sit patiently for brides on their special day, an indulgence of their last girlish foible, but the groom must be prompt and punctual. A groom must endure his bride's lateness right at the front, with several hundred eyes fastened onto his back. Instead, the group at the table stared into Dan's face, right into his eyes.

As he came closer, they could see tears glistening in his eyes. He wrung his hands together as though trying to pray, and there were scratches along the length of his shins, bare beneath his mud-streaked shorts. There was pain in his eyes, but wildness seemed to simmer there too, a spark about to fly. He staggered across the flagstones to them like a man wounded. Anna looked for blood or an injury, but his hurt was on the inside and stung all the more for it.

"Dan!" Effie cried, as if roused from a stupor, her eyes now flitting between Lizzie's and Ben's faces around the table, even though Anna knew her friend had been avoiding looking their way. "My God . . . Dan!"

Anna could see a glint of satisfaction in her friend's face that the clandestine couple might yet be publicly dressed down.

"Hello, mate." Charlie rose warily from his seat, still chewing a mouthful of food. "What can we do you for?"

Across the table, Steve began to stand too, and Bertie. Ben, meanwhile, remained in his seat, wearing an expression of amused disbelief and with it—*was it really?*—an idiotic sort of smirk, as though tickled by the turn of events.

"Stop where you are, please," the bride's cousin called into the darkness toward the groom. "Or we'll call the police."

This time it was Dan's turn to be amused. "How?" he laughed wryly. "You know Lizzie and I chose this place because you can't get a phone line out of here to anywhere. You couldn't call the police even if you knew who it was you should be calling them about."

"Dan, please." Lizzie's floral dress billowed slightly as she stood and moved toward him: one arm reached out, her palm wide in a stop sign. Her voice was sorrowful but final. "There's nothing you can do."

"I came to tell you all the truth," he replied, calmer now and his breath less ragged. He swayed slightly in the gloom and turned his own palms to the sky: a question, a plea.

"Why don't you come and—" Instinctively, Anna tried to make a space for him at the table, but Steve put a hand on her shoulder, and she stopped.

The tears on Lizzie's face welled from her eyes in rivulets and ran down her cheeks like the first raindrops on glass. "It will be so much worse if you go through with this, Dan. Please."

He bristled, pulled himself upright from where he had wilted in sadness and seeming exhaustion. He walked taller now, continued his slow steps toward where they sat, waiting for stage directions.

"I have all the pictures," he spat, pointing a finger at Lizzie where she stood in front of the table, at its head like an honored guest. She closed her eyes as the words hit her—not in a blink but in a death-mask's expression of resignation at forces beyond her control.

"I have all the pictures and I am going to finish this."

53.

Lizzie

I saw a couple of the photos—not out of curiosity, you understand, but because Ben sent them to me to threaten and blackmail, prove he wasn't bluffing. I closed the images almost as soon
as I had clicked on them, as soon as I realized what they were.
The knowledge that I was no longer in charge of just my own
fate hit me like a bus; I felt like my heart was beating outside my
body.

But I had seen enough to feel briefly—so briefly—proud of my
friend. *Go, girl,* I thought madly, paying no heed yet to the consequences.

Because she looked like she was having a great time—and for
the first time, I'd wager. Certainly since awful, drippy James, who
had never really valued her, never adored her the way she deserved. Never made her feel beautiful, either. What a shame
that it had taken a man like Ben to make her realize that she
was.

That was when I became determined to untangle her from
the mess I'd made of my own life so she could carry on feeling beautiful, meet someone else if she wanted to, have their
children if she felt like it. Raise all those little girls at her

school to be better at looking after themselves than I had proved to be.

I almost sent those emails canceling my wedding with a smile on my face—even though, inside, I thought I might not survive the loss.

I had to do this for Effie, because of what she had done for me.

54.

Effie

Pictures? What pictures?

Effie could see Lizzie's desperation to shut her former fiancé up.

"You shit!" Dan suddenly shouted, flecks of spit flying from his mouth and landing in the lavender beds. "You utter, utter shit!"

On the other side of the table from Lizzie, the true target of Dan's wobbling pointed finger stood up: Ben. His chair rasped on the stone as he pushed it back behind him, hands spread in front of him as if fighting flames.

"Mate," he tried nervously. "Buddy, slow down."

Effie turned her head to him so quickly her neck cricked in protest. Anna's eyes flew over too. His usual can-do slickness and easy charm were crumbling under Dan's reproachful anger.

"You see what he's really like?" Ben said shakily, glancing around the table.

It was true: Dan, dusty and half-crazed on the grounds of what should have been his wedding venue, seemed a darker and more savage shade of his usual buttoned-up accountant self. But there was something to the heat of his anger that spoke of genuine and irrepressible emotion, Effie thought; nothing cruel or calculated, the way Ben had described him yesterday.

Ben, on the other hand . . . Ben, who despite arriving with Effie now intended to leave with Lizzie—his smoothness had begun to seem almost shifty. Effie was surprised to find that her sympathies lay not entirely with the frantic-looking man on the terrace but with Lizzie as well; despite the rift between the two of them, she wouldn't have wished this awful scene on her.

"Lizzie, be careful. Stay back!" Ben reached a hand to Lizzie's shoulder as she stepped away from the table and toward Dan. "You don't know what he might do!"

She was now equidistant between the two men, contemplating her choices, the way her life might pan out. The midpoint, the most dangerous spot on any tightrope walk. Between Dan's zeal and Ben's studied calm, Lizzie exuded a nervy fatigue with it all: the jangling exhaustion of someone who hadn't slept well for months.

"Oh, stop it, Ben," she said. She sounded weary, but her voice for the first time that week was steady and free of tears. "I'm not taking orders from you anymore. Leave Dan out of it."

Ben bristled, the concerned expression wiped clean from his face and replaced with another: mounting irritation.

"What is going on, Lizzie?" Bertie's kind face was a haze of confusion and unease.

Lizzie stepped farther from Ben, one more pace toward her former fiancé. "Ben is the real monster in all this, not Dan," she said, looking into Dan's eyes.

There was a shift around the table, although nobody appeared to move—a wobble in alertness, as if a predator had attempted a feint. The group sat rigidly in their chairs like a rabbit watched by a fox.

"Hang on," began Charlie, rising from the table now too. "What about what you said about Dan—the control, the abuse—"

"Is absolutely not true in the slightest," Lizzie said. "Ben made it all up."

"I found it all on his computer," Dan spat, his face purpling with the force of conflicting emotions, tangled loyalties. "Actually, I found it all on yours"—he turned to Lizzie—"and then looked for the truth on yours." He whipped his head back to Ben.

"I've been staying at Ben's while I move out," Dan explained, his face softening as he spoke to the woman he had asked to marry him. "I was round at ours packing up my stuff, and I needed to use the computer—when I opened it, your email was open, and—I'm sorry, Lizbet, but I looked. I thought maybe you'd started seeing someone else."

Dan's voice cracked—Lizzie, eyes closed, looked as though someone had pulled out her heart and stamped on it, Effie thought—but he straightened his shoulders once more, cleared his throat. The anger returned.

"I just wanted to know," he said. "So I looked at everything."

Dan's voice, as he explained what he'd found, was quieter now, softer and less brutally torn from him by the emotions that still pulsed beneath his skin and made one of his eyelids flicker irregularly.

He told them how he had then logged on to his oldest friend's laptop, surprised that Ben hadn't taken it with him on the sudden business trip that had come up in the wake of the wedding having been canceled, but had left it in the flat where he, Dan, was staying to ride out the heartbreak of having been jilted by the most wonderful woman he had ever met.

Anna shifted in her seat. The poor guy looked harrowed by the discovery of Lizzie and Ben's secret love. "Do you want to sit down, Dan? Want a drink?"

"No," he replied steadily. "I just want the truth out in the open."

"Do you want to do this inside, mate?" suggested Ben, florid from the wine and in rude health from the sun, whereas Dan was pale and tired. "In private?"

But Dan only laughed cynically. "No thanks, I don't think you can demand privacy from anyone anymore."

Where she still stood between them, her dress billowing like the sails of a ship in rough seas caught between two ports, Lizzie's eyes clicked open like a porcelain doll's, from resigned despair to determination. She turned back toward the table.

"Ben has been blackmailing me for months," she said. "He has . . . some photos that I didn't want to get out."

55.

Anna

Over the scorching reverb of the crickets and the flutter of moths'
wings against the lanterns that still flickered around the dinner
table, Dan began to describe what he had found in his bride-to-
be's in-box: a folder marked with an asterisk, full of emails from
Ben.

Scrolling down the list, Dan had seen an attachment—a fuzzy
picture, sent from his oldest friend to his would-be wife. He had
felt the bone-chilling, finger-numbing onset of heartache, jealousy, impotent and embarrassed rage. A man scorned, a man
tricked: his best mate and his girlfriend, the oldest one in the
book.

But then he had read what else the messages contained—
threats and begging notes, manipulation dressed up as a grand
love affair—and he had gone back to Ben's flat, its keys on loan
and in his pocket, and looked on his friend's computer too.

"You gave me the password in case I needed to use it," Dan
scoffed at the man across the table, who remained silent, expres-
sionless. "You didn't think I was even a threat."

Ben smirked. Anna shifted her weight uncomfortably in her
chair. By guessing it all wrong, she had only isolated Lizzie further in her attempts to protect Effie.

On Ben's laptop, among the computer games and the corporate training modules, Dan—a man who ran audits of people's lives for a living—had found another folder, one packed with grainy images, stolen moments, of limbs entangled and bare skin, cherubs in repose. A hundred or so. Long-haired, short-haired, slim, stocky, tall, short, their skin golden or black or white. All hair colors, and all eye colors too, he supposed, except they were all asleep when the photos had been taken. A diary of sorts, a catalog.

An unknown and unauthorized portrait of every woman Ben had spent a night with.

"You fucking creep," Iso said, looking up, appalled and in revulsion, at the handsome man standing next to her. Her words broke the shocked spell the others had all been put under. "That's disgusting."

Effie too watched Ben in violent disdain as he stood, ramrod straight, denying nothing.

Dan turned to his bride again. "There was only one photo of you, Lizbet," he said, then turned again to his oldest friend. "I deleted it and all the others too."

Though her head had been sunk in shame, Lizzie now lifted her face to her former fiancé. She seemed almost hopeful. "Only one . . . ?"

"But there's still this." Her fiancé dug in his pocket and pulled out a portable hard drive wrapped in a jaunty orange case.

Anna could tell from Lizzie's face that the other woman recognized the discovery of it as yet another betrayal. "You said you'd delete them completely," she spat at Ben. "You'd already backed them up."

"No matter," Dan said simply. "We can delete these soon enough too."

He spun where he stood and pitched it, the case glowing as it arced through the night sky before landing with a satisfyingly deep splash in the pool. The surface rippled crazily like a broken mirror, then began to settle back to calm once more.

A muscle spasmed in Ben's cheek, the only indication that he had heard what Dan was saying or seen what his friend had just done. To Anna, he seemed to be trying not to laugh.

"Well, what a display," he said sardonically. "Chivalry isn't dead."

Anna growled with anger at him. "Was it you who uncanceled the booze and the flowers and all those bloody chairs?"

Dan's eyebrows rose. "What?"

"Did you leave the message in Bertie's notepad?" asked Charlie, wide-eyed. "And the writing in the mirror?"

"Why did you even come here?" Lizzie whispered. "I did everything you asked."

"Her," Ben said unapologetically, his chin thrust out and a finger raised to Effie.

"Me?" she shrilled in response.

"You'd do anything for her. Anything to protect her," Ben said to Lizzie sullenly. "She's your weak spot."

56.

Effie

She pulled herself taller and tried to quiet the voice that kept telling her that of course it had all been a sham with Ben. A familiar dread began to nibble around her outline.

The pictures.

Of course he had never been attracted to her, because he looked the way he did and she looked the way she did.

He has pictures of me, too.

She's your weak spot, Ben had said, and Effie's voice was careful and calm despite it all: "I think we can safely say after this that there is nothing whatsoever about Lizzie that is weak."

"Especially not Effie," said Anna, a table's width away, without even looking toward the man who had wronged them both but fixing both friends with an expression so fierce her face seemed to glow in the moonlight.

Effie reached out an arm to Lizzie, made to approach her with wet eyes.

"No, wait!" Lizzie's voice was ragged, and she held up a hand to halt Effie's progress, a plea to be heard. "There's more, I'm afraid."

She looked to each side, at Dan and then at Ben, her blond hair swinging wildly with each turn of her head. She had her arms raised at each of them, a tragic Greek pulled between two impossible choices.

"Ben had been blackmailing me with those photos," she said. "But they weren't the reason I canceled the wedding." She paused for breath. "I didn't care what he did to me."

Lizzie looked up at the stars to clear the tears pooling in her eyes. "But I was so fucking . . . *stuck*. Eff, I'm sorry I lied to you about me and Ben, but I just couldn't risk you having it out with him, because . . . because . . ." She blinked and breathed in deeply.

"Because?" Effie prompted, and felt her stomach plummet. *Here it comes.*

"Because he has photos of you too," she finished, brokenly, her voice fading out like an old gramophone record.

Inside Effie's head, the static cut out. The stillness in her brain and on the terrace felt even more oppressive than the usual feedback loops. A greasy block of terror began to form in her stomach, and her palms were suddenly slick with shame.

The pictures he took, and the ones I sent when he asked.

In the depths of her panic attacks these last months, she had spiraled with the worry that it would be details from one of the blurry nights that would reach out of the past, out from the blank spots in her memory, to claim her dignity. Instead it was a series of carefully posed, sharp-focused, ultra-high-definition decisions she had made while fully in control and only too conscious. She had been so hungry for affection—*no, attention*—that she had given everything away willingly. Her humiliation was complete.

One eyelid began to tremble as Effie thought of the girls—*my girls*—in their boaters, rucksacks bobbing behind them as they walked in line like little ducklings through the school gates at Coral Hill. Of the other teachers in the school: wholesome, reliable, steady. Of the parents, just about as well versed in worldly sin as the next highly paid metropolitan liberal but insistent that not a whisper of it should reach their children's ears. It would be like the Spanish Inquisition, Effie thought; she would be hounded out of there less with pitchforks than with horrified expressions, muffled voices, all those pairs of eyes on her.

Where would she go then?

Effie's thoughts flickered in her mind like a scratchy old black-and-white film, sped up for laughs: from the Prep, past the other schools with sparkling reputations, down past the ones where she could still make a difference, and to the bottom of the pile. Even there, an HR department would Google her name and stop short at the image search; any potential employer pausing to read the Post-it attached to her CV would crumple the whole thing straight into the wastepaper basket.

I will never be a headmistress. I will never get another job in education again.

"Oh my God," she whispered and began to sob—with embarrassment at her own poor judgment and horror at its ramifications.

How could I have been so wrong about him?

"Oh my God," she said again. Any other words—the words she usually so prided herself on—were no longer there.

"Effie, I am so, so sorry." Lizzie ran across the flagstones to be next to her, to hold her. "I am so sorry he came after you. I canceled the wedding so he wouldn't use them," Lizzie said, looking up from where she had laid her head on Effie's shoulder. "He said he would delete them."

Effie was a blizzard, a static hum. The reverb in her head turned up to fever pitch and then—

Effie's stomach relaxed so suddenly she wondered whether she was going to vomit. Her muscles spasmed, then bunched again in sorrow.

"You canceled your wedding . . . for me?" Effie's brown eyes were pools of gratitude and pain as she took in her friend's ashen face next to hers.

Lizzie smiled forlornly, matched her friend tear for tear as she spoke. "How could I not, Eff? After what you did for me?"

Effie remembered typing. She remembered articulating arguments, framing quotes and ideas, as she heard her friend groaning and crying through the wall. She remembered sitting her own exams, half-waiting to be pulled out of them and interrogated for having put Lizzie's name on an essay she had written. The many sleepless nights she'd tossed and turned ahead of their results being pinned up on the boards by the Senate House. They had gone to read them like criminals being led to the gallows.

"Effie Talbot: summa cum laude," the lists had read. "Anna Hewitt: magna cum laude."

Those two had never been in doubt, though.

But there, just below: "Lizzie Berkeley: magna cum laude."

A pass, and a good one. Not what she deserved, but something she'd work the rest of her life to be worthy of.

They had backed out of the quad as though inching back along the plank and onto the ship, then headed straight to the pub. When Anna had asked her friends why they were crying so much, they'd blamed it on the cheap, acidic white wine.

As they'd graduated, kneeling in cap and gown, both Effie and Lizzie had expected the Latin-intoning scholar to break off when he reached their names and call out their wrongdoing. A month later—after the parties and the balls, the farewells and the swapping of new addresses in London—they had each gone home. Only when the doors to their parents' homes had swung shut behind them had Effie and Lizzie finally dared to breathe out. They had gotten away with it.

It was the out-breath that had confined Lizzie to bed, however. The realization of just how wrong she had gone, how close she had swerved to ruining her life and somebody else's. Even adoring, gentle Bertie couldn't reason her out of the doom she was feeling.

"Maybe you'll need to pay me back one day," Effie had laughed, that day in Lizzie's teenage bedroom, when she came to rouse her and set her back on the right path.

"I had to pay you back," Lizzie whispered to her in the still French night air.

57.

Effie

"You little fucker," Anna said vehemently, breaking the stillness of the scene.

Ben smirked back at her, hands aloft in innocence. "Look, it was all consensual between two adults. . . . I didn't force anything—she *wanted* me to take those photos."

Effie felt a kick in her stomach and a gag hacked in the back of her throat. "In private!" she screamed over Lizzie's brown shoulder, which was—for now—keeping her safe in its embrace. "They were private!"

Her brain spun. Even if Lizzie had acquiesced to Ben, they would still be living under this shadow years later. Blackmail didn't clear up like a thunderstorm; it lingered on like a black cloud on the horizon forever. Though Bangkok would eventually become a distant memory, the hold Ben still had over them meant Lizzie would still wake up with him in her head every morning—and so would Effie.

"I can't let you do this for me," she said to Lizzie. "You can't cancel your wedding for me, for these . . . photos. It's not right."

She thought of adding yet more worry to the bustling cacophony already inside her head. "It will drive me mad. And it will break my heart to know that yours is broken too."

Effie swallowed hard, and her skin prickled with goosebumps. "If that means those pictures come out, then at least he won't have anything over us anymore."

Lizzie gazed at her, eyes boring deep into Effie's, and rested her forehead against her friend's.

"No!" Anna shouted from across the table.

58.

Anna

She had worked with clients on images such as these before—high-profile clients, rich clients, old clients, and young clients. Always women, never men, because the male physique is no sort of currency—whereas a woman's can be both chattel and millstone.

Anna had represented women who had been forced to make the difficult choice between justice and dignity because of "evidence" their exes had had against them. Do you stand up to them and pursue them for what they owe you and your children, or do you back down because they now have the power to humiliate you on a scale more global and more infinite than our mothers could ever have imagined back when they told us to save it for someone special?

That evidence was proof of intimacy gone sadly cold and trust misplaced, not moral failing. Anna had never understood the type of man who could weaponize the reputation of somebody he had once loved like this. Who could turn blissful memories, albeit ones now laced with heartbreak, to curdled shit; could break a life with a few vengeful keystrokes and feel no qualms about doing so.

To use these intimacies, to upload and disseminate them, was a criminal act, and one these men could go to jail for—but it was more likely they'd just be made to pick up litter or clean graffiti for a couple of months. It was the woman who found herself in prison, trapped in panic attacks and flashbacks, public scorn. A conviction couldn't make the rest of the world unsee any of it.

Anna had known women destroyed by such photos, either backed into a corner and worn down like some exhausted, hunted animal or strung out across the internet like a clothesline full of dirty laundry. Even the strongest ones had several months of not being able to leave the house, then years of trauma; the weaker ones simply . . . gave up. The diagnosis was usually depression or anxiety, and the coroner's report always said suicide—but neither of those was ever true: this was an act of terror, and the charge should have been murder.

Anna was not going to let that happen to Effie. "No," she said again, quietly now.

"Ben, if you don't delete those pictures, I will not rest until you are locked up and everyone knows what you are." She was in courtroom mode now. "I am one of the best divorce lawyers in London, and Bertie specializes in privacy law. My firm has the resources to squash whomever you hire in defense, and I will devote every spare moment I have to making sure that you are squashed too."

She could feel not only Effie and Lizzie staring at her in shiny-eyed awe but Steve too, and she felt a momentary flicker of something like pride: this was what she spent her time away from Sonny doing—being good at her job. In the constant negative appraisals of herself as a mother, Anna had devalued how hard she worked day after day.

Ben's haughty expression faltered, and his strong jaw seemed to fail him for the first time, as doubt made his shoulders hunch, his neck curl back into his shoulders. He suddenly looked so much smaller, Anna thought.

Now Bertie, still in his seat, cleared his throat to speak: "Ben, whatever photos you have—in my professional opinion, I've got to say: Anna will eat you alive."

"They'll be out there though, won't they?" he snarled. "It'll still be too late, and everyone will have seen them—you can't stop me doing it."

Across the terrace, Dan's shoulders fell. "But I deleted them," he stuttered. "And the hard drive . . . I thought . . ."

Another scrape of a metal chair on stone and Iso stood up halfway along the table, her dark eyes flashing brighter in the fairy-light glow than even her many strands of gold jewelry and jingling earrings.

"Dan," she said gently, "they're all in the cloud. He still has them—but don't worry, nobody understands how it fucking works."

She yanked her gaze to Ben and spoke more sternly than any of them had thought she was capable of. "Look, you're obviously a creep of the first order—we don't need a judge's verdict on that. Delete those pictures now, or I will make you a viral sensation tonight—and not in a good way."

She stooped to pick up her phone from the table. "I've been taking pictures all week, and you're in plenty of them. I can get your mug shot up to nearly a million people, with a description of exactly who you are and what you've done. You'll be internationally hated by morning. You'll be a Twitterstorm, a think piece. Your twisted little brain will be a discussion segment on the news."

"I mean, technically that is defamation, Iso, and you might, er . . ." Bertie muttered quietly beside her.

"I don't care," she said to him firmly. "If you had any idea how many messages I get from girls whose boyfriends have shared pictures of them, whose friends have turned on them online. Whose phones have made them miserable. They're a fucking disease, these things." She slapped the one in her hand against the palm of the other. "I make a living from it, but that doesn't mean I like what they do to people."

She said it all without even blinking, her rage as effortlessly, authentically composed as her pictures. *Iso,* Anna thought, *you are fucking brilliant.*

"A million angry women," she continued. "You'll never get a date again once they know what you're really like. Give me your phone—let's get rid of them all, you rotten perv. What's your passcode?"

Wordlessly Ben slid his phone from a pocket of his shorts and held it out to the indignant glamazon. When she saw he wasn't going to move, Iso gave a snort of exasperation and walked toward him, the swish of her pale linen sundress the only noise but for the eternal cricket hum.

"Come on," she barked at him, and Effie saw him flinch, craven before Iso despite towering over her. "What's your passcode?"

He gave it to her, and she began flitting around the screen of his phone, nodding and tsking gently to herself as she worked. Swiping and clicking, highlighting, moving to trash, emptying and restoring factory settings until there was nothing of Effie or Lizzie—or even Ben himself—left on the phone or stored in the cloud. Iso handed it back to him.

"Fuck you," she said politely as he took it from her.

Anna burst into applause; Lizzie gave a whoop and rushed to hug her. Effie, trembling, gripped the back of the chair where she stood and wept with gratitude, her every limb shaking with the audaciousness of Iso's save.

"I had a feeling I was punching above my weight," Charlie drawled, happily tone-deaf as ever and glowing with adoration.

"Without a doubt, Chaz," Effie laughed through uncontrollable tears. "Without a doubt."

59.

Effie

Her mind, so often in a tailspin that was fueled by so many dreaded *wheres* and *what-ifs* that she was unable to answer, began clunking into motion like a well-oiled piston. Finally, Effie understood what had happened with Charlie on the wedding night.

Of course.

They had been lying there, together in the honeymoon suite, the rose petals scattered around them. The heart shape someone had carefully strewn them in had been disturbed first when they had thrown each other down on the bed in gales of laughter and then again by the rougher action afterward.

"I've never felt like this about anybody before," Charlie had told her. "Nobody else has even come close."

A pause.

"That's why I'm ready to make the ultimate commitment—finally." He'd smiled into the creased cotton he lay on, reached a hand out toward her cheek, and then . . .

Then Effie had begun the jerky, guttural shoulder twerk that was the prologue to a day's worth of alcohol leaving her system with abrupt and unannounced force. She had run into the en suite and bid adieu to it and to her dignity both, although it was nothing Charlie hadn't seen before—as he had told her, in fact, while he'd patted her back and stroked her hair.

"You will be happy again, Eff," he murmured as she retched with such intensity that her bony knees scraped the floor and she thought her heart was breaking all over again.

"You're ready to be happy again, you just haven't realized it yet. And you'll meet someone who sees how brilliant you are." He smiled at her when she next surfaced from within the porcelain bowl.

Charlie handed her a square of loo roll for her stinging eyes and runny nose. Though her insides burned as though they'd been sandpapered, Effie felt like she had evacuated six months of cumulative misery as she caught her breath and calmed her sobs on the cold tile floor next to the loo.

"Thank you," Effie said to him. The six-foot, emotionally repressed man-child she'd first met when they were both eighteen had turned Tin Man, had finally discovered that there was a heart in there all along. "So, when are you going to pop the question?"

"Final night of the holiday, I thought." He grinned. "But Christ, Eff, don't ever mention this soppy conversation again or I'll kill you."

Charlie helped her up off the floor and sat her on the side of the bed with a tall glass of water. "You need to get some sleep. You look terrible."

He turned to the door. "Oh, and you're covered in sick, so you might want to take those clothes off before you climb in."

Oh.

If Effie's skin had already felt tight with the various mortifications she had inadvertently put herself through recently, it shrank another few sizes, in those moments watching Ben study his newly emptied phone, as the latest humiliation sank in.

Christ, you idiot.

Charlie hadn't been weird with her or flirting with her—or,

rather: he had been both, because that was what he always was with everyone. Although Effie's capacity for overthinking, for overanalyzing, for *obsessing*, for—*let's not beat around the bush*—near-total narcissism was in the moment of realization shocking to her, she was able to see the calamitously clownish elements in it too. Doing so came as a relief, in fact, an antidote to some of the dread she felt she had been drenched with since the drunken wedding night.

The tears rolling down her cheeks were, for the first time in six months, not entirely unhappy, but they acted as a sort of catharsis for everything else inside her. Her emotions had existed so close to the surface for so long, they needed little encouragement to break through. From punch bag to punch line, she thought, and realized—with a force that made her laugh aloud—that she couldn't wait to tell Anna and Lizzie.

"Oh my God, Charlie," she blurted, and her blush was instinctive rather than embarrassed. Effie had never felt more tenderly toward him. "I'm so sorry I was sick all over you."

60.

Anna

"Dan, why didn't you answer your phone?" Anna asked the man whose gaze was now firmly—hopefully—fixed on Lizzie.

"I thought I'd lost it somewhere when I was moving my stuff out," he replied. "But now I'm not so sure that someone didn't nick it."

Bertie scowled at Ben. "You sent the email to Marie about setting up the wedding from Dan's account, didn't you?"

Ben shrugged, his expression deliberately provocative with surly boredom; Lizzie threw him a withering look that he reeled with. She clasped Iso's arm tightly in thanks, then paced uncertainly over to where Dan stood.

"So you were just pretending to make those calls?" Iso shrieked at Ben. "I knew you were lying about getting reception by the pool! I tried over there for HOURS!"

Lizzie had reached Dan and stood, a supplicant in bare feet, one hand on his dusty, tear-stained face, the other reaching for the fingers she might once have slipped a ring onto.

"I'm so so sorry," she murmured. "Can you forgive me?"

He looked at her through filmy, sad eyes and shook his head.

Anna could see that he had felt in the past week every single emotion he thought could possibly exist, from anguish and de-

ame and contempt, and finally gut-wrenching regret,
uickening fear. Now, the drag of pity, of empathy for how
had suffered. It had weighed so heavy on his heart as he had
traveled across the Channel and the length of a country to find
her that Dan thought he might have accidentally left it behind
him in London, beating feverishly in the flat they had shared. He
looked utterly drained, emotionally and physically wrung out, and
he leaned into Lizzie as though he were losing blood.

"There's nothing to forgive," Dan whispered to her. "I just wish
you'd told me, so I could have helped you fix it. You're mine—
remember? Mine to love, comfort, honor, and all that."

The others blushed and tried not to watch too conspicuously as
he grabbed her in a hug and a kiss that was mainly sweat and
travel rime accumulated on this last-minute dash to France. Dust
from the road had stuck to the tears drying on his cheeks.

There was a beat of stillness, and then Charlie turned toward
Ben. The focus of all the accusations, now a target for all their
resentment, their outrage. Their loyalty.

"That was really shitty behavior," he drawled ominously.

Oh no, don't fight. Anna's intestines shriveled at the spectacle
of it, two posh boys in fisticuffs outside a luxury holiday rental as
though they were streetwise kids.

Iso laid a cautionary hand on Charlie's arm, in whose strong fist
a dinner knife was still clasped.

"Shittier than being dumped for your best mate?" said Ben
shrilly. He threw his linen napkin onto the plate in front of him.
"Shittier than your friend siding with some . . . some internet trollop from an app?"

An intake of breath around the table. Even the insects paused
in their humming.

But the phrase only made Lizzie snort with contempt. "Internet trollop! Christ, Ben, what are you—the virtue police?"

Plenty of the men who posted those photos seemed to think
they were, Anna mused. Witchfinders with keyboards. What dif-

ference did another woman make, given the morass of them online? The internet had made female flesh ubiquitous and disposable, bouncing hairless bodies with no feelings attached that were simultaneously lucrative and worthless.

Lizzie would need her and Effie as she patched her life back together, tried to move past the trauma of threat, but for now Anna resolved to be lighthearted. It was a tonic for the ills they had each of them carried to this place with them, along with their luggage. She and Effie rushed to Lizzie, and the three of them melded, as they had so many times over the years, into a squash of tears, hair, and giggles.

"Internet trollop!" Iso howled, a few paces away. "I'm going to put that in my bio!"

The women opened their arms to her and she crept into their huddle, newly appreciated and warmly welcome.

Ben watched them with a deepening sneer. Despite his height and impressive chest span, he deflated like a forgotten balloon in the face of their mirth. For a certain type of man, female laughter is the most terrifying sound.

"I think," Effie said through a tangle of summertime, sun-bleached hair, "that the time has come for you to leave, Ben."

"Seconded," Charlie said, folding his arms. "Go and pack your bags, and get out of here as soon as you're done."

"I wouldn't stay if you begged me to," Ben spat. "And it's not like you haven't in the past—both of you." He gestured at Lizzie and then to Effie, who colored as though she had been slapped. "Bitches, all of you. Bunch of desperate slags."

"Ignore him," Lizzie said, her arms about her friends' necks like a boxer being helped from the ring. "He's pathetic."

"Somebody should go with him, make sure he doesn't do anything else creepy," Iso said.

As Charlie followed Ben inside, she called out again: "And use the landline to book him a taxi *immediatement*!"

Then they sat, survivors of a showdown, and drew up a chair for

Dan next to Lizzie's. Silent and shell-shocked, they gazed down at the table, still laden with hospitality, as though they had never seen it before. The prospect of food and wine that had so recently turned to ash in the mouths of those chewing it seemed to rise again, phoenixlike, now that the source of irritation had gone.

Steve cleared his throat. "Errr. Drink, anyone?"

Was there any other response?

Each head nodded gratefully and Steve ducked inside.

Lizzie began laughing, with the giddy, unnerving hysteria of the relieved. She had forgotten how to feel light. The psychological wounds Ben had given her would take some time to heal, the scars even longer to fade, but right now, Lizzie reasoned, she could medicate convivially. When he had departed, this house would be replete with all of her favorite people in the world; she intended to make the most of it.

Steve returned with yet another cold champagne bottle, poised to pop the cork.

"There's still so much left in there," he said, squinting and aiming it away from the table as he eased the stopper out with his thumb. "Despite our best efforts to put a dent in it."

"We can charge that to Ben," Iso said. "I saved his bank details off his phone."

As Steve poured, Charlie appeared in the double doors. "He's going," he said, jerking his head toward Ben, who was making his way scowlingly across the Hall to the front door behind him. "Any final words?"

"You can have her, mate," he called contemptuously over one shoulder.

"I meant them to you," Charlie snapped.

"Oh, there is one more thing." Ben hove into view once more, framed by the Hall lights where the altar had once stood ready. "I bumped into your ex last week, Effie. James, isn't it?"

Ben's eyes glittered at her through the fresh night air.

"He's getting married."

61

Effie

Well, that's just not possible, she almost said.

James doesn't believe in marriage. Thinks it's a sham. When you love someone enough you don't need a piece of paper to prove it.

But as Effie tried to speak, tried to sit up from where she had slumped in her chair, pinned there by the knife Ben had success-fully launched right into the center of her heart, the center of her being . . . she realized finally that these words—James's words, the ones he'd intoned whenever the subject had come up—were not the sort of solemn vow she had once taken them for.

Oh, she thought as enlightenment washed over her like a sear-ing, stinging scourge.

He just didn't want to marry me.

Effie expected the hole in her chest to fill with battery acid, for her ribs to break with the agony of it. She waited for the stream of tears that had never been far from her eyes these past six months or more to flow again, a salty tide that would irrigate her misery, turn her back in on herself as she questioned over again *why* and also *why not me* as well as *who* and then *why her.*

But the tears didn't come. Instead Effie felt as though an anchor had been lopped off from around one ankle. There was pain—a dull sort of ache, a throb of embarrassment at what she now saw had perhaps always been inevitable—but there was also something far more complex beneath, something far more interesting.

Indifference and another question with it: *What now then?*

For the first time, the thought felt interesting. Exciting.

"What a twat," Effie said conversationally.

"He's lying," Lizzie said. "Ignore him, he's lying."

"No," Effie said, dry-eyed still and marveling at the fact. "He's not lying."

She knew that Ben had told her the truth because, for the first time in months, everything suddenly seemed to make sense. The questions had stopped, the endless internal match replays of conversations. The suspicions, the regrets, the *if only I'd . . .*

"But, Ben?" she called to the man in the doorway. A man she had once thought her superior but had realized, earlier this week in fact, that he was far less intelligent than she was, not to mention far less funny.

I will never again make do with someone.

I will never again persuade myself to like someone.

I will never assume that somebody else's company is better than my own.

"You're a twat too."

Iso squealed and Ben's handsome face briefly cracked with a snarl as he left the stage not to rapture but to ridicule. As he turned and crossed the length of the Hall, a silent chorus of heads swiveled and heard, from inside, the historic creaking of the paneled door before it closed again and, beyond it, an engine revved into readiness.

Anna turned to Effie, seized her hands where they lay in her lap, determined not to be late to her side when she most needed support. *Not again, never again.*

"It's fine." Effie squeezed her friend's fingers, then reached for her glass and sipped. "I'm fine. Weirdly."

She smiled, and when the smile reached her eyes, she touched her cheek to make sure her face hadn't cracked like cold porcelain in a hot oven.

"I might actually be better than fine." She shook herself as though waking from a daze.

"Music?" asked Steve, darting back through the doors and flicking a switch.

Those horns, that Motown beat, the high hat.

"Happiness condensed to three minutes," he said with a smile, and stood beneath the trellis arch, taking up his official role as wedding DJ once again. Anna joined him and wriggled under one of her husband's arms to lean against him and survey the scene on the terrace. The lights twinkled on, but the smiles outshone them in even more brilliant wattage.

Lizzie and Dan stood uncertainly and began to sway under the stars to the beat, the soaring strings. Their first dance, finally.

"My God, Dan!" called Anna, as the groom broke into a series of well-judged steps. "You really mastered that routine."

Next to them, Charlie and Iso clasped together and twirled. Her putty-pink dress billowed as she spun, and when he whipped her back into his arms, Charlie dropped his dark head against hers.

"I was going to ask you," he muttered into her ear, and she laughed and wriggled as his breath tickled the soft skin. "I swear, I was going to ask you tonight, but I don't want to steal their thunder."

Iso smiled and moved off again, shimmying to the rhythm of the song. "I know you were," she called back to him. "And yes!"

By the table, Effie and Bertie stood eyeing the others like a pair of awkward scarecrows, sentinels to the dance floor unfolding before them but unable, in their stiffness, to engage with it.

"Don't you want to dance?" she said teasingly, tapping her foot.

He shook his head quite firmly. "You definitely don't want to see me dancing."

"Oh, come on!" Effie yanked on his arm and spun herself into Bertie's chest, where—as she landed—he scooped her into an elaborate salsa in perfect time to the music.

"*What?*" she yelled gleefully over the tune.

"They made us learn at school," he said apologetically as he twisted and marched her expertly, counting under his breath before executing a perfect if robotic turn and steering her back across the patio like a wheelbarrow.

On the next dip, the ends of her hair grazing the flagstones, Effie threw back her head to look at the clear moon where it floated in the sky on a lavender tide.

When Bertie pulled his dancing partner upright again, he spun her away and Effie's feet, bare on the terrace since she had kicked off her beaded sandals, skittered backward along the ripples of the still sun-warmed granite beneath. She felt herself floating away from the epicenter of the party, untethered and bobbing at the edge of the group. The fairy lights warped in her vision, and the music seemed to slow.

Not again.

This time, she landed. In a pair of arms so strong, so familiar, so warm and protective she could feel the love radiating through them like a heartbeat in time with the music.

Inches from her face, Lizzie's smile beamed through the dark, the dimples in her cheeks such familiar landmarks that Effie felt she had walked through her front door and back into her life.

Effie turned her face, angled her chin, and the lips that pressed on her temple were the same soft touch that baptized Sonny anew after every trip, tumble, and gritty graze. Anna curled an arm round each of them, and the three women swayed together. The same hug, the same huddle, whether minutes had passed or months, weeks or years.

Home.

"In sickness and in health," murmured Lizzie.

Effie closed her eyes and nodded. These women were her past

and her future, so many ends and beginnings, so many lives old and new. Whether false starts or ever afters, the three of them held an eternity in their arms.

"For richer, for poorer," Anna croaked, her throat tight.

The still point of the turning world; there the dance is.

Effie laughed and felt her heart wing up to join the silver orb, full and gleaming, above them.

She bent her head to theirs and whispered, "I do."

ACKNOWLEDGMENTS

The first draft of *The Wedding Night* was written in what now feels like another lifetime and a different world—one where we could socialize and travel freely, celebrate en masse and meet each other without having to think through the consequences. By the time I finished the final manuscript in 2020, a holiday like the one in its pages had become logistically impossible and in some countries actually illegal.

Sometimes I can't believe how much I used to take for granted. But *The Wedding Night* is a novel about the things we assume will always be there—our friends, our loved ones, our privacy— and how close we can come to losing them. I hope its message resonates, despite curtailed horizons, almost as much as I hope we can have group holidays (and hangovers) again soon.

There are so many people to thank for getting this book out into the world during unprecedented times. My brilliant agent, Laura Macdougall—with love to Thea. My editors at Ballantine and Hodder, Hilary Teeman and Kimberley Atkins—your ideas and enthusiasm were a driving force—and to Caroline Weishuhn: Your dating insights brought me into the digital era! To Denise Cronin and the Random House rights department: Thank you for repping me far and wide. There are so many others at PRH and Hodder who have polished my words and put them out there—Colleen and Debbie, Vero and Alice in particular. To Kate Miciak, who gave me the chance to do something I love—I am forever grateful and always learning.

To Alex—tops pal—for providing the time, space, and happiness to write, and then listening to endless anxieties on the subject. To Freda and Dougie for keeping my heart full. To my parents, first readers again and always the most important, and my sisters: my champions; my Dooms.

To Anna and Nicola, who have taught me confidence and made me strong. To the Mexico gals, my Loose Women, and *The Times* fashion desk, who all toasted and Zoomed *The New Girl* into existence in a closed world last year—and, of course, to the amazingly kind community it found out there. Thank you so much for reading.

THE
WEDDING
NIGHT

HARRIET WALKER

Random House Book Club

Because Stories Are Better Shared ™

A BOOK CLUB GUIDE

QUESTIONS AND TOPICS FOR DISCUSSION

1. As the novel opens, we see Effie and Anna reminiscing on how their friendships have changed since their university days, as they've all grown older and their lives have changed. Have you ever had similar thoughts about old friendships? Were you able to maintain those friendships, or did they fall away?

2. One of the things Anna struggles with throughout the novel are her feelings about becoming a mother, and how becoming a mother has affected how she sees herself, her husband, her friends, and even her career. Have you ever found yourself in a similar position, where a dramatic life change has affected how you view your life, and how others in your life view you?

3. Throughout the novel, we see Effie struggle to find a healthy way to cope with her recent breakup, even as her friends try to help as much as they can. Have you ever felt similarly, or have you ever helped a friend who was feeling similarly? What effect, if any, do you think societal pressures have on Effie's coping mechanisms?

4. Lizzie, too, is struggling with the dissolution of her relationship and calling off her wedding. What do you think of her friends' decision to take her mind off things by going to the château anyway? Do you think it would help or hurt?

5. As the novel progresses, we see Lizzie's ex continue to psychologically torment her, even though she's ended things. Why do you think that is? What do you think motivates her ex to treat her this way—is it embarrassment, or pride, or something else altogether?

6. As secrets begin to come out, we learn to what lengths Effie has gone to for Lizzie, and in turn, what lengths Lizzie has gone to for Effie. Would you go to similar lengths for your best friend? Why, or why not?

7. At the beginning of the novel, Effie and Anna are quite intimidated by Iso and find it hard to warm up to her, but despite not growing close with the women, Iso stands up for Effie and Lizzie and is a key part of the novel's resolution. How did you feel as you watched the women band together? What do you make of the fact that society often pits women against one another instead of teaching them to band together?

PHOTO: © CLAIRE PEPPER

HARRIET WALKER is the fashion editor of *The Times* (UK) and author of *The New Girl*. Born in Glasgow and raised in Sheffield, Walker studied at Trinity College, Cambridge, and lives in South London with her husband and two young children.

harrietwalker.com
Twitter: @harrywalker1
Instagram: @_harrywalker1